SOULLESS

LAWLESS PART 2

KING BOOK 4

T.M. FRAZIER

Copyright © 2016 T.M. FRAZIER
Print Edition
All rights reserved.

This is a work of fiction. Any similarities to persons both living or dead is purely coincidental.

Acknowledgements

Where do I even start? Of course I want to thank my wonderful husband and beautiful baby girl for always supporting me and loving me.

I want to thank my author friends for all their wonderful wisdom and advice and for that extra push when I really need it. Crystal, Monica, Rochelle. I love you guys.

I want to thank Vanessa and Manda over at Prema for being amazing as always.

I want to thank the best group of readers in the entire world, my Frazierland crew. You keep me going each and every day and I can't thank you enough. I love you guys.

Thanks to my agent Kimberly Brower for putting up with me and my schedule craziness. I promise one of these days I will get my act together…maybe.

Julie you are my spirit animal. I don't think I would have finished this without you. Thanks also to Jennie, Kimmi, Julie, Clarissa, and Jessica for putting up with my craziness while writing this book!

Special thanks to Lane Dorsey and Josh Mario John for the beautiful cover photo.

Dedication

For Frazierland, my tribe

How well I have learned that there is no fence to sit on between heaven and hell.

—Johnny Cash

PROLOGUE

BEAR

I WAS MAD at the world, at the whiskey for not being strong enough, at the drugs for not lasting long enough, at the fucking whores I banged for not getting me off when it was my fault my dick was fucking useless after a bucket of fucking blow. I went so far as to be pissed at random people on the street for laughing or smiling when I felt like I'd never be able to smile or laugh again.

How dare they?

How fucking *dare* they move on with their lives like my friend hadn't just died.

I was on the verge of losing what little sanity I had left when I rode out of Logan's Beach and set off to find a place, or places, where I could numb myself against the feelings that followed me from town to town, cheap motel to cheap motel, girl to girl, high to fucking high.

Then, this pink haired girl from the past came barreling into my life and it was like for the first time, I'd found a purpose. A real genuine purpose and not just some shit Chop spewed out as orders, that I and every other member of the Beach Bastards took as bible, but a true reason to live again.

To WANT to live again.

Someone to live for.

Ti was my chance at some sort of real happiness when Lord fucking knows I had no idea what that really was before her. The only glimpses of real genuine happiness I'd ever had came courtesy of Preppy, King, and of course Grace. Like when King tattooed us for the first time and we loved them, even though they were crooked and downright fucking awful. Like when Grace made me my very first birthday cake. Like the time King, Prep, and I sat at the top of the water tower and thought the world was ours to take.

Because at that time, it was.

Then there was Ti, and my new happiness became the first time I saw her smile. The first time I kissed her. The first time I tasted her pussy by the fire. The first time she let me inside of her, shamelessly pushing through her virginity in a frantic need to make her mine.

Because that's what she was.

That's what she would always be.

And I will kill every motherfucker who dares to try and take her from me.

Mine.

BEAR

THIRTEEN YEARS OLD...

I WENT INTO my old man's office to let him know that the shipment he'd been asking about for the last month was finally at the gate. The second I opened the door, I instantly regretted forgetting to knock. Chop was leaning back on the faded green chair in the corner of the room with his jeans down around his ankles, a beer in his hand. A redhead BBB named Millie, or Mallie, or Jennie, was on her knees between his legs, her head bobbing up and down on his dick. "Shit," I muttered, remembering how much shit he gave me the last time I interrupted him with a chick. The black eye took two months to go away, and after that, he'd put me on gate duty for an entire fucking month.

Grabbing the door handle, I slowly retreated backwards, hoping he hadn't noticed me.

I wasn't that lucky.

"What the fuck have I told you, boy?" he bellowed. I froze. "You fucking stupid or something? You remember what happened last time you showed me disrespect? I tell you to fucking knock and you just walk in like you own the fucking place?" The girl lifted her mouth off his dick with an audible *pop* and I cringed. "Don't fucking stop, bitch. Did I tell you that you could fucking stop?" Chop grabbed the back of her head and shoved her back down on his dick, holding her there.

"Sorry, Pop," I said, a slip of the tongue and something else that was sure to set him off.

"Pop? Pop!" This time he yanked the girl's head off his lap and threw her to the side, she landed on her hip and winced. He stood, tucking himself inside his jeans, zipping up as Jodi ran past us out the door. "What are you supposed to call me, *son?*" Chop spat, getting in my face. I could smell the beer on his breath.

"Prez," I answered, looking to the floor as I'd been instructed.

"That's right. Prez. The Daddy and Pop shit was for when you were a kid, and you ain't no fucking kid no more," he said. "Why do I want you to call me Prez?" he asked, poking me in the chest.

"Because you are the Prez," I said, reciting the words he'd made me say ever since I'd officially turned prospect, and he'd decided that Pop was somehow a term of disrespect.

"That's right, prospect. *Me.* I'm your fucking Prez. I'm not your dad, or your pop, or your fucking old man." Chop grabbed me by my blank cut and tugged me down the hall and then down the stairs into the common room. A few of the brothers were sitting on stools at the bar. Most of the others were playing pool, their bets stacked up in high piles on the rim of the table, indicating the high stakes of the game.

Although it didn't really matter how high the stakes were because the second Chop entered the room they put down their cues and turned their attention to us. He stood behind me and pushed me forward. I braced myself on one of the tables to keep from falling, sending a stack of bills scattering to the floor.

"Tell them. Tell your future brothers who I am, prospect," Chop ordered, taunting me like he was waiting for me to snap. I was pissed but I wasn't fucking stupid. All I had to do was bide my time as a prospect because once I was a patched member he'd have to show me some respect.

I hoped.

"He's..." I started but faltered under the gaze of the brothers.

"I'm what, *BOY*?" Chop leaned down and shouted in my ear. "And stand up fucking straight. I know whores who spend all day on their knees and on their backs who stand straighter than you." He grabbed a fistful of my hair and tugged me upright.

"The Prez," I said a little louder this time, wincing as he continued to pull on my hair like I was a fucking puppet and he was holding the strings.

"Who?" he barked like a drill sergeant.

"You are the Prez!" I screamed, hoping it would be good enough for him to let me go and for all of this to be over, which was all I wanted when Chop went off the deep end, which was more and more often.

"And who are you?"

"I'm nobody. I am a prospect."

"What about the rest?" Chop prompted and my hands shook, my fear slowly turning to anger. I took a couple of deep breaths to try and suppress it. No good would come of me lashing out.

Just remember last time. Stay calm. A few more minutes. I told myself.

"Tell them what I have you tell me, you little twat. Tell them what you should already know, but seem to keep forgetting over and over again when you show me disrespect."

I glanced up at the men who all seemed to be amused, smiling and elbowing each other as if they were watching some sort of comedy show, all that is, except for one. A silver haired man in the back of the group stood straight faced, showing emotion that I could have easily have mistaken as sympathy if I thought a brother could have sympathy for a prospect.

I cleared my throat. "I am a prospect in the greatest MC in the state of Florida," I said through my teeth. "The Beach Bastards. I am not a son. I do not have a father. I am a soldier in the army of the lawless, and I am nothing more."

Chop grunted his approval, "Hopefully this will teach you a lesson you seem to have a hard fucking time learning. I do not need or want a son. What I need is a good fucking soldier." He released my cut and pushed me to my knees. Kicking me in the tailbone with his boot, I fell flat onto the floor, my cheekbone smashing against the black-and-white checkered linoleum. "Man the fuck up and start showing me some fucking respect before I send you to the same place I sent your cunt of a mother."

Chop stormed from the room, pausing to exchange a brief annoyed look with the silver haired man. The rest of the brothers resumed their drinking and their game like we were never there.

The silver haired man knelt down and extended out his hand, and I shot him a look that must have conveyed what I was thinking, which was 'is this a trick?' because he laughed, grabbed my hand and pulled me up off the floor. I put my hand over my face where my cheek throbbed, and judging from the new red stain on the white square I'd landed on, it was bleeding as well. "It get's better." He said, slapping me hard on the back.

"Does it?" I asked, and I genuinely wanted to know. *Needed* to know. I saw what the brothers had, and it was what I wanted. The parties. The girls. The bad-ass bikes.

A little fucking respect.

But at that moment I needed to know if what Chop was putting me through was really going to be worth it someday.

"Sure does, kid. I'm Joker," he said, leading me over to the bar.

"Joker?" I asked. "You a comedian or something?"

"Nah, I just really like Batman movies, but Batman didn't seem all that subtle a road name, so they started calling me Joker." He laughed, taking a swig of his beer. "I always liked the villains better, anyway." He signaled to the BBB behind the bar, and she handed him two bottles of beer. He slid one over to me.

"I ain't seen you 'round here before," I said, taking a swig. It was in no way my first beer. "I'm used to knowing most everyone who hangs around here."

He shrugged. "Figured since our clubs are friendly for this second in time, and we got some business going, thought I'd come check things out," he said, spinning around so I could see that his cut read Wolf Warriors instead of Beach Bastards.

"Your club treat your prospects like shit?" I asked, taking a seat on the stool I knew was already on the highest setting so I wouldn't embarrass myself by having to adjust the seat. I may have been the spitting image of my old man, complete with blond hair and ridiculous freckles, but at thirteen I'd barley hit even half of his height.

"Fuck yeah we do," he said with a laugh, taking a swig of his beer. He leaned in close and lowered his voice. "But we don't treat our *sons* like shit. Family is everything, kid. You remember that. *Family* is the entire point of all this fucking bullshit," Joker said, waving his beer bottle to everything around us.

Finishing my beer, I stood up and set it on the bar. "Well, Joker, you heard the Prez yourself. I'm not his son." I turned to leave, my shift at the gate about to start when something Joker said made me pause and spin back around.

"When the gavel is yours, kid, you'll change all this. It's in your blood. You'll make it right again. I know you will. I have faith in you."

I crinkled my nose. "Who are you again?" I asked the stranger who seemed to know not only who I was, but what I was destined for.

"I'm just a biker looking out, kid." He put a reassuring hand on my shoulder and gave me a squeeze. He looked at me thoughtfully and nodded his head like he was confirming something to himself before strolling out the door.

I never saw him again.

CHAPTER TWO

BEAR

ECHOES OF INMATES cries floated through the cell block at night. Most of these guys were hard gangsters by day and puddles of useless misery at night. It seemed that lights-out was the only time acceptable to wallow in the shitty hand you've been dealt.

Not me.

In my game I was both player and dealer, and I knew what cards I held before anyone else did.

Especially Ti.

It pained me to remember the look on her face when they slapped the cuffs on me she thought were meant for her. Her face scrunching up in confusion, followed by her eyes widening in surprise. When she called out for me I almost didn't look back, thinking that she might never forgive me for what I'd done. But I had to. One last time for only who knows how long. And when I did, I didn't expect her to leap into my cuffed arms and press those perfect pouty pink lips against mine.

Those fucking *lips*.

I thought time away from Ti would make me forget. Not about her, just about the little details. The things that might drive a man crazy when he couldn't be with the one he wants most. I thought that maybe as time passed her beautiful face would start to grow blurry and it would be harder for me to picture her. That maybe I wouldn't remember the incredible way she smelled.

Her soft moans.

The way her cheeks flushed when she was about to come.

No, that didn't happen.

What did happen was that I remembered everything, and in bright vivid detail. The more I thought about her the more I remembered.

With so much time on my hands, it was possible I remembered her in even more detail than I had when she was standing right in front of me. Like the way she shifted on her feet when she was uncomfortable. The way she bit the side of her thumb when she was nervous.

I'd never had the need to claim a bitch my entire life. But then I tasted her by the fire and I knew there was no turning back. Not for me. Not ever. That first time with her in the truck, I swear I was chanting MINE in my head as I pushed in and pulled out of her incredible pussy.

If I thought long and hard enough I could still smell her on me.

I often had to remind my cock of where we were and of the immediate threat at hand, because it was easy to get lost in the memories. Naked. Writhing. Panting.

Fuck.

AS EASY AS it was to get lost in the thoughts of her, it wasn't easy to forget about the immediate threat that could be looming beyond every turn. No cell was safe. No hallway. No bathroom. Not even the yard.

When Bethany told me they had enough evidence to arrest Ti, there was no way I was going to let them take her and spared no fucking second thought about taking her place. Which is all the more reason to make sure my guard is up and that each and every Bastard who thought they could come at me in County would end up mangled or dead. Didn't really matter because either way, it wouldn't be Ti.

Unable to sleep, I stood at the cell door and leaned against the bars. Across cell block, through the high window, the ONLY window, was the full moon obscured by thin passing clouds, offering the only glimpse of freedom I was sure to have for a long while.

If ever.

The D.A. announced shortly after I'd been arrested that they were pushing for the death penalty.

The clouds parted and the light of the moon lit up my cell like a spotlight. Oddly enough illuminating the graffiti on the cell block wall above the toilet.

BEACH BASTARDS, LOGAN'S BEACH was tagged in thick marker.

I sighed. Even in my fucking cell I couldn't escape their reach, even if it was only in ink form.

For now.

The Beach Bastards used to be more than just a motorcycle club, more than my home even. They were a brotherhood, bound by loyalty. At the time nothing compared to the feeling of belonging to something bigger and more important than myself.

Something I believed in with everything I had and was.

When I left the MC, I never thought I'd have that again, but

I was wrong. Although the packaging was a little different. Instead of leather and tattoos, it was a smart mouth and a body I wanted riding my face every fucking second of the day.

When I was a Bastard, I'd lived and breathed by a code. The very foundation the MC was built around.

Code dictated that although the Bastards might rip your eyeballs from the sockets in retaliation, they wouldn't kill your wife and kids in the process.

Innocents were left untouched.

That was until Chop laid his hands on my girl.

MY Thia.

The Bastards were now more like a terrorist organization, bound not by loyalty, but by the orders spewed from the mouth of a power-hungry, soulless tyrant. My brothers used to be soldiers, but somewhere along the line they turned into nothing more than obedient dogs tethered by Chop's very short leashes. The kind of thugs who do the dirty work, tag cells while they're inside, and contribute little more to the overall good of the club.

There was no more "good-of-the-club."

The brotherhood part of it was long gone, and in its place was a dictatorship dripping in motor oil, leather, and lies.

When I took off my cut, I didn't know who I was anymore. The man in me was lost throughout years of thinking that my old man was somehow more than a mere mortal because he was the one who held the gavel and passed down the orders.

Until Ti.

She made me realize that I didn't need the club to be a biker.

I can live and I can ride.

I can love and I can kill.

It was both the man and the biker in me who was going to put a bullet in Chop's skull and end this shit because I knew he'd never stop until I was in the ground.

"You first old man," I muttered to myself.

Code dictated that a brother couldn't kill another brother.

It was a good fucking thing I wasn't a Bastard anymore because if and when I got free of those cell bars, the hurt I planned to inflict upon my old man would make what Eli and his pussy ass men did to me look fucking tame by comparison.

Then there was the little matter of my mother suddenly coming back from the dead.

Sadie.

My mother's name was Sadie Treme. For some reason I hadn't remembered that until I found myself sitting across from her in the visiting room wondering how the fuck she was even alive.

The bitch could at least have given me the courtesy of staying dead.

I didn't trust it.

I didn't trust *her*.

I had enough shit going on without having to think about the woman who gave birth to me escaping the fucking reaper, only to crawl her way back to the land of the living.

Throughout the years I rarely allowed my thoughts to wander to the woman who gave birth to me. Chop said she was a traitor, so I believed she was a traitor. Rats didn't have a place in the club or a place among the living. "We don't give rats a second thought after they've been put down. Rats are pests and the only good rat is a dead rat." He'd said that the very night he'd caught Sadie trying to escape Logan's Beach with me in the passenger seat. Hours later, he dragged her into the woods and put her down like a fucking rabid dog.

What's weird is that I don't remember crying then. A son

should cry for his mom when she dies, shouldn't he? I racked my brain to try and remember any sort of tear shed, but the memories never came.

What did come back were other memories, like the way her long brown hair had almost touched her waist back then. The way her hazel eyes had lit up when my old man paid her any sort of attention. The way she never wore any makeup around her eyes, but her lips were always painted bright red. The way she never sung me lullabies, but was always humming tunes by Tanya Tucker and Waylon Jennings everywhere she'd go.

Those memories couldn't have been of the same Sadie who sat in front of me in that visitation center. No, the woman who twisted her fingers and kept peering down at her lap was just a shell of the free spirit I remember dancing to the Willie Nelson song she kept playing on repeat on the club jukebox.

She was alive and breathing, but there was something about her. Maybe it was her sunken cheeks or sallow complexion. Or maybe it was the defeated vibe she was giving off that made me wonder if maybe my old man had succeeded in killing her after all.

Sadie and Chop had gotten together when Sadie was only sixteen years old. She was a runaway turned club whore. Five short years after I was born she was gone and that was that.

Then there she was. Almost twenty five years later, sitting across from me, looking me over with her mouth agape as if I were the fucking ghost at the table.

"Why are you here?" I'd asked, not sure of where else to start the conversation or even if I wanted to have one.

"Honestly, I thought I knew and now, actually being here, I'm not really sure why I came," she'd said meekly, biting her lip and looking everywhere else but me.

"I thought you were dead," I countered, stating the obvious.

She nodded. "I thought I was, too. Turns out, I was wrong."

"What does that mean?" I was already over the vague answers, especially when all it caused were more fucking questions.

"It means when your father pulled the trigger I thought I was dead, but I woke up and was surprised then that I was alive as you are now, but I wasn't free. I was locked somewhere." She pinched the bridge of her nose, "but the details are fuzzy. I escaped, but honestly I don't even remember how. As soon as my mind started to clear, I sought you out."

"You think Chop kept you somewhere all this time?"

Sadie nodded. "Yes, but I don't know where."

"How the fuck didn't you know where you were for twenty fucking years? You don't think that sounds a little fucking crazy?"

Sadie lifted an arm onto the table, palm up, and pushed up her long sleeve. Her forearm was littered with pockmarks in varying stages of scarring from pink to white. "I do know it sounds crazy," she said, her eyes finally meeting mine, "but that's the truth."

"Say it is the truth, there is still the little matter of why the fuck he would do that," I pointed out. "Chop has a reason for everything, even the fucked up shit had a fucked up reason. This?" I said, using my hand to gesture to her arm. She pulled her sleeve back down. "I can't think of any reason for this."

Sadie continued to tug her sleeve over her hand. "The why doesn't matter now, Abel. It's not important anymore. The why doesn't let me move forward."

"So why aren't you already moving forward then? Why come? You don't think Chop will know you were here? He's got eyes everywhere, or did twenty-five years of being drugged and locked up make you forget all that?" I said sarcastically, throwing her ridiculous story back in her face. Bitch could have been a junkie who'd recently found sobriety and just wanted to make excuses for her absence in my life for the last three fucking decades.

Ding-dong motherfucker. Chop shot her. Came back out. Told everyone she was dead. Bitch looks alive to me so even if her story isn't the truth your old man is balls deep in whatever did happen. Ghost Preppy chimed in. I'd been hearing him a lot less since I met Ti and was glad the little fucker was still around. I placed my elbows on the table and covered my mouth with my hands to cover my smile.

Preppy was right, but there was no way I would ever know if she was telling the truth. I wouldn't put long and prolonged torture past Chop, but why would he lie to everyone about it? There was more to the story, and I didn't know if Sadie was lying, or if she truly didn't remember.

She cleared her throat and my eyes fell to her long hair which she was twisting in her hand. It was a lot longer than it was in my memory, touching her waist, and the almost black was now streaked with white. The wrinkles around her eyes were more prominent, her signature red lipstick was gone, her lips bare as well as the rest of her face.

"I signed in with a different name. Plus, after I leave here today, I'm disappearing. For good. I just…I just needed to come, I guess. I had to see you first before I was really gone for good this time." She picked at her nails.

I no longer had to hide my smile because it had disappeared as quick as it had come. "What do you expect from me? A big hug and an 'I missed you, Mommy'?" I leaned back and crossed my arms over my chest.

She ran her fingers over a long faded scar on her forehead

that ran into her hairline. She shook her head. "No, that's not what I was looking for by coming here. It was selfish of me to come, but I had to. I had to tell you what he'd done do me. You needed to hear what kind of man your father is."

"I know all to well what kind of man he is." I said, leaning forward.

Sadie shuffled in her seat. "I think he did it. Kept me alive I mean because he thought I told on the club, but I didn't. Maybe he thought death wasn't good enough a punishment. It wasn't good enough to end my life, he wanted to take it and make me suffer more instead of putting me out of my misery." Sadie sniffled and that's when I noticed her glassy eyes. "You know? I hope to Christ I never do remember what really happened. I pray that it always stays a mystery." She pushed her chair back from the table, scraping it along the linoleum, but remained seated. "Because something tells me there is nothing he did to me I'd want to remember." She wiped her cheek with the back of her hand and suddenly the void look from earlier was back. The sniffling stopped.

"Why the getup?" I asked, gesturing to the light blue scrubs she was wearing.

She glanced down and pinched the hem of the top. "If anyone questions who your visitor was, or if Chop gets wind, hopefully they will be looking for a nurse."

"Why even risk it at all?"

Sadie ignored my question. She sighed and looked up at my face like she was observing me. "You have his eyes," she said, staring right into my eyes. I shifted uncomfortably on the hard plastic chair. "You look so much like him, when you first came out I thought you were him."

"I'm nothing like him," I barked.

"You're in here," she argued.

"I'm here because I chose to be here. Don't get it twisted in that doped-up mind of yours. You don't know me. You don't know the shit I've done that's bad, and it's worse than you could ever imagine. You don't know the shit I've done that's good either, and it's better than you could ever know."

"It's for a girl," she said. It wasn't a question. The corner of her lip turned up in a half smile.

"So what if it is?"

"It means you might just be human after all." She pointed out. She seemed to relax, satisfied with her new discovery. "You got that from my side of the family, no doubt."

"Family?" I asked, scoffing at her casual use of a word she knew nothing about.

"I AM your family," she argued, "I just wanted to be—"

"I've got family," I interrupted. "You don't gotta be nothing."

"Andria? Is that who you're talking about?" she asked, I hated the way she said my half-sister's name, like it disgusted her. Andria was family, even though I hadn't seen her in many years. She was the product of a brief affair Chop had with a waitress in Georgia. Andria should thank her lucky fucking stars she wasn't born a boy because I had a feeling that if she would have been born with a dick she would've been wearing a cut just like me. "Yeah, but she's not who I was talking about."

She again looked down at her lap. "My Abel. My boy. I think that you and I should—"

"McAdams!" a deep voice bellowed. "Time's up. Stand," the guard ordered. By pulling on the back of my chair, he forced me to obey.

"You should know I'm not a Bastard anymore," I said to the

ghost of my mother. "I took off my cut and laid it at that motherfucker's feet. I might not be a monster, but I am a dead man, so I guess it's good you came to see me, even if you don't know why you came." I stood up, sliding the plastic chair against the concrete, startling Sadie who looked up at me with big hazel eyes filled with sadness and naivety, as if she was still the teenager who gave birth to me almost thirty years before. "Get a good look at me now while you can, *Mom*," I said, emphasizing "Mom" and holding my arms as wide open as the cuffs attached to my wrists would allow. "'Cause it might just be the last chance you're ever gonna get." The officer yanked on the chains connecting my cuffs, dragging me away from Sadie.

From my mother. Even thinking of her as my mother didn't feel right.

Because, I realized. I already had a mother, even if I didn't address her as mom she was someone who'd earned the title.

"Oh," I said, shouting back to Sadie over my shoulder, "And you can go wherever you need to go and disappear to because I already have a mom. Her name is Grace."

"Grace?" Sadie asked, sounding as confused as I was when she'd showed up. The guard buzzed me out of the room and lead me back to my cell. I don't know why I felt the need to be hateful toward her, but maybe it was because she'd come back from wherever she'd been and her first instinct was to run away. Maybe it was because no matter what had happened to her the fact was that she'd let Chop break her.

One thing was for fucking sure, it didn't matter what that motherfucker ever did to me.

I would never fucking break.

CHAPTER THREE

BEAR

THIRTY MINUTES AFTER the visit with Sadie, I was out in the yard thinking about our conversation about family when it occurred to me.

Dead men don't have families.

Suddenly, the thought of never having one with Ti, never seeing her grow round with my kid, hit me in the chest like I'd caught a fucking bullet.

A feeling I'd been familiar with a time or two.

Dizzy with the unwanted thought, I slipped up and hadn't been scanning the yard for potential threats like I should've been. The only bastard I'd seen since I'd been locked up was Corp, and considering the condition I left him in I knew at least he wouldn't be a threat again any time soon.

Or eating without the aid of a straw.

But they were coming. I knew that as well as I knew my own name. I could practically smell it in the air.

"You look like you could use one of these," a voice said. I snapped out of my Ti induced thoughts to find a black guy around my height, but double my body weight, his jumpsuit ripped at the collar and arms to make room for his protruding muscles.

"Thanks," I said tentatively, reaching for the smoke he extended out to me from the open pack. I figured if this guy was sent to kill me he'd already done it, probably by flexing my head between his forearm and bicep. The stranger lit a match and cupped his hand around the flame, lighting my smoke and then his own before waving out the match and tossing it into the grass. He set the pack on the table. "Keep 'em," he said.

"Thanks," I said, and although I was pretty sure he didn't want to kill me, I was still skeptical of anyone who was willing to do you favors in jail. Favors never came without a price.

"I'm Miller," the stranger said. "A mutual friend asked me to look out for you."

"Friend? Well that narrows it down then, because it seems like I don't got much of those these days," I admitted.

Miller straddled the bench of the plastic table and it bowed under his weight.

"It's important to have friends in a place like this. Word is a bunch of bikers caught a bullshit misdemeanor case and are on their way in. Our friend figures that reason is you." His voice was so deep it almost echoed when he spoke. He took a long drag of his cigarette. "Our mutual friend helped me out when I was in Georgia State, and I owe him one. Shit, I owe that motherfucker twenty at the very least. Figured that preventing a bunch of white boy Beach Bunnies, or whatever the fuck ya'll call yourselves, from carving you up ain't shit compared to what he did for me."

"I don't think I gotta guess who this friend of ours is anymore," I said taking one last drag of my cigarette and putting it out on the tabletop. King had done his three years up at Georgia State. He stood up and the bench kept the Miller shaped indent.

He stubbed his smoke out on the table. "He gave me a message for you."

"What would that be?"

Miller shielded his eyes from the sun. "He said not to get yourself killed and that the girl is safe."

Thank fuck. That meant King had her at the grove and that the protection I'd set up was with her. Ti staying at King's was not an option. Even though I was the easier target in jail, Ti could still be at risk and without me there to protect her, King's family was more at risk then ever. Although I told King he was taking her back home because it didn't look good for my confession if the DA could link us in any way. If King recognized differently I knew he'd insist that she stay, and I couldn't do that to him after he'd done so much for me.

"Guess I'm just in time," Miller said, tipping his chin to the fence on the other side of the yard. I stood and turned around just in time to see the gate slide open and three men enter the yard.

Three of my former brothers.

CHAPTER FOUR

THIA

TEN YEARS OLD...

IT TOOK ME two whole hours to convince Bucky to bike with me the twelve miles to the pawnshop. After kicking rocks around with his shoe for five minutes, I told him I'd give him my best rod and reel, and he finally agreed.

"How much will you give me for it?" I asked the tall scraggly man with ears that stuck out sideways. I stood on my tippy-toes so I could lean across the scratched glass display case that doubled as a counter and gave the man my best "I mean serious business" face. The man behind the cage on top of the counter wore a nametag that said TROY. Troy looked down at me with one eyebrow cocked like he'd never seen a ten-year-old walk into a pawnshop and try to negotiate before.

"What the heck are you doing, Thia?" Bucky asked, leaving the display of model cars he'd been ogling to join me at the counter. When I roped him into riding his bike to Logan's Beach with me, I forgot to mention the real reason why I wanted to go so badly. Bucky's eyes widened in horror as they darted to the object I'd plunked down on the counter. "That's your Donnie Mcraw buckle, Thia! You can't sell that!"

"It's mine, so I can do what I want with it," I argued. I'd won the buckle when I'd gone to the rodeo in LaBelle with Bucky and his dad last year. Well, not so much WON, seeing as I was the only eight-year-old even willing to try and ride the sheep, but they gave me a prize anyway.

"So?" I turned back to Troy who held the buckle in his hands. He turned it over and banged it against the counter.

"It's hollow," Troy pointed out. Grabbing a small glass tube he closed one eye and held up the buckle, examining it through the tube.

"I don't need cash. Just a trade," I said. "For that." I pointed to a chain in the display case. Troy didn't look to where I was pointing.

"This thing's silver coated. Ain't worth much. Sorry, nothing I can do for you," Troy said, taking the toothpick out of his mouth, pointing it as me as he spoke.

"What the heck do you even need that chain for?" Bucky asked.

I sighed, growing annoyed with his questions. "I got something I wanted to put on it, is all." I shrank back down onto flat feet and Troy slid my buckle back across to me, adding yet another scratch to the top of the glass case.

"What do you want to put on it?" Bucky asked.

"It's nothing," I said, my shoulders falling in defeat. I eyeballed the silver chain through the glass for the last time before turning back around to Bucky.

"*Tell Me!*" Bucky demanded.

I reached into my back pocket and produced the skull ring and held it up for him to see, but only briefly because I didn't want to lose it. I placed it back into my pocket, patting it to make sure it was in there.

"Where did you get that?" Troy asked suddenly, squeezing his lanky frame through the hatch in the cage as far as he could, his waist resting on top of the counter.

"Can't tell you that," I said, considering sticking my tongue out at him. "Come on, Bucky." I grabbed his arm and we turned to leave.

"Wait!" Troy called out. "I was being hasty. You seem like nice kids. The buckle for the chain is a fair deal."

"You didn't even see which one I was pointing to," I said, crossing my arms.

Troy shook his head. "Doesn't matter, actually, keep the buckle. We have too many chains anyway, now show me which one it was again." Troy slid open the case and grabbed the chain I pointed to. He tossed it through the cage as if I was going to bite off his hand. It hit the floor by my feet. I bent over to pick it up, dusting it off. "Are you sure?"

"I'm totally sure," Troy said, waiving us off. "Now run along and make sure that if anyone asks you that you tell them Troy at Premier Pawn was good to you, okay? You gonna tell them that, right?"

"Yeah," I said, although I didn't really think that anyone was going to ask me to rate my recent trip to the pawnshop anytime soon.

Troy nodded so hard I thought his head might fall off. "Good. Now off you go," He waved us off, snaking back down through the hatch in the cage, slamming it shut.

We left and Bucky was close on my heels as we rounded the building to where we'd left our bikes leaning up against the alley wall.

I took the skull ring from my pocket and slid it onto my new stainless steel chain, securing it around my neck. I popped the ring into my Future Farmers of America T-shirt.

"You gonna tell me what that is?" Bucky asked as we picked up our bikes.

"That's my secret," I said with a sly smile. The truth was that I had been dying to tell Bucky ever since Bear and his biker friends visited the Stop-N-Shop, but I wanted to wait until I was sure we were out of range of the ears of the small town gossips.

Which in Jessep, was pretty much everyone.

"I can keep a secret," Bucky said, keeping pace beside me as we walked our bikes toward the street.

I stopped and turned to Bucky. I held out my pinkie. "You have to pinkie swear first and only then I'll tell you, but only because you're my best friend and I know you won't tell anyone."

"I'm your *only* friend," Bucky reminded me, rolling his eyes.

"Don't make me punch you in the gut, BUCKY," I said. He might have been older than me, but he was small for his age. Kids made fun of his size as much as they made fun of me for my pink hair. We'd bonded over being outsiders in the second grade and became fast friends. And now we were swearing, the most sacred and serious promise in the world, so that I could tell him all about the blue-eyed man with tattoos who changed everything.

Bucky grabbed my pinky with his own. "You have to swear you won't tell a soul what I am about to tell you, and when you're old and grey that you will take this secret to your grave, and even then you won't tell like other ghosts and stuff," I said.

Bucky nodded, shook my pinky, and spit on the ground, sealing his swear. "I promise, now spill it Pinky," he sang, throwing my own hated nickname in my face. This time I did stick out my tongue as we dropped our pinkies.

We didn't get on our bikes when we got to the road. Instead, we pushed on the handlebars and continued to walk beside each other. I pulled the ring back out of my shirt so Bucky could see it, turning it over so he could get a good look of the skull.

"Is that a real diamond."

"I think so," I said, unable to help the huge smile that spread across my face.

"So how'd you get it?" Bucky asked.

"This here?" I asked, holding up the chain, "This is a promise."

"Like a pinkie swear?"

I shook my head. "Nope, it's way more powerful than that."

"How'd ya get it? You steal it? Looks like it cost a lot of money." He reached out to touch it and that's when I tucked it back into my shirt.

"No, I didn't steal it," I corrected. "It was *given* to me."

After a long dramatic pause, Bucky shrugged and waved his hand around. "By who? You gonna tell me or not, Thia?"

I patted the ring under my shirt as I recalled the day Bear walked into my life. In my excitement, I may have embellished a little, not realizing then how close to the truth I really was. "This ring was given to me by the biggest and strongest man in the whole wide world. He could've given it to anyone he wanted, and he chose *me*. It means that we're linked…forever."

Bucky's voice got all high, like I'd just punched him in the nuts. "Forever?"

Just then, an older man riding a motorcycle, a big silver one with a tall windshield flew by us on the road. A small woman with grey hair sat low next to him in a sidecar. We fanned the dust away from our faces, and while Bucky was busy coughing, I watched the bike drive off, completely fascinated and in awe of the sound it made, how fast it was going, and how the old lady looked so comfortable in her little seat she could've been knitting instead of barreling at break neck speeds. I stared after it until long after it had disappeared around the bend.

I turned back to Bucky and smiled my biggest smile.

"Yep. Forever."

Chapter Five

THIA

There isn't much out there in the world that scares me. Life is way too scary to waste time being afraid of the unknown when the known is frightening enough. I was never scared of the boogie monster or anything lurking under my bed or in my closet at night when I was a kid.

The only thing I was scared of were things that could actually happen.

Like tornadoes.

It's not like Jessep, Florida, my hometown, ever saw the kind of tornadoes that inflicted real catastrophic damage. The kind we got were the small ones. The occasional shingle-shifter or tree-toppler.

Yet somehow, all of my nightmares since Bear went away have revolved around the descending spirals of doom. Leveling buildings, farms, towns…

Lives.

The afternoon storms had been rolling in with a vengeance over the past several days. Darker. More menacing. Like they were trying to send me a message of darker days ahead.

The clouds were at war with the sky, just like I felt as if I was at war with myself. Love and hurt both existing in equal measure inside me. It turned physical and after a few days had developed into a devastating full body ache.

A dark line of clouds approached, encroaching on the blue sky as the afternoon's impending storm made itself known. Rolling and billowing toward me, my nightmare coming to life.

I was swept up in the fear that—at any second, I was certain—spiraling clouds would descend from the sky right above my head. I found myself waiting for the moment that the tornado was going to strike and inflict more damage than most people could possibly imagine.

Than most people could handle.

I could almost feel the wind, the wreckage. The sensation of being picked up and slammed back down over and over again.

To me, a tornado has always been the force of nature capable of the most damage.

Until I met a force of nature that would make a tornado seem like a morning breeze. One that picked me up, made me feel like I could soar as it tossed me around, sent me reeling, and threw me back down to the ground, leaving me broken and fighting for my life.

And his.

Bear.

Before my brother died and well before my mother went off the mental deep end, my father used to stay out in the orange grove late into the night. I'd assumed he was fixing the always broken irrigation system or any of the other run-down and failing equipment.

One night I grew curious and snuck out of the house, but instead of finding him attached to the generator or the broken pipes, I found him on his knees in the dirt. The full moon shining down on his face, illuminating his watery eyes as he looked up at the trees as if they were more than just fruit on branches.

It wasn't even the sight of him talking to the trees that surprised me.

It was that he was begging them.

Begging for a good harvest. For the Sunnlandio Cooperation to miraculously increase the contract, for gas prices to drop, for the workers to stop striking for more money, for the forecasted record frost to skip over our farm.

Then finally, for my mother to love him again.

My heart broke for him right there.

That was the night I realized that all the "Everything is fine, sweetheart" remarks my father gave me every night at the dinner table was the lie I'd always suspected it was.

On some of those nights when my dad was out late, my mother would come and drag me from my bed and into hers. We'd cuddle up and watch cheesy romantic comedies.

It was those movies, and not my parents' cold/colder relationship, that gave me my first glimpse into what love was. I got so upset when the couple faced an obstacle that could prevent them from being together. I lived for the big romantic gesture at the end. The one that would finally bring them together forever.

Every single time when the movie ended and the credits rolled, my mother would sigh and brush my hair off my forehead. "You know that none of that is real, right? Movies are make-believe. That kind of love doesn't exist."

Unrealistic is what she'd call it.

Except, that was another lie, even if she didn't know it at the time.

Because that kind of love did exist.

What I felt for Bear had simmered under the surface since I was ten years old, and when we met again, albeit under shitty circumstances, it had exploded into something more powerful than any cheesy romance could ever depict.

With one major difference.

Our story didn't have a happy ending.

There was no chasing after me on horseback or confessing our feelings to one another in front of a crowd of teary-eyed people.

No, our story ended with Bear in jail, hell-bent on taking the rap for the murders of my parents, which my mother was ultimately responsible for.

When Bear's lawyer, Bethany Fletcher, explained that Bear had signed a confession to spare me from facing the same threat from his former brothers, one that he himself now faced within the walls of the county jail, I didn't want to believe it.

He threw himself onto the fire for me.

King is taking you home.

Stay there. Wait.

Trust me.

Bethany passed me a note in Bear's handwriting minutes after he'd been arrested while I was still looking down the road as if he'd be back at any moment. I held on to it with shaky hands and turned it over and over wondering where the rest of it was.

"I don't understand," I said to Bethany through my teary eyes.

"Do what he says," she'd said, you don't need to understand. You just need to listen.

"Why did he do this?" I asked.

Bethany cocked an eyebrow at me like I should already know the answer. "The reason why any man does anything foolish and ridiculous. For love, of course."

"It's not safe for him there. We need to get him out!"

"Thia," Ray said, coming to stand beside me. "Don't you see? They were going to arrest you. Bear's at least got a fighting chance where you wouldn't. He grew up in the club. He knows how to handle himself. He knows what he's doing. Bethany's right. As hard as it is, you have to trust him, and in the meantime she's going to do everything she can to get him home. We all will."

King came to stand beside Ray and placed his hand on her shoulder.

I shook my head. "It should be me. He didn't do anything. I did!" I turned to Bethany. "I'm the one who shot my mother. I'm the one who killed her. It should be me! Please, we can't let him—"

Bethany clucked her tongue and waved her index finger back and forth. "That's not what happened, my dear. Bear crashed his bike into their grove. He went up to the house to use their phone since his had no service. When he got up to the house, your mother was standing outside ranting about killing your father, waving a shot gun around. Bear grabbed a pistol from the porch and shot her with it in self defense before fleeing."

"That's not what happened," I said flatly.

"According to his confession that's exactly what happened," King said. "You need to trust him."

Trust?

Trust is a funny thing. Especially when both my patience and my sanity had already reached their limit, and the man I love had been arrested for something I did, leaving me with an empty heart and an infuriating note, ordering me to go back to the place I hated most in the world. I trusted him and I knew in my heart he was doing what was best for me.

What I didn't trust was that he wasn't going to get himself killed in the process.

"Get some rest. I'm taking you back in the morning," King said, and that was that.

I didn't even try to sleep right away, knowing full well it would be impossible when I would probably still be able to smell Bear on the sheets. Instead, I sat in the same little rowboat where Bear confessed his feelings for me, except this time, I left it tied to the seawall, not having the strength to fight the current.

I took a swig of the half empty bottle of Jack I'd found in the garage apartment and looked out over the water of the bay. The amber liquid burned my mouth and throat, bypassing my newly broken heart and igniting a fire in my stomach.

With each swig, I swore I could still taste Bear's lips on the bottle.

It was late. The air was stagnant. The humidity so high that little drops of water beaded up on my arms and dripped into the creases of my elbows.

Everything happened so fast, yet it was like no time passed at all.

How was that even possible?

How long had I even known Bear before he decided to sacrifice himself for me?

Days? Weeks? Months?

Time blended together until it slowed to a stop and I watched in horror as Bear was dragged away.

It hurt that he didn't tell me what his plan was although I understand why he didn't tell me.

He knew there was no way in hell I would have let him do it. If I would have known, I would have driven to the sheriff's station and beat him to the confession.

It's not like I loved him from the moment I first laid eyes on him. No, I was a just a kid, but I was infatuated. Something inside me changed that day. It may not have been love, but more like an extension of myself walked through that door. From that day on, with Bear's skull ring tucked under my shirt, it was like I could breathe.

Like I was complete.

I'd reached for Bear's ring every time Erin Flemming bullied me in the fifth grade, and I drew strength from it on the day I'd finally had enough and socked her square in the stomach. I was sent home from school and didn't even flinch when my mother grounded me for a month.

It had been totally worth it.

I'd rubbed it for good luck before my shooting matches. I still held the record for most blue-ribbons in three counties. And late at night, I laid in my little twin bed, and held it against my lips, wishing it could somehow make my parents stop fighting.

Even after I learned that the promise I'd been wearing around my neck for eight year's was an empty one, I was no less elated when Bear had given it back to me.

I pulled the ring out of my shirt and looked down at the one eyed skull. The light of the moon reflected off the diamond, making it look as if it were winking up at me.

The longer Bear was in jail, the more likely it was that he was never coming back out, yet no one would tell me exactly what it was I was supposed to be waiting for.

My heart twisted and bile rose in my throat, the whiskey burned its way back up just as it had burned on the way down.

I couldn't linger on that thought. I couldn't let my mind go there.

But I couldn't just *wait* either.

Promise me that no matter what, you won't give up on me. Promise me, Ti.

Fuck waiting.

I launched the bottle into the air with a guttural roar. It spun around and around until landing in the bay with a splash, causing a ripple in the glass-like surface of the water. By the time the ripple reached the boat, I decided that although I trusted Bear, there was no way in hell I was just going to sit back and let his fate rest in the hands of others. I was going to do something at the very first opportunity.

I just had to figure out what exactly that something was.

CHAPTER SIX

THIA

I'M IN BEAR'S *apartment. It's late. Too late for the burner phone on the nightstand to be ringing. I roll over and answer it.* "Hello," *I say, my voice scratchy and rough from sleep. I clear my throat and the voice on the other end chuckles.*

Chills break out down my spine and I sit straight up in bed.

"Baby, it's me. Don't say a fucking thing. Just let me talk. There is so much I need to say to you but I don't know where to fucking start. I'll just start with this. I think about you. Even though it's only been hours I miss you more than I've ever missed anything. I never knew what missing anything even meant until now. I don't know when we are going to be able to talk again, so I wanted to tell you all of this now, while I still can. Are you still there, Ti?"

"Yes," *I say breathlessly.* "Yes, I'm here."

"I love the way you moan when I make you come. I love the way you get wet just from hearing my voice. But I'm also going to miss the way you chew the ends of your hair when you don't know what to say. I'll miss the way you look at me like you're trying to figure me out, when really I'm a simple guy, I'm usually just thinking about how fucking gorgeous you are and how to get you naked. I'll miss the way you always say you're never hungry when I ask, but then eat half of whatever it is I'm eating. I'll just miss you. I do miss you. I miss the way you make me feel like a person of the world, instead of a problem in it.

"Until you, I felt like nothing. I was nothing. You gave me everything and I plan to do the same for you. You're too good for me, but I plan to make that up to you with how good I'm going to be for you. With you. Because of you.

I remain silent as I was told, but I can't silence the tears forming in my eyes.

"The world was dark and you turned on the fucking light switch and now it's so bright, I'm walking around blind. I'm in fucking jail...and I've never been happier. How fucking ridiculous is that? I sound like such a pussy, but in case something happens to me, I just thought you should know all this. You NEED to know all of this."

"I—" Bear cuts me off.

"No, no talking. I'm crouched in a corner of the most disgusting bathroom I've ever been in, in the middle of the night, talking on a burner phone I fished out of an air conditioning vent, so please, Ti, just listen."

I nod as if he can hear it.

"I have a confession. Every time we've fucked, I've come inside of you. I've been in here for months, longer than you and I've been...well, whatever we've been. I'll be really fucking disappointed if you're not pregnant. If and when I get out of here, I plan on fixing that. I plan on filling you with so much of me that you have no fucking choice but to carry my kid.

"I may not ever be a good man, baby, but unlike my piece of shit old man, I think I'd be a good dad. I want a girl. Pink hair, just like you.

I cover my mouth so Bear won't hear my sob and hold the phone away for a second so I can sniffle.

"Don't worry about me," he continues, his voice cracking ever so slightly. "And for fuck's sake do what you're fucking told. There is a *plan in place. Bethany is working on getting me out. But it's gonna take time. Trust me. Trust us. Can you do that for me, baby? Can you trust me?"*

Yes. I can.

"Now we can talk, tell me something about you. Something I don't know. Something that's not jump-off-a-bridge depressing 'cause there ain't a lot of shit in here worth smiling at."

I smile into the phone and say the first thing that comes to mind. "I've always wanted a dog. A big one. We had one when I was younger, a Great Dane. My parents never let me get another one after he died, but I've always wanted one."

"I'll get you one, baby. The biggest one they've got. The second I get out."

"Do you really think you're coming home?" The question is twofold. Is he really going to get out? And will he really be able to survive this?

"I don't really know that. But I know this, a lot of people in my life have tried to take me out when I had nothing to live for and they've never succeeded, and I see that as a good thing."

"I don't understand," I say.

"It means now that I have something to live for, they are going to have to come after me with a fucking nuke strapped to their chests in order to take me out, 'cause I'm not going anywhere, Ti. I'm not leaving you. Not now. Not ever. I promise."

"I believe you," I say, because I do.

"Now tell me where you are," Bear says, his voice dropping an octave. *"Are you in our bed?"* he asks and there is something about his voice mixed with the OUR BED that already has me laying back on the bed and snaking my hand down the front of my stomach.

"I'm in our bed," I say, practically purring.

"Panties and a tank top?" he asks, citing my preferred sleeping attire.

"Yes," I say.

"Good, now listen to me, baby. You remember that first time I took you in the truck? Remember how I pushed my cock inside of you. You were so tight, I think it hurt me more than it hurt you when you gave me your sweet virgin pussy."

I snake my hand down lower. "I remember," I say and it almost comes out as a moan as I dip my fingers into my panties.

"Are you touching yourself?" Bear asks.

"Yes, I am."

"Good girl," he says, his voice straining. "Push your panties down and spread your legs for me."

I tear off my panties and spread my legs wide as if he were between them viewing what's his. "Okay," I say.

"Do you remember the first time I tasted you? The first time my tongue touched your clit, your pussy? Do you remember what it felt like when I fucked you with my tongue until you couldn't take any more?"

Closing my eyes, I circle my clit with two fingers remembering in vivid detail every single thing that Bear is mentioning. His warm wet tongue, the tightening in my lower stomach when he relentlessly fucked me with it. Faster and faster I circle until I'm already close to the edge. "Yes," I say.

Bear chuckles. "Keep those legs spread wide. Remember what it felt like to hold on to my hair while my face was between your thighs." Closer and closer I inch toward the edge, faster and faster I circle my clit. Then harder, until even the slightest of breezes might tip me over. "Bear," I moan, "I'm so. I'm so…"

"I can't wait to do that again. But I'm not going to let you come on my tongue next time," Bear says, and suddenly I'm disappointed.

"You're not?"

"No, because just when you are about to come in my mouth, I'm going to sit up and pull you onto my cock and slam into you. I'm going to fuck you. HARD. Until we're both fucking screaming and coming, and coming some more."

I fall, I fall, and I fall, and just as I am about to crash over the edge into the most beautiful orgasm I've ever had using my own hand, there is a commotion in the background. "Fuck. I gotta go, Ti."

"Wait," I pant, my eyes spring open. "When are you...?" I say, unsure of what exactly I'm going to ask.

"Love—" The "you" is cut off and the line goes dead. I hang my head between my knees. "He's going to be okay," I say aloud, trying to reassure myself.

I am high. I am sad. I am happy. I am anxious.

The phone call with Bear makes me one thing I haven't been since he's been gone and that is the thing I want to cling to until the second he's with me again.

Hopeful.

I hang up the phone and hand it back to King who puts it in his mouth and swallows it in one big gulp.

That's how I knew the entire call was nothing more than a dream. The reality was that Bear had issued a no-contact rule. I was not to reach out to him and he was not to reach out to me. No calls. No visits. King explained that visiting the man in jail who was accused of murdering my parents didn't make me look like the innocent Bear was trying to make me out to be.

When I opened my eyes, it really was King who was standing over me, his ginormous body cast in dark shadows, no evidence that he'd ingested any electronic devices. Thankfully, unlike my dream, I was fully dressed in a T-shirt and sweats, although I was still breathing hard, not yet fully recovered from the orgasm I'd almost had in my sleep. "Time to go home."

Home? I sat up and rubbed my eyes. King instructed me to

meet him outside in ten minutes and left the room. I tossed the covers off and made my way to the bathroom to take a shower.

A cold shower.

Home.

Where the fuck is that?

CHAPTER SEVEN

BEAR

A HORN BLASTED overhead, calling yard time to an end and not a moment too soon. Miller and I went to the nearest exit, never taking our eyes off our new company. "Not you, McAdams," the guard manning the gate said, pushing me back out into the yard after Miller had already gone back in.

"What the fuck?" Miller asked, looking back as the guard slid the gate closed leaving me alone in the yard with my three former brothers who were making their way across the yard. Miller shot me a sympathetic look as another guard shooed him back inside the building.

"Thought you guys needed a moment alone. A little reunion of sorts," the guard said with a sneer.

"Fuck you," I spat, the mother fucking guard knew exactly what the fuck he was doing and I had no doubt he'd been paid off to do it. "Why don't you come in here and we'll see how fucking funny you think this is." The guard chuckled at the hilarity of three against one, twirling a set of keys around on his fingers. With a mock salute he followed Miller back into the cellblock, whistling as he went. The heavy door echoing across the yard as it slammed shut.

I cracked the bones in my neck, preparing myself for the fight of my life. I met the pussies at the picnic table I'd just vacated, and to my surprise, Wolf leaned against the table while Stone and Munch took seats. I'd kind of just assumed they'd get on with it already. Although Miller had just given me a pack of smokes, when I spied a pack in the front pocket of Wolf's jumpsuit, I reached in and plucked it out along with a book of matches. "Thanks for the smoke," I said, lighting one and tossing the matchbook onto the table. "You girls ready to try and do this, or what?"

Try being the most important word.

I wasn't scared of these motherfuckers. The only fear I really had was not seeing Ti again.

I was more annoyed than anything.

Agitated.

All those years and all that time wasted trying to make my brothers better outlaws and this was the best plan they could come up with? "I swear I taught you bitches better than this," I said, shaking my head. "Taking me out in an open yard in front of a shit ton of cameras. Chop's been losing his fucking touch for years, but I expected more than this sloppy shit from you three." I expected them to stand up, puff out their chests, and make their threats against me.

Something.

Munch and Stone looked to the ground while Wolf lit his own cigarette. Before the flame met the paper, I punched him in the eye, and he immediately dropped to the ground.

I was always better at offense.

"Chop sent us, but we ain't here to take you out, fucker," Wolf said, rolling on the ground with his hand over his eye.

"Then what the fuck did he send you here for? A fucking

tickle fight?" I breathed out the smoke through my nose, and although I had no idea how the next few minutes were going to play out, I felt relaxed amongst the familiar conflict.

At peace.

At home.

Adrenaline built as each second ticked by until I was positive I could flip a fucking truck over if I had the chance.

Or take on three guys at once and win.

"No, he did send us here to take you out, but that's not what we're gonna do," Munch said, standing up and helping Wolf off the ground.

"You're going to go against your Prez's orders?" I clucked my tongue against the roof of my mouth. "Now I'm actually disappointed. I must have been a real shitty teacher for you guys to make that kind of call."

"We ain't going against Prez's orders," Stone chimed in, standing up from the bench, "'Cause he ain't our fucking Prez anymore."

"Come again?" I asked, unsure of what weird alternate universe I'd just stepped into.

Wolf released his eye, which was already starting to swell, and unzipped his jumpsuit. Pushing it down, he revealed his bare chest, which used to be covered with a full chest piece tattoo of the Bastards' logo. Now, it was an oozing wound, tissue and strands of damaged skin stretched across his chest, only a fraction of the tattoo remained.

He winced as he zipped back up.

"What the fuck? Chop do that?" I asked, pointing with my cigarette to Wolf.

He shook his head as both Munch and Stone revealed their own recently burned off tattoos. "No, he didn't. We did. We all did."

"Why?" I asked, standing there in complete disbelief that three of the Bastards' most loyal soldiers had turned on their club. "What the fuck did Chop do that made you feel like you had to go all pyro on yourselves?"

"Stone, tell him…" Munch said with a reassuring nod. "He's gotta know if we plan on making this right."

"I can't man," Stone said, punching his open palm and shaking his head. His eyes became glassy and he sucked in his lips, rocking back and forth slowly like he was willing the memories of whatever he didn't want to tell me. Stone got his name because when it came to taking people out he was a stone cold killer. The type of guy who barely had his gloves off, the body still warm, when he'd pipe up and say 'I'm hungry, who wants a sandwich?' To see him reduced to almost tears made me very curious about what the fuck it was they wanted him to tell me.

"You can do it, man. Just tell him," Wolf said.

"The BBBs, they're just fucking whores," Stone said like he was reminding himself of that fact.

"Really? Is that what Em was to you? Just a fucking whore?" Wolf snapped, kicking his foot up onto the bench resting his elbow on his knee.

"Fuck! No," Stone said, dropping his forehead to the table and running his hands over his shaved head, the black triton tattoo on his temple shimmered with beads of his sweat. "She was… Shit!" Stone stood up so abruptly he almost took the table with him. "They're just supposed to be whores. Hangers-on. You know that. We all fucking know that." Stone paced back and forth as he spoke, wringing out his hands and looking between the grass and me. "They're there to suck and ride cock without question. If they question, they are out. They can't say no. They can't deny a brother. Those girls lived for the party. For the adventure of the club."

"Yeah, until they stopped living altogether," Munch chimed in, lighting a cigarette.

"What the fuck are you guys getting at?"

Stone looked at me straight faced but there was more pain in his eyes, more emotion, then I'd ever seen from him and I'd known him for over ten years. "What I'm getting at is Em."

"Em?" I asked, not recalling a BBB by that name.

"Yeah. She had jet-black hair and weird purple grey eyes. She came to the club shortly after you left. She had nowhere else to go, her mom died in some sort of accident. Anyway, after the parties when everyone was all passed out we talked. She wasn't like the others. She listened. She actually liked me. We grew kinda close." He breathed out a sigh. "Too fucking close. She was my girl. Despite what she fucking did with the other brothers before she came to my room at night she was still my fucking girl."

"So what the fuck happened?" It wasn't the strangest thing I'd ever heard. Over the years I'd seen a few BBBs become old ladies. It was no secret that Sadie was one of them.

"Chop caught wind of it, although it's not like we were keeping it a secret. He found out that I planned to take her out of the club and the life, and set her up in a place. He shouldn't have cared. Tons of brothers have done it before. He didn't even know her fucking name. But just like with all the other codes or club law Chop had been adding or taking away to suit his own damn moods, suddenly a club whore as an old lady was forbidden."

"Keep going," I said, although I was pretty sure I knew exactly how the story was going to end. Because with Chop all the stories ended the same way and most of the people in the stories were no longer breathing.

Wolf lit a cigarette and passed it to Stone, who continued. "Chop called me into his office. He asked me to close the door. I did and took a seat and that's when I noticed the stilettos poking out from under his desk. I knew it was Em. I'd bought her those fucking shoes." He paused and ran his hand over his mouth. "I asked him what he needed, although I felt like I was gonna either puke or fucking kill him or both. The fucker smiled the entire time. He made me wait. He knew was he was torturing me and he was enjoying it."

"Cock sucker," Munch said, banging his fist on the table.

"I racked my brain to think of what I could have done to ask for this type of punishment but I came up blank," Stone said. He sat down on the bench again, dropping his head to the tabletop and spoke to the floor. "I was a good soldier. I was the best soldier. I never asked questions. I did what I was told."

"Tell him the rest. It's almost over," Wolf said.

Stone took a drag of his cigarette and a tear fell from the corner of his eye. The guy whistled while killing and he was crying over a club whore? It made no sense. "Then he told me that he didn't need anything from me but that he had something for me. I asked him what he had. He told me it was a lesson."

Stone bit his lip and his face grew redder and redder as his sadness turned to anger. My own heart started pounding. "I panicked because I left my side arm in my room, but I never figured I'd ever need it against my own life with Prez 'cause I was a good soldier," he repeated. "Real fucking good."

"I know you were, brother," I said.

"He grabbed a fistful of her hair and yanked her mouth off of his dick. 'Don't be rude, Em. Say hello to our guest.' She turned to look at me and her lips were still all wet from him. Her eye was swollen and her bottom lip was split open with blood dripping down her chin. I thought I was going to be sick right fucking there until I saw the fear in her eyes. It wasn't just fear though. It was like she was blank. Like she'd already given up. Whatever happened before I got in there had to have been bad enough to make her think there was no fucking way out. I think that might have been the most brutal thing of all. Because she was right." Stone was now sobbing.

Munch put his arm around his shoulder. "We'll get that motherfucker, I promise."

Stone continued through the tears. "He told me that what he wanted was for his soldiers to be soldiers and not fall in love with the 'cum-dumpsters' every single brother in this place had sprayed his shit on a hundred times. I asked him why he was doing this. I didn't understand. He was my Prez. A fucking king to me. The Bastards took me in off the street and gave me something to believe in. I wouldn't have ever crossed him, no matter what. Even when you left and I thought he was wrong, I stayed by his side. Not because I thought he was right, but because you taught me not to question my Prez, so I didn't."

"Skip to the end," I said. I hated that I had to wait for what I already knew was coming.

"'Because whores aren't your family,' Chop said. 'Your brothers are your only family. Whores are fucking disposable.' I didn't even realize he had a gun in his lap until he held it to her head 'See? I just came down her fucking throat' he said, 'and this whore thanks me by bleeding on me.' Then he pulled the fucking trigger."

"Fuck!" I said. Now I stood up and started pacing.

"That's not all," Wolf said. Leaving Stone and Munch on the

bench as he walked over to me and lowered his voice like he didn't want to upset Stone any further.

"How is that not all of it? That cocksucker killed Stone's old lady right in front of him to teach him some sort of sick lesson about his views on family?"

"Not even close to all of it."

"Just fucking tell me already," I said, thinking about how Chop roughed up Ti made my own stomach start to churn. It could have been her. He could have killed her.

"He didn't just kill Em," Wolf said, looking back at Stone who was face down between his elbows.

"He killed another one?" I asked, wondering why the fuck Chop would kill two BBBs.

Wolf shook his head. "No, brother...he killed them *all*."

"Holy Fuck," I said, taking a seat on the bench. Wolf sat next to me.

"We took off our cuts and burnt the fuck out of our skin because a Prez, a real Prez, wouldn't do that kind of shit. He wouldn't kill people you love," Wolf said, looking me square in the eye so I could see he was telling the truth. "And I get it now. Why you left. 'Cause he asked you to chose between the club and people you think of as family and that shit ain't right." He shook his head. "It ain't fucking right."

"Executed," Munch piped in. "In the court yard, one by fucking one. We tried to stop him. He shot a prospect in the leg and told us to mind our own fucking business while he took care of his."

"Why the fuck would he kill BBBs?" I asked, thinking of the innocent fucking girls whose only crime was wanting to be part of a world they shouldn't have wanted to be a part of.

"We got no clue. All we know is that he called them all out

into the courtyard and put a gun to their heads. He kept yelling at them, asking them where *she* was, and when they would ask who he was talking about or tell them that they didn't know, he'd lay them out and kick their bleeding bodies into the pool."

I held my face in my hands. "He didn't stop until they were all gone," Wolf said, lighting another cigarette with the one in his hand.

"It happened so fucking quick. One minute he was fine and the next minute he was murdering all the club whores. When he was done, he walked around muttering and then locked himself in his office. When he came back out, he acted like nothing had happened. He told the prospects to clean up the mess and he played a game of pool. It was real fucking bazaar," Munch said.

"He killed my old lady," Stone wailed.

I pulled on my beard and glanced over to Stone. "Chop's been trying to go after my old lady since before she was even mine," I admitted. "I can't tell you I know how you feel brother, but I can tell you how it feels to be afraid of that happening every fucking second of the day." Remembering the bloodied mess Gus had dropped off at King's doorstep that was Ti made me grit my teeth until I thought they'd crack.

"First of all, I'm shocked as shit that you, of all fucking people, have an old lady, but we'll talk about that shit when we have less pressing matters beating on our fucking doorstep," Wolf said, with a small smile that reminded me of how close we used to be. The familiarity of us sitting at a table, no matter how shitty the subject was we were discussing, was a welcome feeling.

"There are nine of us. Nine who burnt off our tats the night after the BBB thing. The three of us, Gus, Chump, and a few of the others. When Chop gave the orders to come here and take you out, it was the perfect opportunity," Munch said, looking around to make sure no one was listening. There was only one guard and he was by the gate on the other side of the yard where they had come in. Well out of earshot.

"Opportunity for what?" I asked, still unsure of why they would follow Chop's orders to come to County if they were no longer Bastards.

"Chop wants to go to war with you," Munch stated. He held out his open hands and stretched his arms out to his sides. "You're gonna need an army."

Stone looked up from his arm for the first time. "We're your army."

"I appreciate that, but if that war ever happens it might be in here because I got something in the works to get me out, but if it doesn't come through I'm looking at hard fucking time," I said, wiping the beading sweat off my forehead.

"You in here because of the girl, aren't you?" Munch asked. "'Cause killing two civilians ain't really your style."

"Yeah." I inhaled deeply, needing the nicotine more than ever. "Better me than her. Would fucking do it again in a heartbeat. I signed a confession, so it don't look like I'm going nowhere anytime soon."

"You leave that to us, brother," Munch said with a slick smile. The kid could always figure his way around shit, so I wouldn't put it past him to really be able to get me out somehow. "We already have something in the works."

"What Munch means is that a chick he used to bang got herself a job sorting evidence for the county," Wolf said.

"That right?"

"Yep, and it seems that the guns used in the murders have just up and disappeared," Munch said, making a poof with his hands. It's not like those guns had my prints on them, but it was still enough to cause a big ripple in the prosecution's case.

"They still have my signed confession."

Wolf laughed. "They don't anymore. Funny thing about that too. The prosecutor assigned to the case seems to have lost all traces of it. And the judge—being old and senile and not to mention deeply in debt to us for running his daughter's fiancé out of town—swears he never even saw it." He winked.

Wolf shook his head and smiled. "We also think that hot shot, shady as fuck lawyer of yours had the coroner's report altered to say a whole bunch of conflicting things about the murder. She filed for a case dismissal, so now we just wait."

Munch cracked his knuckles and slid an unlit cigarette behind his right ear. "That bitch is shady as fuck, and I'd like to show her how much I appreciate the way she looks in those tight skirts by way of fucking her cougar ass sideways. She prosecuted a couple of cases where I wound up on the wrong side of the courtroom, and I swear I didn't care how much time I got as long as she kept bending that fine ass over her table to sort through her papers."

The three of us laughed and even Stone smiled briefly. It all felt normal.

Well, as normal as I'd ever known.

Somehow I had a feeling that it wouldn't be the last time Bethany Fletcher and I would be working together.

The prospect of getting out and seeing Ti made my heart beat stronger, faster, and more powerful.

And then suddenly it hit me.

"I think I know how to get to my old man," I said, taking a long slow drag from my smoke, my thoughts firmly on my surprise visitor from that very morning.

"How?" Munch asked, leaning in close.

"Not how. WHO," I said.

"Okay who?" Wolf asked, also leaning in.

"You said Chop was asking the BBBs where SHE was." I stubbed out my smoke and pulled on my beard. "I think I know who SHE is."

In the yard of the county jail on a day where the sun relentlessly beat down on us like it was trying to punish the occupants of the earth, a broken piece of me was put back together.

"So what do you say, brother? You want some new soldiers, so we can all wear a cut again? So we can all believe in shit again?" Munch asked, stubbing out his smoke. "We can be our own club, do shit right this time."

I cracked my knuckles. "I ain't putting a fucking cut on again. That part of me is fucking dead. I won't be your leader. I won't be your Prez, but I'll be a soldier with you. We'll go to fucking war together, and we'll bring that motherfucker down."

We may not have been an official MC.

But we were officially at war.

CHAPTER EIGHT

THIA

"I THOUGHT YOU were taking me to the grove," I said as King pulled up at a motel off the highway, halfway between Jessep and Logan's Beach.

"I am, but Bear didn't want you to be alone out there. He called someone to watch over you. We're meeting here."

"Who?" I asked, but King was already out of the truck and opening one of the motel room doors.

We waited for what seemed like hours, but in reality was probably only minutes when a knock came at the door. King placed his index finger over his lips. He slowly moved toward the curtains, peeling back the thick fabric and peering out the streaky window. Satisfied with what he saw, he removed the safety latch and unlocked the door. He opened it only a few inches and stepped aside to let whoever it was in the room.

What I saw standing there was not what I expected.

It was not who I expected.

What I was expecting was another burley biker. Someone who looked mean and was draped in skull and cross-bone tattoos. What I didn't expect was the blonde petite thing standing before me.

I certainly never expected a *girl*.

"This place is a dump," she said bluntly, pushing past King. She looked around the room as King shut the door, latched it, and took another peek out the window.

"Any possibility you were followed?" King asked. She ignored him, flitting about the room like a fly trying to find an open window.

"Do you know how many people a year contract diseases from places like this?" she asked, eyeing the bathroom with a look of pure disgust. "Statistically, given the age of the motel and approximate patronage—based, of course, on available parking spaces and number of maid carts in the hallway—there is essentially not a single spot of this room, or any of the other rooms in this building, that hasn't at one time or another been defiled by semen or fecal matter." It's like she didn't breathe between sentences.

She walked around the room, appraising everything from the chord leading up to the lamp to the base boards. She wasn't much older than I was. "Did you know that two thirds of all cases of food poisoning aren't actually food poisoning at all, but just the side effect of some little murderous, single-celled, bullshit organism waiting on your hands to jump onto your food and then into your mouth and digestive track to cause you, if you're lucky, hours of indigestion and spastic colon problems, and if you're not lucky, your sudden and untimely demise?" She shook her head. "Death by diarrhea."

I was getting a headache.

Country-slow was a term I was sure was invented in Jessep, where life moved along slower than a tractor driving down the main road. This girl was motoring around the room at such a high rate of speed that she looked and sounded like she was stuck in fast forward.

"Rage!" King snapped. The girl spun around from where she was inspecting the doorframe of the bathroom. "Do you think you were followed?" he repeated.

The girl scoffed as if what King was suggesting was impossible. "If I were being followed, I would have thrown them off. If I were being followed, I wouldn't be standing in this disgusting motel room right now wondering what microbial being is going to do me in." She rested her hands on the strap of the bright blue duffle bag slung across her shoulder, that read LEE COUNTY HIGH SCHOOL across it in big white block lettering. She looked up at the old popcorn ceiling. "You know me better than that."

"Your name is Rage?" I asked, trying not sound as surprised and confused as I was. She was barely over five feet tall. She wore a pink fitted T-shirt that said something about wearing pink on Wednesdays, cutoff white shorts, and white Keds. "Are you a friend of Bear's?" I asked, trying to put together what the fuck was going on.

The girl turned her attentions from King to me like she was just realizing I was in the room. She looked me over and smiled sweetly. It wasn't the kind of smile that screamed friendly or outgoing as her casual attire and perky personality would suggest. This was a pageant smile. A rehearsed smile.

Badly rehearsed.

She looked as if she were in pain.

Rage moved back to the door and opened it. I thought at first that she was leaving but she unhooked the plastic do-not-disturb sign hanging from the inside of the door and moved it to the outside, before closing it again and turning back toward us. "Yes, my name is Rage, and no I'm not a friend of Bear's. I'm a friend of whoever pays me the most, which right now is King and Bear." She pointed her thumb to King. "And by the way, Rage is short for Ragina."

"No, it's not," King said, calling her out.

"Okay, it's not," she said, dropping the fake smile. "The truth is that my name might or might not have something to do with a possible minor-to-major extreme anger management issue I may or may not have had at one point, or possibly still have now."

I looked at her but didn't say a thing. I couldn't. I was stunned into silence.

"We aren't staying here are we? I'm not a fucking gross biker. I can't just snuggle up and sleep in a bed that I know is breeding living and breathing organisms and is full of crusted leftovers of failed impregnations." She shuddered. "Don't even get me started on the fucking towels."

"You sleep now?" King asked.

"No," Rage answered flatly, still searching the ceiling. She wrinkled her nose. "Maybe I should tell you I *was* being followed so I can get the heck out of this Bates motel situation over here." Her eyes went wide. "Oh my God, I see mold!" she exclaimed, pointing to a few black specs around a crack in the corner by the door. She bent over at the waist and put her hands around her throat like she was suddenly suffocating. Each intake of air sounded like a very loud, very phlegmy struggle to breathe. "I can't breathe. The mold triggered my asthma. I'm having an attack! I need my inhaler!"

"What can I do?" I asked, springing up and over to her, in hopes of saving her life.

"The warehouse explosion in Ocala. That you?" King asked, unfazed by Rage's predicament.

Rage stood up straight and smiled, and I had to lean to the

left in order to avoid being whipped by her ponytail. Her asthma attack suddenly forgotten and her eyes turned dark, her pupils grew large, like she'd just snorted a line of something. "That was beautiful wasn't it?" she said excitedly, jumping up and down, clapping her hands together. "My best work yet. A symphony if you will. It was magical."

"You blew up a building, Rage. You're not fucking Mozart," King said sarcastically.

She looked off dreamily into the distance. "Mozart was a visionary. His brain saw things, the world, differently." She raised and lowered her arms, holding an imaginary baton as if like she were a conductor, instructing her orchestra, "And so do I."

It was King's turn to roll his eyes.

Rage dropped her arms and tapped her foot. She held her bag tightly to her chest. "I don't know you, but unfortunately if we stay here any longer, I am going to blow up this fucking motel, and you might be collateral damage if that happens, and I super love your hair so that would be a real shame, since I've been put in charge of keeping you safe and all."

"Her?" I asked King, not caring if she could hear me. King's knuckles were white and it looked as if it pained him not to set the girl in her place after she'd insulted him.

"Oh. My. Shit," Rage exclaimed. "I think some of the mold in the corner just moved. Let's motor before I decide that babysitting Jem over here is a really fucking bad idea."

King opened the door and we filed out.

"This is going to be fun!" she announced sarcastically, as she got into the truck and tossed her bag to King who set it in the truck bed. She shifted to the middle as I got in beside her and we headed off to Jessep.

Bear was in jail for me, *because* of me. If he wanted me to go home and he wanted Barbarian Barbie to accompany me, then I would do it.

Rage popped her gum in my ear, and I bit my lip to the point of almost drawing blood. "It smells like sweat in here," she complained, turning all the air conditioning vents toward herself.

Trust, I reminded myself.

After all, it wasn't like it was going to be that long.

I mean, it couldn't be that long because Bear was going to get out soon and everything would be okay.

I started saying it over and over again. By the time we breezed into Jessep it almost sounded believable.

Almost.

CHAPTER NINE

THIA

IT WAS ANOTHER lifetime ago when I was last in Jessep. At least that's how it seemed, although in reality it hadn't been very long at all.

Yet the stench of rotting oranges was more pungent than I remembered, so strong that Rage covered her mouth too just as we passed the WELCOME TO JESSEP sign. If possible, the dirt roads had gotten even harder to navigate, as evidenced by the truck bouncing from side to side as I tried—and failed—to dodge crater-like potholes and large rocks.

Home.

Is that still what this place was?

It didn't feel that way.

We passed the small cross on the side of the road marking where Kevin Little rolled his John Deer, trapping himself under the shallow water of a retention ditch. I never knew Kevin, but I knew his family. The cross had been there for as long as I could remember. Wilted wild flowers were piled up on the ground around it. Limp balloons tangled with each other, the strings were probably the only thing holding the warped wood upright.

That cross used to be the first sign that I was coming home.

It was the first thing to give me that warm and fuzzy feeling of familiarity whenever I turned off the main road and onto the first dirt road that lead into Jessep.

Coming into town this time was different.

It seemed familiar, but it no longer felt like home.

I don't know when that happened. Was it when my parents died and I skipped town? Was it before that and I just hadn't noticed?

In Jessep, the children of farmers either became farmers themselves or married farmers. I'd known from very early on that it would fall on me to take over Andrews Grove. It was all I knew. It wasn't that I liked the idea. I never really even thought about it as a like or dislike. It wasn't a choice. It was just what was going to happen. There were no plans for my college education. The closest thing to college I would ever hope to get was a few nighttime business classes and certification courses held every few months in the cafeteria of the combined elementary/middle school.

But then my parents checked out, and I was running the grove before I could even sign up for the courses. I tried my best with the knowledge I knew from growing up in the grove to save it, but it all went to shit so fast, it was like I blinked and it was all over.

I'd failed.

★ ★ ★

"I DON'T WANT to go in there," I said, staring at the front porch.

"I had the power turned back on," King said, misunderstanding my reasoning's for not wanting to go into the little house of horrors of my past. Rage on the other hand skipped up the steps and kicked open the front door, disappearing inside.

"It smells in here," she shouted, making a long and loud gagging noise.

"Is she really the one you guys wanted to watch out for me?" I asked King. "I mean, I know you said she blew up a building but are you sure she wasn't just trying to deodorize the place or something? She seems to have a thing about smells."

"Don't let the pink fool you," he said, his voice deep and hard. "That tiny psycho germaphobe in there is the deadliest fucking person, well, maybe second deadliest, I've ever known and it's because she doesn't take sides. She has no conscience. It's good that we got to her before Chop did or you'd be meeting a whole other side to Rage. One that ends up with you not breathing."

"Oh," I muttered, not sure if I should be happy or sad about Bear choosing to leave me in the care of Rambo, prom queen edition. King strode up to the porch and shouted something to Rage who appeared again in the doorway, twirling the end of her ponytail.

"Ray or I will call to check on you," King stated as he walked right past me and got back into the truck. Within seconds he'd already backed out of the driveway and disappeared down the road. I couldn't see the truck but I could make out the dust billowing behind his truck and over the trees as King made his way out of Jessep.

I glanced up at Rage who pressed her lips together and frowned. I couldn't help but wish I was still in that truck with him.

I shuffled up to the house but stopped just short of the broken down deteriorating steps.

"You shoot?" Rage asked, holding up one of my first place blue ribbons.

"Yeah. A bit."

"Wanna have a little competition?" she asked with a mischievous smile, pulling two guns from her duffle bag.

Rage may be able to blow up buildings and if what King said was true, a lot more than that. But in a shooting competition I had a strong doubt that she could beat me and maybe a little distraction from reality was what I needed. After all, I had no idea how much time we had on our hands.

"Okay," I said, pointing behind her. "There's a fence on the back of the property. Might still be some of my old targets out there—"

"Nope. Not exactly what I had in mind," Rage interrupted, checking her reflection in the chrome of one of her guns. She tossed me the other which I thankfully caught. "Come on," she said, heading back up into the house.

"I can't," I said, twisting Bear's ring in my hand.

Rage narrowed her eyes at me, "I figured that when I saw the look on your face when we first pulled up, but I have an idea. At least come up the steps."

Reluctantly, I took the steps slowly, one by one, cringing with each familiar creak. I stopped "What bothers you most about this place?" Rage asked from the other side of the screen.

"Everything," I admitted.

"Be more specific," Rage said, letting out an exasperated sigh. "I already know that it holds some bad memories, yada yada, killed your parents here, yada yada."

"Something tells me the last one wasn't exactly a guess."

Rage smiled sheepishly. "I know everything about everything."

"Good to know."

"So tell me what you hate about it. You know, besides the

obvious, being-a-shit-hole, reason."

"Well," I started. "I hate that this is where my brother died, but I was young, so what I really hate is that my mother never changed his room or got rid of any of his stuff. It was like a ghost lived with us, one she liked better than me or my dad."

"Keep going," Rage said. "Close your eyes." I did as she said and the images of all that was wrong with that place flooded my mind. I heard the squeak of the screen door open and started to open my eyes again. "Keep them shut," she ordered.

I took a deep breath. "I hate the family portrait in the living room because my mom had it painted by one of her friends years after my brother died and instead of it being of the three of us my mom had my brother painted in. I loved my brother, and we had lots of pictures of him all around the house and I loved them all, but I felt like it was a slap in the face to me and my dad. We were alive, yet she treated us like we were the ones who were dead."

"Good," Rage said, tugging on my arm, making me take a step forward. "More."

"I hate the rocking chair in my brother's room where she was sitting when I realized she killed my dad. I hate that I know the exact place in my parents' room where my father died. I hate the table in the kitchen where we had Sunday dinner and would all smile and talk about our days like there was nothing wrong. Those weren't dinners. Those were lies."

I felt another tug and took another step. "Okay, good. Now open your eyes." I did.

"Wow," I said. I was standing in the middle of the living room. "How did you do that?" I asked, noticing the panicked feeling was gone.

Rage replied with, "Because recently someone taught me

how to overcome a fear, and I thought maybe I could pass that along to you."

"Yeah, but how?"

"Easy peasy," Rage said. Turning suddenly she aimed her gun at the family portrait hanging above the mantle of the little fireplace in the living room and fired, shattering the glass, sending it raining down to the floor, leaving a dusty rectangular mark on the wall where it had hung. She turned back around. "You take the power back."

It was like suddenly something inside of me broke and without thinking I took a step past Rage, walking around the broken portrait in the living room in complete and total awe. "Yes," I said, looking back up to Rage. "Let's do it."

Rage and I spent the rest of the afternoon making a competition of setting up vases, photos, stuffed animals, plates, and other objects of my hatred, taking turns obliterating each and every one of them.

Neither one of us missed a single shot.

"Have you ever missed?" Rage asked from her perch on the counter, as she watched me sweep glass into a dust pan.

"Yes," I admitted, remembering the park and how I almost got Bear and I killed because I hit Mono's shoulder instead of his chest. "Once, maybe twice."

Only when shooting at people.

"You?"

Rage swung her legs back and forth and scrunched up her little nose. "Just once, although I'm starting to think I did it on purpose."

We were both quiet after that as I cleaned up the mess, and Rage cleaned her guns. She'd been right. In order to overcome my fear I had to take the power back, which meant I couldn't just sit around and do nothing when it came to my fear of losing Bear.

I had to do something.

Unfortunately, in order to do something I had to wait for Barbarian Barbie to turn her back.

At least long enough for me to borrow one of her guns.

Which I realized very quickly was going to be hard when she didn't leave my side. When I showered, she sat on the toilet with the lid down and filed her nails. When I cleaned out the freezer, she did a bizarre series of stretches in the middle of the kitchen. When I went outside to throw away the trash, she kept pace beside me and complained about the heat.

That first night when I went to sleep in my little twin bed in my old room, Rage surprised me by getting in right beside me. "What's going to happen to this house?" she asked without a trace of tiredness in her voice.

"Bank will probably take it back soon." I said, yawning.

"Good. That means we can blow it up when we leave," she said, sitting up and hopping up and down on her butt and clapping like she'd just been crowned prom queen, which she most certainly could've been with her blonde hair and tanned skin. However, I had the nagging inkling that Rage's past was more colorful then prom court and pep rallies.

"Deal," I agreed, enjoying the idea of watching the place go up in an explosion of flames. "But do you really have to sleep in here? You can sleep in my brother's old room. Or on the couch. It pulls out. The extra linens should be in the hall closet." I didn't mention anything about my parents' room, preferring instead to pretend like the room where I'd found my father's bloodied body didn't exist.

Rage ignored me, her silence telling me all I needed to know about her plans for going to find another place to sleep.

"Is what King said true?" I asked. "You don't sleep?"

"No, I don't. Not really. Not for a long time, anyway," she said, staring up at the ceiling.

"How do you survive?"

"I don't really know," she answered with an audible sigh, although she seemed like she was talking about more than just her lack of sleep.

"I have to help Bear," I admitted. Testing the waters to see if there was any way I could get her to help me instead of hindering me.

"You can't help him," Rage said, taking me by surprise.

"Why the hell not?" I asked, turning on my side to face her. Rage did the same. Her blue eyes sparkled but were lacking something which I soon realized was what King had been talking about when he'd dropped us off.

"Because you can't leave the house. Those are my orders."

"But why?"

"All I know is that I'm here to make sure you don't try anything stupid."

"How are you going to stop me?" I asked, growing bold.

Rage giggled like a schoolgirl with a secret, she rolled onto her back, again turning her attentions to the ceiling. "That, Thia, is entirely up to you."

CHAPTER TEN

THIA

I HAD A dog.
   Well, sort of.
I sort of had a dog.
   I first spotted it one night when I was sitting out on the porch in my grandmother's old rocking chair. Rage, who I was supposed to believe was a killer, unabomber, babysitter of sorts, spent the afternoon baking muffins. Really good muffins as far as I could tell from the one bite I'd had. But before I could grab it off the plate again, which I'd set on top of the old wooden toolbox, it ran away in a flash of teeth and brown fur. I stood up an looked out over the railing at the tiny thing who was barely out of the puppy stage, happily munching on my muffin. He was all skin, ribs, and bones. The second he took his last swallow, he hightailed it between the trees and into the grove.
   The very next night I left out some food again, this time on purpose and this time it was a few pieces of breakfast sausage. I sat in the same spot, watching and waiting. Sure enough, he crept from his hiding spot in the trees and stole my food all over again.
   Night after night it played out the same way, except I'd

switched to feeding him actual dog food that Rage had delivered from the feed store. Everything else we needed was magically stock piled in the refrigerator and pantry, even the deep freezer in the garage. We weren't just hiding out. We were all set for the zombie apocalypse.

"You should name that thing," Rage said, taking a seat on the top step. You spend enough time with it.

It's not like there is much else to do.

"I should just name him Muffin since that's what he took from me the first time.," I said.

Rage turned up her nose. "Nah, if you're gonna name him a breakfast food then name him something good at least, like Pancakes, or Waffles, or something like that."

Pancakes.

I fed Pancakes for weeks. Every morning and every night, I put out a bowl of dog food and another with water and stand back and watch him suck it all down, keeping a distrustful eye on me the entire time. And without fail, each night after he'd finished, he'd scurry away again. Eventually I started standing a little closer while he ate and finally instead of running away, he began to linger for a few minutes after his meal.

One night I didn't wait for him. I just set out his food and went back inside.

I was in a bad mood, unable to shake thoughts of Bear never coming home, and the hope of doing anything to help him faded away minute by minute as I sat there being utterly useless.

I didn't wonder where Rage was. She was always close by. I stopped talking to myself out loud because even though I didn't see her all the time, she was usually close enough to answer me back. The first few times it scared the crap out of me, once I fell off the porch.

I really wish that bitch slept.

By the time I reached my room I thought that Pancakes would be long gone.

I was wrong.

Not only did Pancakes not wander back off into the wild, but he followed me into the house, and when I plopped down face first onto my bed, the mattress dipped slightly and a wet snout came to rest across the back of my knee. I lifted my head and there he was, looking up at me with big, yellowish-colored eyes like his behavior was perfectly normal. After a few seconds of staring at one another, he fell asleep, like he'd never been afraid of me at all.

"I guess I have a dog, now," I muttered into the pillow, drifting into my own nap as Pancakes' warm doggy breath tickled the backs of my legs.

He was a poor substitute for Bear.

Too hairy.

Too skinny.

No tattoos.

But he would have to do.

CHAPTER ELEVEN

THIA

SIX MONTHS.
 Six loooooong fucking months with no end in sight. Not a word from Bear. What was worse was that each time Rage's phone rang, my stomach lurched and my heart dropped. The world around me stopped spinning until she gave me the, "It isn't *that* call" look and I could breathe again.

At least until the next call.

I felt nauseated at least three hundred times a day.

I became jumpy. Paranoid. My hands shook whenever Rage mentioned Bear's name.

I couldn't eat, and just like Rage, I couldn't' sleep. Afraid that at any moment I would lose the one thing in my life that ever brought me real happiness, I became someone I was really starting to hate.

Bear could have asked me anything else. Anything at all, and I would have done it. Rob a bank, become a flying trapeze artist, learn Japanese. At that point I would have gone to the MC and put a bullet in Chop myself if it meant that I could take a breath again without wanting to pull my own hair out strand by pink strand and DO NOTHING.

But no. He asked me the worst thing he could possibly ask me.

He asked me to WAIT.

He might as well have asked me to sit while someone removed my fingernails one by one with tweezers because waiting was a torture in and of itself.

"How many of them went in there?" I heard Rage ask in a whisper. I stopped in the hallway and pressed my ear to the door of my room. "Four? Shit, do you know anyone on the inside who can protect him? I know that one guy but anyone else? Yes, it is my fucking business, because I'm here babysitting his old lady in little house on the motherfucking prairie out here, so if you want me to protect her, you will tell me what the fuck is going on." There was a pause. "Really? Well, that's something I didn't know. No, of course I won't tell her. She's going to be fucking pissed though. Yes. Okay, fine I got it." She ended the call and I leapt into the kitchen. With my heart in my throat, I threw open the little cabinet above the refrigerator and searched through my mother's prescription bottles until I found the one I was looking for. I poured two glasses of soda and when Rage came back out I was leaning over the counter, pretending to be interested in the cookbook I'd just opened. I handed her one of the glasses.

"Thanks," she said. "Cheers." Rage raised her glass to me and took a sip.

As much as I couldn't stand the girl when we'd first met, I really started to like Rage. We talked. I mean I talked and she mostly gave vague responses back, but it was companionship nonetheless, and lord knows that being in that house alone would have driven me up the biggest cliff in crazy town until I was sailing off the edge.

Which is why I almost felt bad when I crushed three Ambien into her Dr. Pepper.

Almost.

Ten minutes later her eyes closed and her head fell back against the pillow. "Sleep well," I sang as she began to snore softly. I quickly dressed in my best sundress. A short, light blue, spaghetti-strapped number with tiny white flowers that made my legs look a lot longer than they were and my chest a lot bigger than it was.

The serious nature of what had to be done required a serious dress.

I grabbed a bike from the shed that probably hadn't been ridden since the seventies, pumped some air into the tires which were seriously lacking tread, and peddled into town with my constant companion, Pancakes, running close behind my back wheel for the fist mile before growing bored and running off behind some trees in search of better entertainment.

Trust me, his note had said. And I did trust him. I trusted him enough to know that he would die for me, and six months was pushing the limits on borrowed time. After hearing Rage on the phone, it didn't sound like there was much hope for month seven.

I was done waiting.

There was a certain deputy sheriff I was going to see, and although the last time I'd seen him ended with him locking me in a cell, and Bear almost murdering him, I had to at least try.

And I hoped the good deputy would be agreeable to what I had planned, because I wasn't leaving until I got what I'd come for.

I patted the messenger bag I'd slung across my chest that held the gun I'd taken from Rage.

No matter what.

CHAPTER TWELVE

THIA

I DROPPED MY bike in front of the hardware store and looked around for Buck's police cruiser. When I didn't see it, I popped inside where I found Ted standing behind the counter in his usual attire of overalls, and not much else covering his huge belly. He was polishing something with a dirty rag. When he heard the door chime, he set whatever it was down and came around the counter. "Thia," he said, with a sympathetic smile. "I was so sorry to hear about your parents. How you holding up?"

"I'm all right, Ted," I said, appreciative for his concern. Most of the people of Jessep were raging gossips. It's the small town way. Ted's always been the first one to ask me about *me* without joining in on the rumor mill. "You seen Buck around?" I asked, needing to see my friend ASAP.

Or my *ex* friend.

Or whatever he was.

Ted shook his head. "Not yet today, but sometimes I see him parked behind the diner 'round this time. You could check there."

"Thanks, Ted." I spun around to rush back out the door, but Ted stopped me.

"You know, I met your Bear last time he was in here," Ted said. "He's a good one. I can tell. We bonded over bike parts and being outcast bikers." Ted smiled and I could tell it meant a lot to him to meet one of his own. Bear had told me about their conversation and I'd been surprised. I'd known Ted my entire life and in our small town I'd never heard a soul utter a single word about him being an ex member of the Wolf Warriors MC.

"He told me," I said, offering him a tight-lipped smile.

"Good," he said, straightening a stack of *Auto Trader* magazines by the door. "He's a good kid and I know he didn't have nothin' to do with the way your parents went out, but from the look in your eyes I can see you already know that." It sounded so weird to hear someone call Bear a kid, because to me he was the furthest thing from it.

"I do know that," I admitted with one hand still on the door handle.

"I'll tell you the same thing I told him when he came in here. I may be an old man and retired, but my club knows I'm still here, just inactive, and I've still got friends in the life. If Buck can't give you the kind of help I think you're looking for, then you come see me." Ted walked toward the register and reached behind the counter. He pulled out a shotgun, resting it high on his shoulder like he was a soldier going to battle. "I can still be pretty persuasive when I need be," he said. The evil glint in his eye made me instantly believe him. It was like I was seeing Ted for the first time and it made me realize something, if I were being honest.

I liked this Ted.

"Thanks, Ted," I said. With that, he tipped his hat and put the shotgun away. He went back to his polishing as if Biker Ted had never been there, slipping easily back into the role of

Hardware Store Ted.

"You tell him I said hello," He added, as if I just came in to buy a quart of oil.

I was touched by Ted's offer, but what I really needed right then was someone who had a connection.

A way *in*.

There was only one person I knew who could help me. With one last wave to Ted I rushed out the door in search of the only person in Jessep who had such a connection.

And who may or may not hate my guts.

★ ★ ★

I FOUND BUCK in his cruiser behind the diner, exactly where Ted had said he would be. He wore mirrored aviator sunglasses, and although I couldn't see his eyes, I knew they were shut. His head was tilted back against the reclined seat, his mouth wide open as he snored away. The sun reflected off his badge as he breathed in and out, making it look as if it were a light bulb being turned on and off.

"Bucky!" I shouted, slamming my open palm on the roof of the cruiser, startling him back to consciousness. His head connected with the headliner as he jumped up in surprise.

"It's Deputy Douglas," he mumbled the familiar correction as he came out of his haze, catching his sunglasses as they fell off his face and rubbing the top of his head. "Thia?" he asked, squinting against the sun.

"The one and only," I said, leaning up against the cruiser. Buck reached for the handle and I stepped back to let him out, but before he did so he put on his ridiculous wide-brimmed sheriff's hat that made him look like Deputy Dog from the cartoon we used to watch as kids.

"So, the prodigal daughter returns," Buck said in his slowest and thickest southern drawl. He hung his sunglasses from the collar of his shirt and assumed a very wide "I'm a police officer" stance, tucking his thumbs into his gun belt. "You know, last time you left I thought I'd never see you again, especially after your *boyfriend* decided to try and kill me," he said the word boyfriend like he was waiting for me to correct him, and although I didn't think that word was accurate enough to describe what we were, I didn't have time to go over the specifics of our relationship.

"In all fairness Buck, you were being an ass by locking me in that cell, but never mind. There isn't time for that. I need your help. That's why I'm here."

"Oh, *now* you need my help? We used to be friends, but six months ago I get a call that your parents are dead and that you're on the run, but I didn't hear it from you. I had to hear it from the sheriff himself. Then I find out that the guy you ran off with last time is now in jail for murder and you *still* never came to me. So tell me, Thia, why I should help you now, when my oldest friend couldn't be bothered to come to me in the first place?" This time he didn't seem pissed. The sarcasm that he put up when I first banged on the roof had faded away. His shoulders fell. The front he tried so hard to put in place was shattering.

Buck wasn't angry.

He was *hurt*.

Suddenly, I felt bad, although what he was saying wasn't entirely true. "We'd grown apart, Buck. It wasn't like you were the best of friend to me either. Once my family started falling apart and the entire town started calling me Crazy Thia Andrews, it was like I didn't exist to you anymore."

"I might be the law, but you could have come to me." Buck

dropped the official stance, mirroring me and leaning up against the cruiser. "You have to have known you could have come to me, Thia." Buck and I used to share everything, and me not going to him when my parents died was because of one very simple reason. I never thought to. I thought of Bear, getting to him, and nothing else.

"I'm here now," I said. "And I promise, I'll tell you everything you want to know."

"Might be too late for that now," Buck said, scratching his head and looking down at his feet.

"Just listen, and if you don't want anything to do with me ever again, I'll disappear and you won't ever see me again." I put my hand on his shoulder, a gesture I hoped would be reassuring. He looked up at me, his dark brown eyes searched mine. "I'll disappear for good this time."

"Get in," Buck said, opening the driver's side door. I rounded the cruiser, barely able to contain my excitement. I got into the passenger seat while he took off his hat and settled into the driver's seat. I opened my mouth to start to tell him the truth, in hopes that he'd return the favor, when he held up his hand to stop me. "Something we got to get out of the way first," he said with a straight face. My stomach sank. Every second that ticked by was another second too many.

"What?" I asked with as much calmness as I could muster.

"First, you have to pinkie swear," Buck said, holding out his pinkie. I took it in my own and we both kissed the backs of our hands, like we had a thousand times before.

"I promise I will tell you the truth if you promise to keep an open mind," I said.

"Deal," Buck agreed, a small smile creeping onto his face. We dropped pinkies and I began to tell him everything, from my parents' death—the real story—to Bear, to the club. The entire time, I clutched the ring I no longer hid under my shirt for support. I had to force the words from my mouth, but I kept my part of the deal while Buck kept his, listening to every word. After a few minutes it got less difficult and the words flowed smoother. The air around us grew lighter, reminding me of the once easy going friendship we used to have.

When I was done talking and the truth was out there, I sat back against the seat and waited for Buck to say something. "Do you love him?" he asked, surprising me. Of all the questions he could have asked about what I'd just said, that's the first one that sprang to his mind?

"Yeah, I do," I admitted. "Very much."

Buck sighed and scratched the stubble on his chin. "Then where do we go from here?" he asked, meeting my gaze for the first time since I'd arrived.

"You'll help me?" I asked, trying to combat the hope that was threatening to explode inside of me.

"I pinkie swore, didn't I?" Buck asked, wagging his pinkie in the air.

"Thank you!" I squealed, launching myself at him and hugging him close.

"You're strangling me," Buck choked out. I released him from my sumo hold.

"Sorry," I said, settling back into the seat.

"That's okay," Buck said, looking rather amused. "Now, I know you wouldn't come here without some sort of plan. So spill it. What do you have going on in that pretty pink head of yours?" He had the same mischievous look on his face that he'd had when we were kids, right before we did something that resulted in neither of us being allowed to see one another again until whatever grounding period that had been bestowed upon us was over.

"Well," I started, not knowing what his reaction would be to what I was about to suggest. "Are you still friends with Dr. Hurley?"

"Dr. Hurley…the coroner?" Buck asked, scrunching his face. I nodded. "Sure, I still play poker with him every Tuesday, but…where exactly are you going with this, Thia?"

"Where I'm going is anywhere and everywhere that can lead to Bear getting out of that jail cell as soon as possible. Stealing evidence. Botching the coroner's reports. Maybe we can get Dr. Hurley to say that even though Bear confessed that there is no possible way he could have done it. I don't know. I hadn't thought through the specifics, but I just need to do something. ANYTHING." I twisted my hands in my lap. "Before it's too late."

Buck looked at me with an eyebrow raised and his jaw resting thoughtfully on his hand. "I get it. I do. But…" He paused and looked out the front windshield as if there was something out there to see besides the dumpster and the back wall of the diner. "Why *him*? Why you think that this guy is your hero or something? I hate to say it Thia, but in a way, don't you feel like you're betraying your parents by being with this guy? Like maybe you're only with him because you're pissed that they're dead and this is your way to get back at them."

"Buck," I started, as calmly as I possibly could, trying to ignore what he'd just said about Bear being some sort of post mortem rebellion. "You can ask me all this and I can answer you, but can we do that while we drive to Dr. Hurley's office? Please. I'm begging you."

"I told you I'd help you and I will but answer me first," Buck demanded. "Don't you think if your parents could see you now that they'd be pissed at what you're doing...with *him*?" He scrunched his nose and said *him* as if he'd gotten a whiff of skunk spray.

Any control over my calmness I had snapped.

"What do you want me to say, *Bucky*?" I asked, throwing my hands in the air. "Do you want me to tell you that I wish I'd just died with my parents? Because I won't. My father used to be a great man, but for the last few years he'd been everything *but* great. He fell apart because my mom fell apart. He was weak because she was weak. And when they faded away and I was working three jobs to try and hold it all together, I had NO-BODY. Tell me Buck, where were you then? Because I don't remember you coming to my rescue." Buck opened his mouth but I wasn't done. "I'm not like them. I won't crumble. I won't make excuses. I refuse to wish away my life because they didn't know how to live theirs, without yielding under the weight of their own bullshit. And I'll tell you something else, I lived through the most horrible night of my life, because I was *strong* and I'll survive this now because I'm *strong*."

"Thia—" Bucky started, regret written all over his face.

"You're wrong about one other thing too," I said, reaching for the door handle. "I don't think Bear is my hero. I don't need him to be my hero. Love isn't about wanting a hero, it's about wanting to be one for the other person."

I made a move to get out of the car but Buck reached over and held onto my arm. "I want to be yours," he said, taking me by complete surprise. "It's all I've ever wanted."

"What?"

"Ever since we were kids I thought it would be me and you in the end. Then suddenly it was like you got that *ring*"—more skunk smell—"and at first, I thought it was a silly kid thing like when you had that weird crush on Al Pacino and wall papered your room with posters from *Scarface* and *The Godfather*. But then he showed up here, and I knew it was him right away. That's when I knew I'd lost you."

"Bucky," I said, sympathetically placing my hand over his which was still on my arm. "We can start over. Be friends again," I offered, hoping it would be enough.

Buck shook his head, and although I took my hand off of his, he didn't release my arm. "Thia, that's not what I'm talking about and you know it."

I sighed. "That's why you stopped coming around," I said, realizing the reason for the gradual rift in our friendship wasn't because he couldn't handle my family's drama or hardship but because he wanted to be more than just my friend. Which only managed to piss me off. "Wait, let me get this straight. You wanted to be more than my friend and you knew that wasn't what I wanted, so you decided that our friendship wasn't worth it?"

Buck nodded. "Yeah, and I'm sorry, it was stupid of me, but I couldn't handle it. I didn't know what to do."

I couldn't believe what I was hearing. "Oh, you knew what to do all right. You abandoned me during the hardest time in my life because you had a crush. How noble of you." I rolled my eyes and made another move to get out, but Buck's hand tightened around my arm. "If you're not going to help me get him out then I'll just do it myself. He's in trouble Buck, I have to go so stop—"

"Thia," Bucky interrupted, putting his hand up.

"What?" I asked, blowing out a frustrated breath at his interruption.

He quirked an eyebrow at me and searched my face. "You really don't know, do you?" Buck asked.

"Know what?"

"This whole time I thought you were lying to me. Trying to get me to do something for you but I couldn't figure out what. I didn't think you didn't know though."

"Know what, Buck?" I repeated.

"Bear, or whatever you call him. He's not in jail. He's out. He's *been* out."

"What?" A weight started to lift off my shoulders...until it crashed back down on me with more force than ever. "No, that can't be true. He would of..."

"It's true. And he didn't," Buck quipped, cutting me off. He leaned back, the leather seat creaking underneath him.

I wanted nothing more than to punch the smug look off his face.

"How long?" I asked, my disappointment quickly turning to anger. I tightened my grip on the door handle once more. Any harder and I'd be snapping it off.

Buck shrugged. "Just about two weeks or so. Case was dismissed. The DA botched the paperwork. The signed confession went missing along with pretty much all of the evidence collected at the scene. Finger prints, even the two guns. Something tells me that lawyer lady had something to do with it. I did some research on her. This wasn't the first case she was involved in where evidence magically disappeared and it's not like..."

Buck's voice faded off into the distance. The only words I registered were playing over and over again in my head. An echo of TWO WEEKS. I was going to be sick.

Bear was out. Free.

He was okay.

I took a deep breath.

He hadn't come for me.

My chest tightened.

The realization I came to next was dizzying.

Bear *wasn't* coming for me.

I was so lost in my thoughts, I barely registered Buck taking my hand in his or how close he'd shifted over to me, or even the arm he'd slung over my shoulder. I didn't notice a damn thing while I tried to process how I was feeling when he lurched forward and pressed his cracked thin lips on mine. His cold tongue attempted to snake its way into my mouth.

I froze. My eyes open, witnessing the horror that was Buck kissing me. It only took a few seconds for me to remember my limbs and what I could use them for. I pushed against his chest, but he didn't move. I shouted against his mouth, but he still didn't budge. I pulled my knees up between us and kicked on his chest. That seemed to do the trick because suddenly the door flew open and Buck was gone.

I was strong, but there was no way I was *that* strong.

I shifted over to the driver's seat and spied a very frightened looking Buck on his butt in the dirt. A very large, very blue eyed, very shirtless, very muscular, very tattooed, and *VERY* angry man was attached to that gun.

Bear.

CHAPTER THIRTEEN

THIA

MY HEART LEAPT and sank all at the same time. My focus wasn't on Bear's nostrils as they flared out with his ragged breaths as if he were about to breathe fire. Or his knuckles which were white with tension, or his teeth which were bared like a wolf's. It wasn't even on the frightened deputy on the other end of his anger and his gun.

It was on the freckles that lined the tanned skin below his beautiful eyes. It was on the way his chest rose and fell, reminding me that not only was he was alive and breathing, but he was right in front of me.

He was free.

And he was fucking pissed.

Fully expect me to break his fucking wrists or end his fucking life. Bear had said to me the last time our paths had crossed with Buck.

Shit.

Buck's life was on the line. Bear could put a bullet in his chest or head at any second, but instead of fearing for my old friend's life, I couldn't help but admire the straining muscles of Bear's biceps, and again my attentions were on the way his chest rose and fell as he breathed through his anger. Maybe it was fucked up of me, maybe it was just because I hadn't seen or spoken to him in over six months, but Bear being angry to the point of wanting to kill for me made my heart flutter and the place between my legs throb. And when a memory flashed though my mind of the last time we'd been alone together. Naked. I had to bite my bottom lip to keep myself from writhing on the seat.

My Bear.

My entire body recognized him, and from what I was feeling I knew it had missed him as much as the rest of me had.

Bear squatted down, looking at Buck with pure hatred in his eyes. "I told you not to lay hands on my fucking girl again or I'd end you," Bear seethed, fire dancing in his eyes. He cocked his gun and aimed it straight at Buck's chest who was visibly trembling, his mouth wide open, scrambling backwards in the dirt road. A wet spot formed on the front of his pants.

"I'm the la-la-law," Buck stammered, reaching for his gun. Bear stood up, lifted his foot, and stomped his boot over Bucky's holster.

"I'm not," Bear countered. If I didn't do something, I knew Bear would be seconds away from making good on his threat.

I slid out of the cruiser. "I came here for his help," I said.

"Looked like you were doing a real good job of convincing him to give it to you," Bear spat. "That dress for him too?"

"What?" I asked, the reunion I'd envisioned for us looking nothing like what was unfolding.

"Get in the fucking truck," Bear snapped, jerking his chin to King's truck which was parked right behind the cruiser.

"No," I said, crossing my arms over my chest. "And you know what? I don't have to defend myself to you or anyone else.

I didn't do anything wrong. Only guilty people need to defend themselves, and I wasn't guilty of anything but trying to help you."

I stomped over and shooed away Bear's boot, which he reluctantly removed from Buck's holster with a deep growl. I unsnapped the gun and handed it up to Bear. I held out my hand to help Buck up, but he waved me away.

"I can't believe I was actually going to help you," Buck muttered, standing up and brushing the dirt from his pants and palms.

Bear took a half step forward, making Buck jump back. "The only thing you shouldn't be able to believe right now is that you're still fucking breathing. I'm having a pretty hard time with that one myself. So GO before I change my fucking mind," Bear said, his jaw clenching and unclenching. The chords in his neck straining as he tried to maintain control.

Buck shuffled to the cruiser but I wasn't done yet. "If the condition of you helping me was what you just tried to pull then you weren't going to ever help me," I pointed out, needing him to know that what he wanted wasn't ever going to happen between us.

"Get the fuck out of here, now!" Bear shouted. A warning I knew he wouldn't be repeating again. He pointed with the barrel of his gun to the cruiser.

Bucky wasted no time jumping in and turning the key. "You're going to regret all of this, Thia," Buck said, his voice shaky. "Maybe not now. But someday, when you realize he can't give you the kind of life you really want. A normal life. You'll regret it then." He put the car in gear. "And I won't be here when it all blows up in your face."

I looked back at Bear, and even though his eyes screamed

rage and murder and every other frightening emotion a person could possibly possess, I saw something else. Something more. Something that told me what Buck was saying was complete and utter bullshit.

Because where Buck probably saw a criminal with anger issues and violent tendencies.

I saw a fierce loyalty.

I saw love.

"I think there's something you aren't really understanding about all this," I said to Buck, leaning in through the window of the cruiser. I could feel Bear's disapproval at my back.

"And what would that be?" Buck asked, his attitude firmly back in place now that he was safely behind the metal of the car door. But he couldn't fool me. I could still smell the urine on the front of his pants.

"I needed help just now, someone to protect me, from you of all people, and *he* was here," I said, waving back to Bear who stood like an angry stone statue. "Where were you when I needed help, Buck? Not today, but when the grove and my family were falling apart and I needed a friend more than anything? Where were you when I needed *you*?" I looked back at Bear. "Because I know where he will be when I need him, which is a lot more than I can say for you." I pushed off the car and took a step back.

Buck opened his mouth but there was nothing he could say that I wanted to hear. "Bye Bucky," I said, effectively cutting him off.

"I almost forgot," Bear said, stepping in front of me. He reached into the cab of the cruiser, grabbed Buck's wrist off the steering wheel and pulled his arm out the window. In a quick flash of movement, Bear dropped his elbow down onto the center of Buck's forearm. *CRACK.* A scream tore from Buck's throat, his arm dangling at an unnatural angle.

His broken arm remained hanging out the window as he drove off. His screams echoed over the small buildings as he raced away, fishtailing across the dirt and disappearing in a cloud of dust.

"You didn't have to do that," I said, turning around to meet Bear's glare. And his sweaty chest. And his eyes that although were dark and angry, seemed as if they could see right through me.

Suddenly I became very conscious of what I was wearing, pulling down on the short hem of my dress as if Bear were staring at me naked.

"I told you I'd either break his wrist or end his life if he laid his fucking hands on you. I was being…nice. Now why don't you tell me why I get out of jail and go to see my girl, only to find that instead of waiting for me like she was told, I find her in a cop car with the fucking law's motherfucking tongue down her fucking throat?" It started out as an angry question and ended as an angry roar. I swallowed hard. Bear took a step forward.

I was scared.

I was turned on.

I was pissed the fuck off.

I fought against the need to throw myself in his arms.

"You should have done what you were fucking told. I'm going to snap that little girl's neck who should have been fucking watching you," Bear seethed, running a hand through his hair.

"I'm not a fucking lap dog," I snapped. "And Rage is… sleeping." It wasn't *exactly* a lie.

"Rage doesn't sleep," he argued.

I folded my hands behind my back and rocked on my feet. "She does after a cocktail of Dr. Pepper & Ambien."

"You *drugged* her?" Bear asked with disbelief.

"A little?" I admitted, although it came out as a question. "Why the fuck do you care? You've been out of jail for two weeks while I've been sitting there waiting and worrying like some love-struck idiot. There are a lot of things you can do to me, Bear, but I won't have you make a fucking idiot out of me. I won't." As strong as I was trying to be, my voice cracked.

"I'll deal with you when we get back to the house," Bear snapped, his words loaded with so many different meanings I trembled with both fear and anticipation.

"You're going to *deal* with me?" I asked. "How are you going to *deal* with me?" My attitude and confidence faded with each word until the last was merely a whisper.

"Yes, DEAL with you," Bear warned, suddenly pausing to take in my appearance. Slowly, from top to bottom, like he'd only just realized I was standing there. His eyelids hung heavy over his sapphire blues as they licked over my body, drinking me in like he was thirsty.

No, not thirsty.

Hungry.

When he licked his lips I could have sworn he was about to eat me alive. I tingled all over. The awareness of him in such close proximity after so long washed over me. Angry or not, my body didn't care. *I* didn't care. I wanted to reach out and touch his face, reassure him that he had no reason to be angry, but part of me liked that I could draw that kind of reaction from him. He came alive when he was pissed, and something inside me loved that he became this primal possessive beast out to remind me who it was I belonged to.

Bear clenched his jaw and the muscles in his neck tensed and strained. He looked as if he were ready to either kill or fuck. All I knew was that, one way or another, I was about to be devoured.

I pressed my thighs together, trying to manage the pulsing

between my legs, but the contact only ignited it further. Bear chuckled and glanced down to where my ankles were crossed. He closed the gap between us in two short strides, taking me off guard. I stumbled backward, tripping over a lose rock in the road. He reached out and roughly grabbed my arm before I could fall, pulling me flush into his hard chest. His warm skin radiated through my thin dress. I bit my lip, suppressing a moan. My legs grew weaker and weaker as he lowered his head, inching closer and closer, until I was sure his lips were going to meet mine, when without warning he released my arm and spun away. "Get in the fucking truck, Ti," he called back to me.

I stood there, unable to move, and trying to catch my breath while he headed over to King's truck like that moment never passed between us. When he noticed I wasn't behind him, he growled and stalked back over to me. He grabbed me by the waist, his fingers digging into my skin. He lifted me up, my short dress bunching up over my butt cheeks and slung me over his shoulder like I was a rolled up rug.

Wack.

He slapped my ass with his open palm. Hard. The bite of the smack stung where I was sure he'd left his mark. He tossed me into the truck with a caveman grunt and slammed the door behind me.

I was confused as all hell.

I was so angry.

I was also elated.

I was in lust so hard that I was in physical pain.

I was really fucking angry.

I was head over heels in love.

Motherfucker.

CHAPTER FOURTEEN

BEAR

I KEPT MY mouth shut during the entire five-minute ride back to the grove. I was too fucking angry to talk. The overwhelming need to both fuck her and punish her occupied every inch of my being. I cracked the joints in my neck and shoulders, trying to find some sort of relief from the agony in both my mind and my aching cock before it was too late and I took it out on Ti... and her pussy.

When we got to the grove, I told Ti to wait in the truck while I went inside. Rage was rubbing her temples, I assume just waking up from the drug-induced sleep Ti had put her in. If I wasn't so fucking pissed off that Ti defied me and sought help from that cock-suckin' cop, I'd actually be kind of impressed.

"Bear, don't you fucking start with me, this wasn't my fault," Rage said with a groan. "I didn't know your fucking girlfriend was psycho enough to drug me." She stood and shook her head from side to side like she was trying to clear the fog. "On a brighter note,"—she stretched her arms over her head—"so that's what sleep feels like."

"I need some time with Ti. Be back tomorrow morning," I barked.

"Tomorrow?" Ti asked from the doorway, again not doing what she was told.

Bear, Yo bitch be feisty! Me likey. Ghost Preppy chimed in.

I scratched the back of my neck. "Yes, tomorrow. I have shit to do and I need you here for one more night. Do you think you can listen to me for once and do that one thing for me, Ti, and just stay fucking put?" I turned back around, but Rage was gone. The back door flapped against the frame.

I guess I didn't need to tell her twice.

"Don't bother, Bear," Ti said, I turned around in time to see her lips form a straight line as she made her way back down the steps.

Fuck. My blood started to boil. This was not how I saw this going.

I caught up to Ti in a few strides, spinning her around and holding her by the elbows. "I'm on the fucking edge of my control right now. If you stop acting like a spoiled brat for two fucking seconds, I could explain to you why—"

"Why you've been out for two fucking weeks but haven't bothered to contact me? To come for me?" Ti interrupted. Her brows narrowed, the lines of her forehead marring her perfect pale skin. I paused, not realizing she'd known about my release being secluded out in the sticks. "Deputy Douchebag tell you that?" I asked. It wasn't as if I wasn't going to tell her about it. I'd come to her as soon as I could.

And now that I was finally with her, I wanted to choke her.

While my cock was inside of her.

"It's okay, Bear. You aren't under any obligation to me. You don't have to protect me anymore. I'm fine on my own. If you don't want me then…" She struggled against me, but there was no fucking way I was letting her go as her anger turned to sadness. Her voice cracked. Tears sprang to her eyes.

"You think I don't fucking want you?" I asked. For a smart chick, she could be dumb as shit.

She nodded. "Why else would you—" I cut her off and although I knew she was upset, for some reason that only enraged me more.

"I don't know, Ti. Maybe because I'm about to go to war with my old man and I had to meet with some of my old brothers who want to fight on my fucking side. Maybe because I think the key to winning the war might be my dead fucking mother who by the way showed up to visit me in County. Maybe because it wouldn't look good if the first thing I did when I got released was go and see my girl whose parents I confessed to murdering so I thought a week or two to let that shit blow over was the best course of action. Maybe I felt like keeping you out from behind bars and in my sight where I could protect you was a little more fucking important then my raging undying and motherfucking overwhelming need to be with you!" I yelled. I seriously considered shaking some sense into my girl. Ti bit the side of her thumb.

"You don't think it was fucking painful for me in there? Not to hear from you? Not to see you? I almost caved and called you a million times, but when I thought about what harm that could cause you…I couldn't," I finished, searching her face waiting for some sort of reaction.

She twisted her mouth the way she does when she's thinking. The redness in her cheeks faded to pink. Her tensed muscles relaxed under my grip. "Well, when you put it that way," she mumbled, looking off into the grove and then up at me. "Your mother really visited you in jail?"

I nodded. "Shot by my old man and tossed into the bushes

on the side of the road, and she shows up twenty-five years later to say good-bye to me." I laughed, because the entire thing was fucking absurd.

"Where's she been all this time? And why find you now?" Ti asked. They were the very same questions I'd asked when she'd showed up.

I shrugged and told Ti how my mom thought that Chop somehow kept her captive, the idea that she'd been drugged all this time, and how Sadie said she wasn't clear on any of the details.

"She's why you have to leave again?" Ti asked, leaning into me instead of away from me like she had been. My cock jumped.

"Yeah, if she was important enough to my old man to keep locked up all that time, having her in my pocket wouldn't be a bad thing. We might be able to use her to get to Chop and end all this."

"We?" Ti asked.

"We," I confirmed, and then I filled her in on the conversation I'd had with the brothers in the yard.

Ti smiled. "You have a club again," she said, beaming up at me. Her reaction took me off guard. She seemed happy that I might find my way back into club life, when I thought it would be the last fucking thing she'd ever want.

I shook my head. "I wouldn't go that far. I can't. I don't trust them anymore," I admitted. "I'm not trying to run a mutiny. I'm still not a Bastard." I paused, searching my brain for the right way to explain what I was trying to do. "This is more like banding together for the sake of revenge." I told Ti the story of what happened to the BBBs and she gasped, covering her mouth with her hand.

"Holy shit," she said, wrapping her arms around me.

The moment was interrupted when something with fur flew past us in a blur into the grove.

"What the fuck was that?" I asked.

"My dog?" Ti asked, squinting against the sun.

"You have a dog?"

"His name is Pancakes. Rage named him although I wanted to call him Muffin, or maybe Donut," she said watching the spot where he'd just disappeared.

At the mention of donut my thoughts immediately went back to Deputy Dangley Arm. "We'll talk about the dog later. Right now you just need to listen." My anger started to boil again. "I told you to trust me, didn't I?" I asked, squeezing her arms a little too tightly.

Her eyes snapped to mine. "Yes, and I did trust you. I'm here, *aren't I?*" she asked. Her defensiveness only egged me on more.

"You weren't here when I found you in town with that lawman's tongue down your fucking throat," I spat, and as I remembered looking through the windshield and seeing him practically on top of her, the anger I felt washed over me all over again. I pulled her closer.

"Bear, let me go!"

"No," I growled. "No broken arms next. Next time I break his fucking neck."

Ti pulled back again and this time I let her go. "I went there to help you! Bucky kissed me, but I didn't kiss him back. Deal with it! If you can't handle it or if you don't believe me you…you can go fuck yourself!" she said, staring me down. Challenging me. Taunting me.

I fucking love this girl.

It was with those words that my anger and lust finally broke free. Any sort of control I thought I had shattered in an instant.

"I'd rather fuck *you*," I said, my own voice rumbling in my chest. Reaching behind her neck, I threaded my fingers up through her crazy pink hair, yanked her face to mine, and crushed my lips to hers.

MINE

CHAPTER FIFTEEN

THIA

KISSING BEAR WAS like getting a taste of a drug I needed to survive, a drug I'd gone without for way too long. I'd grown weak without it. Desperate. With one press of his lips to mine I went from being a junkie on the streets to a rock star, high on a drug I'd never planned on quitting in the first place.

Bear moved from my lips to my jaw, "You're here, Ti," he murmured when he reached my ear, his lips tickling my skin as he spoke like he still couldn't quite believe it. He then licked and sucked the sensitive skin behind my ear, nipping it with his teeth. I gasped. He chuckled. I felt all of it deep in my core. "And you're real. All the things I've waited so long to say are fucking useless sentences lost in the back of my mind somewhere, because the only thing I can think about right now is how much I need to be inside you again. How much I need to *FUCK* you," Bear said, slowly emphasizing the word FUCK. His words sent a flush of wetness between my legs, my body unaware of any prior argument. Its only awareness was of Bear and what he was doing to me and my body. "This little fucking dress," Bear said. He reached down and ran his warm palm up the side of my thigh, starting at my knee he, lifting the hem up to my hip along the way, and settling his hand on my ass.

His blue eyes darkened to a glistening black. The air around us changed, growing thicker, heavier, charged with energy.

I shook my head, trying to remember my train of thought. Trying to remember why I was so angry at the beautiful creature who at that moment only wanted the exact thing I wanted. So why couldn't I just let this go and give in? "I may love you, Abel McAdams," I said, breathlessly, using his real name for the first time, "but I am no fucking pushover. So don't you ever pull that shit again. I won't be able to take it. I won't be able to—"

Bear cut me off. "Shut up."

I wanted to be angry. I wanted to lash out at him and give him the verbal beating I'd planned the entire drive back in the truck but had somehow forgot. The last thing I wanted was for his demand to shut up to make me want to grab him by the beard and yank his face between my legs. I tried the anger route one last time, closing my eyes for a moment in an attempt to break free of the lust-fog that had taken over. I stomped my foot on the ground and took a deep breath and kept my eyes shut. "You can't just tell me to—"

"Shut up," Bear repeated again.

My eyes sprang open to find him gazing down at me, his eyelids heavy, his breathing erratic. Without thinking, I reached out and ran the pad of my thumb over the line of freckles under his eyes and much to my surprise he closed his eyes and leaned into my touch. He grabbed my hand and brought my thumb to his mouth, briefly sucking on the tip.

My nipples hardened, begging to be touched.

"Bear," I started again, desperate to say my peace.

"Fuck me," Bear said.

"What?" I asked like I hadn't heard him, but I had. Loud

and clear. My body had too, every part of me impossibly turned on and aching for relief from the torturous arousal Bear had ignited. My core clenched and I pressed my lips together, trying not to give away how affected I was by him.

"You heard me. I know you did," Bear said, slowly, seductively. He tucked a wayward strand of hair behind my ear. "But just in case you didn't, I don't mind saying it again." He dipped in close, his lips brushing against mine when he said, "*fuck* me," again.

My hands, with minds of their own, slid from his face down his chest, landing on the ridges of his defined abs. "Or better yet," he said, craning his neck to suck my earlobe. "I'll fuck you. We'll fuck each other. Doesn't really matter, baby. I've been thinking of nothing else but fucking you in every position invented for six long fucking months and I'm not about to let anything get in my way, not even that smart mouth of yours."

I hadn't even realized we were moving until my back hit the side of the house and I was trapped between the wall and the heat of his hard, shirtless body. "I've fucking missed you," he said, his voice raspy and deep. "So fucking much." He rubbed his nose against mine then trailed it down my neck, sending shivers down my back and need between my legs as if he'd already touched me there. "So that's what I'm gonna do. I'm gonna fuck you, baby. I'm gonna make you come harder than you've ever come before." Bear rocked his hips against me like he was sealing the promise, his hardness prodding against my stomach.

Bear continued fucking me with his words. "That dress you're wearing makes me want to push my cock between your fucking tits." His erratic breathing became harder and faster. "I can see your hard nipples." He licked his lips. "Are you thinking about me tasting them?" He ran his fingertips over the rounded mounds of my breasts, then snaked a finger into the top of my dress, grazing a rough fingertip within millimeters of my nipple.

Tease.

Bear pulled back slightly and looked down at me. His gaze was dark. A mixture of lust and pain. His eyebrows knitted together. "It's been too fucking long since I've touched you," he said, the pad of his thumb finally making contact with the hardened peak of my nipple. As much as I tried to contain myself, I couldn't. I moaned loudly, and it was as much because of the contact as it was because he quickly removed his hand from my dress, and I immediately wanted it back. He reached down, his fingers trailing up my thigh and back into my dress, stopping just short of the edge of my panties.

"I can feel how hot your pussy is for me and I'm not even touching it yet," Bear groaned into my neck. "Let's see if you're as wet as you are warm." Pushing the scrap of cotton to the side, he slowly dragged one long finger over my clit and into the wetness between my folds, causing me to buck against him when he traced my inner lips. "Holy shit. You're so fucking wet, baby. So fucking beautiful," he said, pulling his finger out and popping it in his mouth and I couldn't take my eyes off of him. "Fuck, I missed the way you taste," he said, as if he'd just taken a bite of the most heavenly dessert there was.

His eyes locked onto mine as he gave his finger one last lick before closing the space between us and crushing his mouth to mine. The second my lips parted and I could taste myself on his tongue I was lost in the sensations of Bear and our connection, which had only grown stronger during our time apart.

I'd lost the war of words while Bear had clearly won the battle over my body. He pulled back just enough to speak, but not enough to sever the connection of our lips. His tongue still licking and tasting me between words. "We can still fight if you want, fuck knows I'm still angry enough, but if we are, we're gonna do it with my cock inside your pussy. While I'm filling you. Stretching you. Feeling what's mine."

I shuddered. A full body shudder that was so strong I wouldn't have been surprised if my teeth started chattering.

"Let's go inside," I suggested on a whisper. He smelled like soap, sweat, cigarettes, and need. The hard lines of his rippling muscles contracted rapidly as he struggled for more air. For more me.

For more us.

My breathing matched his as he grabbed the back of my neck and sucked my bottom lip into his mouth, groaning when he released it, pressing his forehead to mine. "There has never ever been anyone like you," Bear said softly. "You're it for me, Ti. Don't ever doubt that. But you've been a bad, *bad* girl." The corners of his mouth turned upward in a crooked smile, his cock throbbing through his jeans against my belly. My insides ached and throbbed and pulsed, and whatever else they were capable of doing at the anticipation of Bear being inside me again. I wondered what was taking him so long to strip me bare and take me against the fucking wall.

Bear was as beautiful as he was hard. He was as complex as he was simple. He was both the storm and the calm. The fear and the solace. The rage and the peace.

My life and my love.

He was also the biggest fucking tease who was two seconds away from making me explode. "What are you waiting for?" I asked, my chest heaving like I was about to have a heart attack, my nipples so hard they felt as if they were about to fall off. My need dripped embarrassingly down the inside of my thigh.

Bear lowered his voice. "I was thinking that bad girls who don't listen should be punished, and that maybe I should make you wait for what you want."

Oh hell no.

I was about to take him up on his original suggestion to keep the fight going while we fucked when he dropped to his knees and dug his fingers painfully into my hips. He lifted my dress, pressed his face between my legs, and inhaled deeply. He licked over my panties, his tongue warm and wet through the fabric. "Your pussy smells like fucking heaven. Never smelt anything so good."

"So fuck me," I said, closing my eyes and leaning further back against the wall. Bear's hold on my waist was the only thing keeping me upright. He stood back up, parted my thighs with his knee and rocked forward, running his shaft over my clit. "Is this what you want, baby?" he asked playfully. "Maybe you should beg for it."

I was painfully aroused, my pussy contracting and clenching around nothing when it should have been massaging Bear's cock as he drove it in and out of me. I was seconds away from giving Bear what he wanted and begging him to fuck me, but I had a better idea on how to end this game he was playing.

In a bold move I reached out and palmed his erection through his jeans. Immediately he threw his head back and hissed as he inhaled sharply though clenched teeth. "Fuck," he groaned, rocking forward into my palm.

I removed my hand and pushed on his chest, catching him slightly off guard. His step faltered, but he quickly recovered. "What are you doing, little girl?" he asked, his deep vibrating voice massaging me from the inside out, a wicked gleam in his dark eyes.

I didn't answer. Instead, I took a step forward and lifted my dress over my head, tossing it to the ground. His gaze darted to my naked chest, and maybe it was the way he was looking at me, or maybe it was the way he licked his plump lower lip and then sucked it into his mouth like he was preparing to swallow me whole.

Or maybe it was just that I was ready to take what was mine and I was tired of waiting.

I rolled my nipples between my fingers and Bear's mouth dropped open. "I missed your perfect tits," he said, nostrils flaring. Again he dropped to his knees, this time to take a nipple into his mouth and suck. Gently at first and then harder making me gasp. He rolled his tongue over it slowly and then faster and faster, the same way he would when he was licking my clit. I held on to the sides of his head for support, threading my hands through his long hair as he moved from one nipple to the other, leaving each sensitive peak for just enough time for them to turn cold in the warm night air.

He stood abruptly and kissed me hard. Wrapping his arms around me, he held me tightly against him, almost too tight. It wasn't just a passionate kiss. It was a message. This was Bear telling me that I was still his. That he wasn't ever letting me go.

I snaked my way between us, running my hand down Bear's stomach. He broke our kiss to look down to where my hand was resting on the waistband of my panties. I watched his expression as I pushed my hand inside and dipped my fingers into my wetness.

"Fuck," he said, the control he was so adamant about having moments ago to teach me a lesson was cracking quickly as he watched me push my fingers in and out of the place I needed him most.

"MMMMMMMMMM," I moaned and although it felt good it felt nowhere near as good as when it was Bear's fingers inside of me.

I was forced to remove my hand from my panties when Bear pushed them down to my ankles. I was completely naked. "So beautiful," Bear muttered, undoing his belt. I pushed his jeans down over his perfect ass and they fell to the ground. He reached around me and lifted me up into his arms with one hand, pinning me against the wall.

Instead of impaling me with his cock, which is what I was sure he was going to do, with his free hand he circled my clit with his thumb and inserted two fingers inside my pussy while trailing kisses on my breasts and stomach. With just that little contact, I was already so close to coming and I knew from the pressure building that when I did come, it was going to be explosive. "Do you want to come on my fingers, or my cock, baby?" My pussy clenched around his fingers, approving of the sound.

"Cock," I answered on a strangled cry, so close to release my core felt heavy and tight.

"Good girl," Bear said, releasing his hold on me just enough so I could slide down and he could align his cock with my entrance.

There was nothing slow about him entering me. The teasing he'd started earlier was over. There was nothing left but pure animalistic need. In one swift and very hard thrust, he buried himself inside me, the pleasure so great that it bordered on a welcome pain. "This is mine. This has always been mine. I took your virgin pussy and claimed it, now it belongs to me," he grunted as he fucked me hard and deep.

Over and over again he thrust furiously, finding a fast rhythm. He'd barely begun when the pressure became so much I began to crack until I was shattering, breaking, falling, convulsing around him in waves. The pulsing was endless as he drove into me harder and harder while I bucked on his cock, riding out the long waves of the most powerful orgasm I'd ever had.

I was still coming when Bear's thrusting became erratic and frantic. Faster and faster, he pounded into me until I didn't know if he was pushing in or pulling out. He let out a long, animalistic groan as he stilled, coming deep inside of me, filling me with his release.

I came down from my orgasm just in time to feel every bit of his as he emptied himself. He fucked me with small shallower thrusts as he rode out his own orgasm.

"Holy fuck," Bear said, collapsing to the ground and pulling me on top of him.

"Yeah," was all I could manage to say. I was lucky I could still breathe after that.

We stayed like that, lying in the grass in each others arms for what seemed like forever, yet would never seem like long enough. When he sat up, he pulled me up with him.

Bear tipped my chin up so I would look at him. The smile on his face reached his eyes, which were lighter and back to their usual blue. "*Now* we can go inside," he said, standing up. I reached for my panties but he swatted my hand away. Bear surprised me by hoisting me over his shoulder and walking back toward the front of the house.

"What are you doing?" I asked, staring at his bare ass as he walked.

"We've fucked. Now it's time to fight. But then, I'd like to fuck again, so no need for all the clothing bullshit." And just like when he'd carried me to the truck, he smacked my ass with a loud *THWAP*.

"Owe!" I cried out.

"Don't be such a little bitch, Ti. I plan on doing more to you tonight then just a few little smacks to the ass." He carried me up the porch steps and into the house.

"That's your dog?" Bear asked, stopping in the doorway. I couldn't see what he was looking at, being over his shoulder and all, but I assumed he was talking about Pancakes who usually took up residence on the couch when he wasn't running around the grove.

"Yep. That's Pancakes," I said. Bear set me down and I turned to see Pancakes on the couch just as I suspected, wagging his tail.

"No, no it's not," Bear argued.

"Uh, yeah, yeah, it is. You're not afraid of dogs are you?" I asked, taking a step into the house. Bear grabbed my arm.

"I'm not afraid of dogs," he said, never taking his eyes of Pancakes who continued to wag his tail and run from one side of the couch to the other.

"Good, then let's—"

"But, that's not a dog," Bear said.

"What are you talking about?"

"Ti, I hate to be the one to tell you this."

"Tell me what?"

Bear pointed to Pancakes. "Your dog…is a coyote."

CHAPTER SIXTEEN

BEAR

AFTER I FUCKED my girl a handful more times, we fell asleep in a tangle of limbs on the living room couch. I learned two things in those first few hours of our little reunion. Number one was that although fucking Ti had always been off the charts amazing, an *angry* fuck with Ti was an out of body experience. Number two, was that Pancakes, the coyote, liked to watch.

The other bit of good news was that I was positive there would be many more reasons on many more occasions for Ti to be pissed off at me in the future.

My little spitfire.

Out the front window the sky was lightening, the sun's first rays were just minutes from turning the dark sky blue. I kissed the top of Ti's head and she stirred. "No, I'm still sleeping," she argued, keeping her eyes shut tight. She swatted around blindly with her hand. I grabbed her wrist and set her hand back down on my chest to avoid being poked in the eye.

"I gotta go, baby," I reminded her. She answered back with a groan followed by soft snores. I laughed into her hair. "Stone has a lead on where Sadie might be. A tip from a women's shelter a few hours north. Gus and Wolf are coming with me. Shouldn't take that long to track her down."

"Maybe she just wants to be left alone," Ti groggily pointed out, lazily running her fingertips over my chest. That little touch was enough to send spasms to my cock, stirring it back to life as if it hadn't just shot off multiple rounds into the naked girl sprawled out on top of me only a few hours before.

MY naked girl.

"Maybe, but whatever she wants, something feels off, and not just the fact that she's actually alive. It just doesn't sit right with me, none of it does," I said.

Ti reluctantly sat up and yawned, rubbing the sleep from her eyes. Her long hair fell all around her face in tangles. A red bite mark sat in the space between her shoulder and neck where I'd gotten a little carried away and I wanted more than anything to get carried away again.

I reached up and ran my finger over the bite mark and Ti smiled, knowing exactly what it was I was thinking. I tucked some of the crazier pieces of her hair behind her ears. "You're downright adorable when you wake up, you know that?" I said.

"I am?" She bit her bottom lip and blushed like she was shy. Like I hadn't taught her how to ride my cock like a fucking champion the night before.

"Yeah, in a 'I'd like you to ride my cock again' kind of way," I informed her, rubbing my palm over my already hard shaft to show her what she was doing to me. What she *did* to me. Her gaze dropped to my hand, her tongue darting out to wet her lips and it was all I could take. I sat up and pulled Ti back down on top of me for a kiss. I had to go. But I had a few minutes. Maybe ten minutes.

Half hour tops.

A throat cleared, and we both looked up to find Rage, in all her pink T-shirted glory, staring down at us and our naked entangled limbs with a mixed expression of confusion and disgust.

Ti cuddled closer, pressing her tits up against me to shield herself from our visitor, yet Rage only seemed bored by our nakedness. She shooed Pancakes off the La-Z-Boy and took his seat. He whimpered, but only moved as far as her feet then dropped down on the floor. He propped his snout on his paws, continuing his creepy coyote voyeurism. I turned my attentions from Pancakes back to Rage. "You gonna leave so we can get dressed, or you joining us?" I asked sarcastically, which earned me an elbow to my ribs by Ti.

"Ugh." Rage rolled her eyes.

"So you've never…?" Thia asked, sitting up without covering herself.

Rage picked at her nails. "Oh yeah. I totally have. I just don't understand what the big deal is."

I gave Ti's ass a squeeze and she jumped. "Then you need to find someone else to fuck," I informed her. "Come on, baby, we got business to finish." I stood up from the couch, my heavy cock bobbing up and down as I scooped Ti up into my arms. She yelped in surprise. "We'll be right back." I carried her down the hall into the nearest open door, which happened to be a small yellow-tiled bathroom. I set her down on the counter and slammed the door shut. I didn't waste a single second before grabbing her knees and spreading her legs. I pulled her toward me so that her pussy was flush with the edge.

"I feel bad that we just left her," Ti said, although the way her head fell back and her mouth parted when I circled her clit with two fingers told me she couldn't have felt *that* bad about it.

"I can go get her if you want her to watch." I wagged my

eyebrows. Of course I was joking. It's not that Rage wasn't hot because she was. I just wasn't attracted to girls who look like high school cheerleaders, but packed enough explosives to level neighborhoods. It wasn't really my deal.

I looked down at Ti's glistening pussy. My deal was wet, ready, and right in front of me.

"That's not what I meant," Ti said, groaning as I pushed my cock inside of her. "Hold on to the counter," I ordered and for once she did as she was told and gripped the edge, using it as leverage to push back against me when I thrust into her.

"I know that's not what you meant," I said, reveling in the feeling of her tight warmth. "Preppy's the only one I'd let watch anyway." I hadn't realized I'd said the last part out loud until Ti responded.

"You'll have to tell me about that," she said, slowly circling her hips to allow me deeper access.

"Fuck, that's good, baby," I said. I learned very quickly that when I praised Ti while we fucked, she took whatever it was I was praising her about and raised that shit to the next level. Which is exactly what she did when she pushed down with her hands, raised her ass off the counter and ground her pussy around my cock.

"Yeah, I'll tell you someday," I agreed, unsure of how the fuck we were having a conversation. The chords in my neck strained as she tensed around me, strangling my cock.

Ti must have been thinking the same thing because then she said, "But not now, Bear. Now, you just have to shut up and fuck me."

So I did.

Hard.

I fucked her until her head slammed so hard against the

mirror that it cracked and pieces of it fell all around us, but we still kept fucking. She sunk her teeth into the flesh of my shoulder and drew fucking blood, probably to get back at me for the night before. Her red, blood-stained lips when she smiled up at me only made me hold on to her tighter. Thrust deeper. Harder. Faster. She ground up against my cock until she was screaming my name and her pussy was tightening around me like a fucking vise. I held back until I was sure she was recovering from coming and then I exploded inside of her so hard I went temporarily fucking blind.

Fuck I love this girl.

After we recovered and showered I took off in the truck, but not before promising Ti that I'd be back the very next day for her. In return I made her promise she wouldn't drug Rage again. Rage who, while my girl and I were saying our goodbyes outside, stared at us from inside the house, through the screen, like we were animals in the zoo and everything we did and said to each other was something out of the pages of National Geographic.

If I hadn't carried Ti off to the bathroom, I was positive Rage would have watched us go at it. She hadn't hidden her curiosity from us, although I don't think her curiosity about sex was a sexual thing, if that makes any sense. I think the girl was more curious about why sex didn't appeal to her or what it was everyone else seemed to get out of it. Which to me was fucking crazy considering I would seriously and gladly hand over a limb, any one of them, except the one between my legs, to be able fuck Ti every day.

Rage was the complete opposite of the one other person I knew who always wanted to watch. Besides Pancakes.

He had watched because he was curious too, at least it started out that way, but his curiosity was definitely sexual in every way.

Well, sexual…and violent.

Preppy.

He was a depraved little shit.

You're no Disney princess yourself, shit bag.

I liked porn as much as the next guy, but the shit Preppy was into didn't get my dick hard as much as it made my nuts want to retreat back into my body and hide out until the coast was clear.

A depraved little shit…who I'd give either of those nuts to have back.

I reached behind my neck and rubbed the PREP tattoo King had done for me. It always seemed to burn when I was thinking about him.

It burned especially hot when I thought back to the first night I'd realized that violence and sex went hand-in-hand for Preppy.

And sometimes, knife-in-hand.

CHAPTER SEVENTEEN

BEAR

EIGHTEEN YEARS OLD...

THERE WAS A party.
There was a party every night.
If not at the compound, then at King's house. The three of us, me, King, and Preppy were always down for a good time and when the sun went down we partied until it came back up. My club was always welcome, the liquor was always flowing, and the girls were more than willing.

"Hey, pretty girl," I said to some chick I'd never seen before with long brown hair and dark, almost black, eyes. She was dressed conservatively for one of our parties, and what I mean by conservative is that she wasn't topless or in the middle of playing a game of finger cuffs with the boys by the bonfire. She was probably a spring breaker. Her tanned skin the first giveaway. Most locals, even if they worked outside, weren't tan unless they were born with it. This girl had a glow about her that said she'd been lying in the sun all day, the tip of her nose slightly reddened. Yep, visitor. Which was great for me because that meant she'd be doing my second favorite a bitch does without much argument or hassle.

Leave.

She was definitely venturing out on the wrong side of the causeway, but it didn't matter because her skirt was short, her legs were long, and in all honesty, my checklist for who I stuck my dick in during those days wasn't much longer than that.

Actually, that was it.

"Hey there," she said, taking a sip from whatever drink was in her red plastic cup. I hoped she hadn't gotten it from Prep, 'cause if so there was so telling what the fuck was in it.

"I got a room here," I told her, cutting to the chase and because I'd never had to put any real effort into talking a girl into fucking me. "Wanna see it?"

"Lead the way," she whispered seductively. I grabbed her hand and dragged her toward my apartment. I laughed under my breath as she struggled to still look sexy while walking across the uneven grass in six inch heels. I walked her into the garage and stopped just short of the apartment door. I hoisted her up onto of the toolboxes in the garage. My favorite toolbox. It was the perfect height for what I needed it for.

"I thought you had an apartment?" she asked.

"I do, it's in there," I said pointing to the door that was so close I could reach out and touch the handle. "But I couldn't wait, baby," I lied, saying the same thing I'd told countless other girls who wondered why they were being banged on top of a bunch of greasy rags in a dark garage that smelled like oil and rust.

Chicks never made it further than the toolbox, and in some cases, never further than the dock, or even that one patch of clearing in the woods. I nuzzled her neck and did the minimum foreplay required not to piss off a chick before sleeving up my dick and shoving on home.

Spring Break Chick was good. Not great.

Great wouldn't come to me for years.

For those days though, she was as good as I got it, although she'd tried to kiss me which wasn't my deal. Making out was for fucking teenagers. I was eighteen and well into my stick-my-dick-in-it or nothing stage.

That night wasn't the first night I felt like I was being watched while I was with a girl. I looked out the garage window to the party-goers and knew for a fact that the people by the bonfire couldn't see in. I always made it a point not to turn the lights on, but still, the feeling wouldn't go away.

"What are you looking for?" Spring Break Chick asked, panting like a small hairy dog left out in the hot summer sun.

"Nothing," I lied. I was looking for something, all right, but it was more like a *someone*. I closed my eyes and pushed hard into her, trying to concentrate. She moaned and put on a good show but I was still distracted by the uneasy feeling that someone was there. I was growing bored of the girl and tired of my half assed attempt at fucking her. I picked up the pace so I could just come and be done with it.

That's when I learned Spring Break Chick was a screamer.

Over and over again she bucked against me when I hit bottom and it rallied me on. It wasn't too bad over the top fake shit, which I'd seen my share of, especially with the BBBs. This girl was honestly getting off by riding on my cock and, I was feeling it.

"You gonna come, pretty girl?" I asked, not because I thought she was really that pretty, but because I had no fucking clue what her name was.

I never did.

"Yes. YES!" she shouted. She gripped my neck and dug her

nails into my skin as I pounded into her. It was then I saw it. First it was just out of the corner of my eye. A flash of movement. But as the shadows in the garage shifted I realized that the it was a him.

When he noticed he'd been caught, he stepped completely free of the shadows and into the one spot of moonlight penetrating through the window. Anywhere else in the garage and he'd be cloaked in darkness.

He'd wanted to be seen.

Preppy.

He wasn't jerking off. His pants were on and his belt buckle fastened. He wasn't even making his usual sarcastic comments.

He was just watching. Not me. But her. His eyes glowing under the light as he looked her over like she was an exhibit at the Ringling Brothers museum.

I paused briefly, Preppy's presence throwing off my rhythm. "Why did you stop?" the girl asked. I could have outed Preppy for being a creeper right then and there, shouted at him to go. But I didn't. There was something in the way he was watching that made me feel like it was okay for him to stay, okay for him to keep watching.

I kept going.

Again Spring Break Chick started to moan, writhing up against me, scraping her nails down my back. Preppy was one of my closest friends and I wasn't a stranger to sharing bitches with my brothers in the club, although it was more of a BBB jumping from room to room without everyone in the same room at the same time.

I got the oddest feeling while Preppy stood there, not making a sound. Almost like he needed this for some reason. Needed to see what normal fucking looked like.

Like he needed to be a part of what we were doing.

Preppy was one of my best friends.

So I let him.

It was the quietest he'd ever been. Since the day we'd met, I'd never known him to go more than a few seconds without talking, but as I thrust my dick harder and harder into the girl, he was almost stoic. When I noticed he was staring at her tits, I yanked her poor excuse for a shirt—a small scrap of silk—up to her neck, so he could get a good look at them bouncing up and down as I fucked her.

His eyes glowed in appreciation and he nodded his thanks.

Figuring out Preppy was hard. From what King had told me about his past, he'd had a rough start in life. We all had. Preppy a little harder than most, but he never talked about it.

Ever.

I didn't fault him for that. I didn't exactly ever want to talk about my old man either.

The thing was that Preppy could get girls.

He *did* get girls.

He wasn't as tall as me or King, but he was still tall. He was still ripped to shreds, which came easier to him than it did for me because he started out a skinny kid, but when he started working out, he went right to ripped and lean. Other than a few inches of height and a few pounds of muscle he had something that both King and I were seriously lacking on some days.

Humor.

Personality.

Wit.

Charm.

When the girl's pussy started to clench around my dick, the squeezing sensation caused my balls tighten. I looked over to

Preppy who was as still as I'd ever seen him. No twitching or shoving his hands in his pockets or running his hands through his hair. Just looking. Watching. Observing.

I was getting close so I shoved the girl down on the toolbox so that her back was flush against the diamond shaped metal. I held on to her shoulders as I plowed into her, making sure to drag my cock along the front walls of her pussy as I pulled in and out. Her larger than average tits bounced up and down, and as soon as she came I followed her over, although it was more like a sneeze than a come because I was more preoccupied thinking about our company and what it meant that he was there, than I was about actually getting off.

"That was…wow," the girl said, sitting up. I pulled out of her and tugged off the condom, throwing it in a nearby trashcan. "Wanna go again?" she asked, wrapping her long legs around my waist and digging her heels into my back, pulling me forward.

"You want more?" I asked, holding her face in my hands. She reached out and licked one of my fingers.

"Yes, please. Give me more," she begged.

Out of the corner of my eye, I saw Preppy making a quiet move to leave out of the side door. "Prep," I called out. He stilled. I unwrapped the girl's legs from around me and took a step back, tucking myself back into my pants. "Why don't you come over here and take care of this beautiful girl? She says she needs more and I'm not so sure I have much more to give her."

At first Spring Break Chick was startled of Preppy's presence in the room and looked at me like she was in shock, but as soon as Preppy stepped into the light, she smiled as if I'd just given her a puppy. He legs were still spread, her wetness glistening for him to see.

Slowly Preppy moved closer and closer, his gaze focused

between her legs.

In my mind, I wasn't just offering to share a girl with Preppy, I was offering him a chance at normalcy. A chance to just fuck and not be so caught up in the hows or whys of it all.

"Have at her bro," I said, clapping him on the shoulder I left him to it and made my way back over to the party. I wasn't ten feet away from the garage when I heard the scream. It wasn't the kind of scream she'd made when I made her come, but the kind of scream that said "Someone just stabbed me," I turned and ran back as fast as I could.

And sure enough...

The girl was no longer on the toolbox, but laid out on the floor on her side, crawling away from Preppy at snail speed, but where a snail left slime in his tracks, the girl left blood.

"He fucking stabbed me!" she shouted, grabbing her thigh which still had a pair of silver scissors sticking out of the top, gushing blood with her every movement. Preppy stared wide-eyed at the trail of blood and at the blood on his fingers, but didn't make a move to help or even flee.

He just stood there with an unreadable expression on his face.

I picked the girl up and carried her out of the garage. One of the BBBs stitched up her leg and called her a cab home. I gave her a few hundred bucks to keep her mouth shut, and Preppy and I never talked about it again.

But I still felt him watching.

The next time I brought a girl into the garage and called him over, he looked worried. "I can't," he said, even after the girl said she was game.

"You want me to stay?" I asked in my most reassuring voice, wondering where it was in his fucked up mind that he went when sex was involved and what was causing the intensity that radiated off of him like he was a different person when he was watching. An entirely different version of Preppy. What shocked me most was that in place of his usual sarcastic and obnoxious demeanor, he was tentative. Shy.

It creeped me the fuck out.

Yet, I wanted to fix it for him somehow.

"Come here, baby," the girl said, parting her legs. I sat up on the toolbox next to her and lifted off her shirt. I played with her nipples while Preppy suited up and pushed inside.

After a few seconds, Preppy looked up at me, his eyes dark and menacing. He looked like a fucking demon. "I want to hurt her," he whispered. The girl, so involved in Preppy's dick, thank fuck, she hadn't heard him.

I shook my head, there would be no more scissor play if I had anything to do with it. "Watch, I'll do it for you," I said. I grabbed the girl's throat in my hands and squeezed just enough to make it uncomfortable for her, but not enough to actually cause pain. She moaned and gagged at the same time.

"She likes that," Preppy said, looking completely dumbfounded. He rammed into her at a furious pace while I held onto her tight. When I grabbed a handful of the girl's red curls in my fist and pulled, ripping a scream from her throat, it sent him over the edge and he came with a groan before collapsing onto the floor.

I picked the girl off the tool box and started to pull her away from the garage. "Is he going to be okay?" she asked looking back, but I didn't let her stop. It was better to let him recover than to leave him there alone with the girl and have to deal with the very real possibility it wouldn't just be a thigh he carved into the next time.

"Thank you," Preppy called out, still hunched over, face first on the concrete floor. His pants around his ankles.

It was the very first and the very last time I'd ever heard him utter those words.

Unfortunately, I couldn't say the same about the stabbing.

CHAPTER EIGHTEEN

THIA

"I'VE BEEN THINKING about it, and I think there's something wrong with your dog," Rage said. She was sitting on a barstool at the kitchen counter, painting her nails. Pancakes immediately took back his spot on couch the second Rage had gotten up, laying on his back with his legs spread and his tongue hanging out of the side of his mouth.

"He's a coyote," I corrected.

She turned up her nose. "Well, that would be what's wrong with your dog then."

"Do you know what kinds of diseases dogs can carry? Never mind coyotes. I heard once that some dogs can carry STD's on their tongues and with one little lick on the mouth..." Rage made an exploding motion with the hand she'd just painted. "Boom, herpes."

I was only half paying attention, my mind and body still humming from my night, and morning, with Bear. "I don't think that's true."

"I don't know, maybe it was parakeets. Don't you think that thing could be violent? You know a coyote is not the same thing as a dog."

"Rage I've heard you say the same thing every day for six months." I pointed to Pancakes who was fast asleep, still upside down, although now he was halfway off the couch, slinking further and further toward the floor with each little snore. "Does that look violent to you?"

"Do I?" Rage asked, blowing on her nails and flashing me her pearly white celebrity looking smile.

"Point made."

"Can I ask you something?" Rage asked, getting up and strolling around the living room as she examined the pictures on the wall like she hadn't been seeing the same ones every day for months. "Well, you drugged me so technically you owe me an answer."

"I prefer to think of it as giving you some much needed sleep." I struggled with the lid on a jar of peanut butter and was about to use my old bang-it-on-the-counter-until-it-submits trick when Rage walked over and grabbed it out of my hand.

"Hey, I—" I started, but stopped abruptly when Rage twisted it off in one try without putting any effort into it, while I on the other hand, was on the verge of popping a blood vessel in my eye when I had tried.

She handed me the jar and continued her stroll. "You and Bear. Did you… was he…" She sighed and I didn't know if she was embarrassed to ask me her question or if she couldn't find the words to ask it.

"Is this a sex question?" I asked, casually, trying to make it less awkward for her.

"Yes," she answered, picking up a photo off the coffee table of me and my dad when I was still in diapers. He held me in his arms and I was reaching for an orange off the tree. She set it back down.

"What do you want to know?" I asked. Pancakes fell to the floor and startled himself awake. He looked around as if he were looking for whoever pushed him off the couch. Within a few seconds he was back up and back asleep.

"Was he your first?" Rage asked, clearing her throat.

"Yes, he was," I said, licking the remaining peanut butter off the knife and tossing it into the sink. I handed Rage her PB&J and sat next to Pancakes whose paws were rotating like he was chasing something in his dream.

"And you...like sex with him?" she asked, popping her lips and folding her hands behind her back. She had set her sandwich down on the table without taking a bite.

"Are you sure you've had sex before?" I asked, wondering how anyone couldn't love what it was Bear and I did when we were alone, together, naked, and he was...

"Yes, I have. And I think that's why I'm so confused," she admitted. "And in my line of work, I don't get to talk to too many girls my age."

"Armed babysitting protection services?" I asked, raising my eyebrows.

Rage laughed and tightened her ponytail. "Protection services," she repeated, "I like that. Actually, I don't protect much of anything these days." She pulled herself up onto the counter, dangling her feet.

"You must have one hell of a good story," I said, taking a way too big bite.

She scoffed. "I don't know how good it is." She looked out the front window and then at me. "But maybe I'll come back and tell it to you one day."

A car door slammed and immediately Rage was on her feet with her hand behind her back on her gun. I pushed off the couch, startling Pancakes who ran out the open sliding glass door in the kitchen.

We walked to the front door and I caught a glimpse of a familiar sedan I never wanted to see again. We both stepped onto the porch, me first with Rage following closely behind. "It's no one," I grumbled, "Just some guy I shot once," I said loud enough for Mr. Carson to hear as he made his way up the walk, stopping just short of the steps.

"Well now, that's not a very nice greeting when I've brought you a present," Mr. Carson said, holding up a manila envelope, bringing memories back of the last time he was here and of another envelope he'd held.

I folded my arms over my chest. Rage stayed behind me, just outside the doorway. "Mr. Carson, you can take your envelope and get back in your car and leave, or this is going to end the same way it did last time."

Mr. Carson smiled and put a hand over his heart. "Ms. Andrews, I forgive you for what happened last time."

"I'm not seeking your forgiveness, Mr. Carson."

He seemed amused by my admission. "Last time, I will admit, I was a piranha. Feeding at the bottom of the barrel. I realize my error now and I have another offer for you."

I scowled. "Make your offer to the bank. In about six months this place will be theirs. I'm sure you can work out a deal that best fits your black soul and their fat wallets."

"You sound bitter, Ms. Andrews. Let me make this better," Mr. Carson said. "Sunnlandio Corporation doesn't want to wait the six months. Time is money and everything like that. So we are making you a much better offer. We would like you to sign over the property now and we will handle all debts and put a sizeable amount of cash in your pocket. Trust me, it will be worth your while." He again held up the folder. "The numbers even surprised me." Out of pure frustration and an overwhelming desire for Mr. Carson to leave, I made a move to go down the steps and grab the file.

Rage stopped me by grabbing me by the arm. "I'll get it," she said. She went down the steps slowly, snatching the file from Mr. Carson's hand. Rage's eyes lingered there, on his hand, for just a fraction of a second.

"And who might you be?" Mr. Carson asked, sounding a lot like he was talking to a toddler.

"Management," Rage answered. She opened the file and quickly scanned whatever was in there. "It's legit, Thia. I think you guys should sit and talk about it," she said, but there was something off about her voice. I'd heard her cheery, I'd heard her bored, I'd heard her complain A LOT, but this tone wasn't like anything I'd ever heard from her before. I searched her eyes for some sort of ulterior meaning, but found nothing.

"Come on inside, Mr. Carson. We were just making iced tea," Rage said, leading Mr. Carson up the steps, passing me on their way into the house. A huge victory smile plastered across his rat like face.

I should have aimed for his fucking head.

"Have a seat. My name is Mandy. I'm Thia's cousin," Rage said.

Her name is what?

Mr. Carson took a seat at the table while Rage opened kitchen cupboards and started taking random things out, setting them on the counter.

That's when I saw it. The very small, very subtle look she shot me. I would have missed it a nanosecond later but luckily I hadn't. She looked between me and then the knives in the butcher block on the counter, and then finally Mr. Carson. The smile never left her face and her attention never left our guest, but the message couldn't have been more clear.

"I'll cut some lemons," I said, grabbing a knife and walking over to the refrigerator. We had no lemons, but on my way back from the refrigerator I managed to slip the knife into Rage's waiting hand.

"Here we go," Rage said, walking around the counter with an empty pitcher. Mr. Carson looked at it and then looked at her, his forehead creasing in confusion. Rage dropped the plastic pitcher and when Mr. Carson's eyes followed it to the floor, Rage grabbed his wrist and set it on the table. In what seemed like no time at all, she raised the knife and ran it through the back of Mr. Carson's hand, pinning him to the table.

He screamed and reached inside his jacket, but Rage was faster. She pushed his jacket down his shoulders, locking his arms to his sides and preventing him from getting to whatever it was he was reaching for. She pointed to the knives and I tossed her another one and she did the same with his other hand. The screaming escalated.

She reached into his jacket and removed his gun.

Then, as if she hadn't just stabbed a man, TWICE, she calmy pulled out her gun, set it on the table next to his, making sure to point both of them toward Mr. Carson. She took a seat at the table while he continued to wail.

"You bitch!" he cried out, throwing his head back.

"You *BASTARD*," Rage said. She reached over and yanked up the sleeve of his jacket, revealing the Beach Bastards emblem emblazoned on his forearm.

"What?" I asked, clamping a hand over my mouth, not believing what I was seeing.

"Thia, why don't you be a doll and get us some rope?" Rage instructed.

"Rope?" I asked. "What for?" Mr. Carson tried to move his hands but only succeeded in making his wounds larger and the blood pour out faster.

All the other variations I'd seen of Rage's personality disappeared and were replaced by the sinister being staring hatred into her new captive. Rage smiled sweetly. "'Cause, Thia darling, this is the South and I'm in the mood for a good old fashioned hanging."

CHAPTER NINETEEN

THIA

I DIDN'T KNOW if she was actually going to go through with hanging Mr. Carson, and not because I didn't think her capable, but because the grove—and Jessep in general—lacked any sort of trees with sturdy enough branches. Orange trees wouldn't exactly get the job done. Regardless, I'd gone out to the shed and found what Rage had asked for. I'd just stepped back into the house when something buzzed.

Rage reached into the front of her shirt and pulled out an older style smart phone. Mr. Carson was passed out in his chair, his hands now covered in red, his blood dripping to the floor off the side of the table. Rage's eyes went wide when she looked at the screen. Her face paled. She abruptly got up and grabbed the rope from my hands, but instead of lynching Mr. Carson or whatever his real name was, she stuffed a pink bandana in his mouth and tied him to the chair using a series of complicated looking knots.

"What's going on?" I asked, hoping whatever it was had nothing to do with Bear.

"It's nothing," she said. "I just sent a text to Bear. He's on his way. Told me not to do anything until he gets here."

I studied her face, her quick intake of breath. "Okay, but your phone. What was that? WHO was that?" I asked again and that's when she looked up at me with glassy eyes and handed me the phone.

It was a selfie of a boy a little older than us. Handsome. Almost pretty. He was smiling into the camera, making a silly face with his hand on his chin.

"He's cute?" I said but it came out like a question. I handed her the phone back.

"He is, but he's also in trouble," Rage said, staring down at the photo and running her fingers across the screen.

"You got that from a selfie? He looks happy to me." I leaned over to look again just to make sure I didn't miss anything, but again nothing stood out to me as being out of the ordinary.

Rage put her phone back into her shirt. "It's his bat signal," she said.

"His what?"

"His bat signal. He doesn't like selfies. Said he would never take one. It's our sign. He was only supposed to send one when he's in trouble."

"Rage...who is this boy to you?"

She bit her lip. "He's...I don't really know," Rage answered quietly.

"You need to go to him," I said, making her decision easier.

Rage started to protest, but I wouldn't let her. "Listen to me, if the roles were reversed and Bear was in trouble, I wouldn't give a second thought to leaving you. You said yourself that Bear is on his way. This dude is tied up and knocked out. I know how to shoot a gun. GO!" I grabbed her by the shoulders and shook her like I was trying to shake some sense into her. "I got this," I assured her.

Rage looked up at me, blinking though tears. In the next second she grabbed her gun from the table and handed me Mr. Carson's. "Everything will be fine," I said again.

She nodded. "Thank you," she said before disappearing out the door.

Everything was *not* fine.

★ ★ ★

BEAR WOULD BE back soon and then I would be leaving that house and that town forever. I stared down the hall at my parents closed bedroom door. Neither Rage or I had opened that door in all the time we'd been there. And although I'd taken back some of the power the house had held over me, I hadn't quite reclaimed it all. I was afraid if I left without making my peace with it, that it might haunt me forever.

I checked to make sure my prisoner was still tied tightly to the table and still unconscious, which he was.

Before I had a chance to think too much about it I was standing outside the closed door of the room I feared the most. The room where my father took his last breath.

My parents' bedroom.

I turned the knob and pushed open the door which creaked as it slowly revealed the room to me.

My father's blood stained the wood floors, which were buckling at the seams under the dried pool of red. Reluctantly, I took a step inside the room.

Maybe this isn't so bad after all. It's just blood.

I ran my fingers over the ornate gold-framed mirror that hung above my parents dresser. One of my mother's favorite flea-market finds. I picked up a bottle of my father's cologne and sprayed it into the air. Inhaling deeply, I smiled, remembering better times. I combed out my hair with my mothers brush and I stared at my reflection in the mirror until I was sure that my reflection had started talking back to me. "Get out of here," I saw myself say. "It's not safe." And then finally. "Look behind you."

I wasn't fast enough. Just as I turned around, large hands clasped around my throat, turning me back facing the mirror. He squeezed, crushing my neck, closing my airway. I struggled and kicked and bucked, but it was no use. I watched in the mirror in horror as the whites of Mr. Carson's eyes bulged out of his head as I struggled for air. I tried prying his fingers apart with my own but he didn't move. "Night, night, you fucking cunt," he whispered in my ear. With my vision rimmed in static like snow that grew larger and larger, I felt my body go limp. I fell sideways onto the floor and although he'd released me, my airway wouldn't open. I couldn't draw breath into my lungs.

The last thing I saw was a laughing Mr. Carson, standing over me, as he faded further and further away until he was gone and the only thing I was left looking at was the broken blade on the ceiling fan. Some sort of commotion was taking place out of the corner of my eye.

Someone screamed.

But it was too late.

It all went away.

Everything.

I was dead.

CHAPTER TWENTY

THIA

L IGHTS. SOUNDS.
Barking?

I woke up with a start like I'd been launched into consciousness from one world to the next. I sat up so quickly it was like an involuntary knee-jerk reaction to be able to pass air into my lungs again. Opening and closing my mouth I gulped for more air, which came much slower than I wanted.

But at least it came. My breaths were short and staccato.

I'd gone from the land of nothingness into a flurry of commotion. The room spun around me as each of my senses was shocked back to life like they'd just been struck by lightning.

My brief death had taken a toll on me. My neck was sore. My head throbbed. I reached for my throat. I swallowed and it felt as if I'd gargled with sand or broken glass, or a cocktail of both.

There was a crash.

Surprised by the sudden noise I stupidly craned my damaged neck around the side of the bed to see where the noise had come from, and was immediately rewarded with a severe stabbing sensation in and around my throat.

I pushed through the pain, dragging myself on the floor instead of causing further injury to my neck. When I'd moved far enough to see around the bed, my eyes landed on the scene playing out in front of me.

★ ★ ★

THE SPINNING ROOM began to slow until it thankfully came to a stop. When I was finally able to take a deep breath I coughed on the exhale, drawing the attention of Mr. Carson, who was on his knees beside the bed. His white shirt torn around his right arm, revealing an open and bloodied gash across his bicep. He pursed his lips and although he was the one on his knees he looked smug, like he'd somehow still won.

The Bear from that morning was not the same Bear who was now in that room, standing behind Mr. Carson with a gun to the back of his head.

Bear looked possessed. A vein throbbed in his temple. His chest heaving up and down. Even the veins running down his defined abdomen, disappearing into his low-slung jeans, looked as though they were pulsing with anger.

"Ti," Bear said, calling me even further back to the land of the living. "You okay?"

"I'm fine," I said, my voice hoarse and scratchy. It hurt to speak, but it was nowhere near the pain I'd felt just minutes before. I grabbed onto the bedpost, hoisting myself into a standing position. "Do you know who he is?" I asked, looking at the man on his knees.

Bear nodded, pushing the barrel of his gun against the back of the man's head. "His name is Tretch. He's a nomad Chop uses on occasion to carry out his dirty work. He's less known than the crew at Logan's Beach and when he's not wearing a cut he looks like a fucking pussy so he's believable as a civilian."

"He's Mr. Carson to me. The guy I shot. The Sunnlandio guy." Bear laughed wickedly and smacked the butt of his gun against the back of Tretch's head, who winced and swayed, but didn't fall.

"This motherfucker is going to wish you killed him," Bear seethed.

"Bear," I started, leaning on the bed for support.

"No, Ti. Don't try and talk me out of it," Bear said, fire dancing in his eyes. He paced the floor, two steps one way and then two steps the other. His eyes didn't meet mine. "This fucker laid his hands on you, Ti. His life ends now. The last fucker got away with a broken arm." Bear leaned down next to Tretch and spoke directly into his ear. "Unfortunately for you, I'm all out of broken arms today."

"Bear," I said again, trying to get his attention.

"Ti, it's not an option, he's—"

"Bear!" I shouted past the pain, possibly tearing something in my throat. Bear's eyes finally snapped to mine as if I'd temporarily brought him out of his murderous trance. "I'm not trying to stop you," I coughed out. "I just don't want you to *shoot* him." I could see the light go off in Bear's eyes. He knew what I meant, just like he always seemed to know what I meant without me having to explain it. "Tretch wrapped his hands around my throat and tried to choke the life from me. I think you need to repay the favor." I pulled myself onto the bed, crawling up to where I could be closer to Bear and look down at the piece of shit who almost killed me.

Tretch may have never worked for the Sunnlandio Corporation, but it didn't matter. The man on his knees in my parents' old bedroom might as well have worked for them, because to me represented the evil of that company, the evil of the MC who'd tried at every turn to bring death to our doorstep, to rip Bear from me and me from Bear. The idea so absurd, I tossed my head back and started to laugh.

I was manic.

I was insane.

Maybe I'd inherited some of my mother's crazy after all.

I wasn't laughing because I was asking the man I love to strangle someone to death, but because I honestly didn't think that even death could separate us.

"You sure?" Bear asked me warily. I abruptly stopped laughing.

Bear was a biker who didn't need a scared little girl, he may not have been in a club anymore but he still needed an old lady.

He needed me.

I nodded, and not just because I thought that's what Bear wanted from me, but because I'd never been so sure of anything before.

"No! No! Let's talk about this!" Trench shouted. He tried to stand but Bear kicked out the back of his legs and sent him back down to the floor.

"Like this, baby?" Bear asked. There was a quiet reverence in his voice. He handed me his gun and I took over the job of keeping it aimed at Tretch. Bear wrapped his big strong hands around Tretch's throat and started to squeeze, just as Tretch had done to me.

Tretch struggled, his legs kicked out from underneath him. The muscles in Bear's forearms flexed and strained while he held tight to the man dying between his hands. My own hands automatically went to my neck, tracing the swollen fingerprints Tretch had left behind.

Bear's eyes found mine and didn't leave. The whites of his eyes turned to red. He gritted his teeth.

Tretch looked to me with bulging eyes, one final plea for his life, knowing I was the only one who could grant it to him.

I didn't want to.

With one last angry roar Bear squeezed the last of the life from Tretch, his eyes rolling back in his head. His chin fell to his chest.

Bear released his hold on Tretch, shoving his lifeless body sideways onto the floor. Bear reached into his boot and pulled something out. He flipped it open, a serrated blade sprang out. I was sure Tretch was already dead, but for whatever reason Bear had, he crouched down and gashed Tretch's throat wide open.

As a former member of Future Farmer's Daughters of America, we'd taken a trip to the slaughterhouse, and the way the blood poured from Tretch's neck reminded me of watching the pigs get slaughtered one by one.

Only this animal happened to be human.

WAS human.

I shifted off the bed and stood on unsteady legs, holding on to the end table for support.

Bear's boots crunched over shards of ceramic from a vase broken in their struggle. He made his way over to the now empty vase stand and picked up a lace doily. He wiped the dark red from his knife before shoving it back into his pocket and threw the bloodied scrap of lace at Tretch's feet.

Tretch might have been dead, but Bear's anger was alive and well.

So much so the room was thick with it.

Bear stood there, silently, for what felt like hours. Finally, he looked down to his hands and stepped toward me, bringing his hands up to my face. I covered his hands with mine.

"He could have killed you," he said, his voice unsteady. His eyes unfocused. I left his hands on my face and reached up for his, rubbing my thumbs over the freckles underneath his deep blue eyes.

"He didn't," I said, my voice sounding more like normal, the pain in my neck subsiding to a dull ache.

"Ti, he tried—" he started again, but I wouldn't let him go there. I couldn't.

"But he didn't," I repeated. "He didn't." I locked my hands around his neck. I stood on my tiptoes and planted a small kiss to the corner of his mouth. His beard tickled my lips.

Bear's eyes locked onto mine and turned darker than I'd ever seen them. He was searching my face. Searching my soul, but I had no clue what it was he was looking for. He craned his neck down and pressed a tender kiss against the swollen and injured flesh on my neck.

Suddenly the air shifted and it was no longer thick with anger, but something else entirely.

Something even more powerful.

Lust. Need.

Bear's chest was damp with sweat. He smelled like pure man and looked like pure muscle. Every bit of him invaded my senses.

Bear forced me backwards onto the mattress. Our lips connected but only for a brief second. He lifted me up by my waist and tossed me further back onto the bed.

The thrumming of my erratically beating heart and the sounds of us coming together filled the silent space. The creak of the bed springs. The smack of our lips. His boots falling to the ground.

His zipper.

Bear grabbed onto the waistband of my shorts, yanking them down to my feet, tossing them over Tretch's body, which laid across the open doorway. He pulled off my panties with one hand and crawled on top of me, pushing his jeans down over his ass until I could feel him. Large, hot, hard, pressed right up against my core. I closed my eyes and moaned, the contact too much and yet nowhere near enough.

I needed more.

So much more.

I reached for the hem of my shirt and Bear lifted up off of me, just enough to allow me to pull it off and chuck it to the side.

Then we were skin to skin.

My softness against his hardness.

Tortured soul against tortured soul.

The feeling of him between my legs, his weight on top of me, the need for him to be inside of me had me shamelessly spreading my legs as wide as they could go, inviting him into the place I needed him most.

Bear kissed the spot where my neck met my shoulder, over the bite mark he'd made the night before and I saw stars. Maybe I was dying again. Except this was a death I wouldn't fight. This was a death I'd go to gladly.

Bear's tongue licking behind my ear, sucking at my skin, kissing, teasing. His hands kneading my breasts and pinching my nipples. I grabbed on to the globes of his glorious ass, pressing him in closer, needing him to close the torturous gap between us.

"You were made for me," Bear said before his lips met mine, and I was lost in the sensation of his tongue dancing with mine.

Tangling with one another.

He groaned and I lifted my hips, again searching for more. Begging.

A few minutes earlier I'd thought I was dead, and now I'd never felt so alive.

Bear rocked against me, running his hard length through my wetness, and I relentlessly ground against him like I couldn't get enough.

Because I couldn't.

I didn't want to.

Not then.

Not ever.

I didn't care about the corpse in the corner or the blood on the floor. Both old and new.

All I cared about was Bear.

He reached between us and ran his fingers over my clit. He wasn't gentle. He wasn't even that nice. He was downright rude to it. Pushing hard and circling it like he was punishing it. Punishing me.

"You want me, baby?" he asked, pulling back and searching my eyes. "You want this?"

I reached out and brushed away the hair that had fallen into his face. I knew he wasn't just asking if I wanted his cock, he was asking if I wanted this life.

"Fuck me," I said, answering his question in a language I knew Bear was fluent in.

He didn't need anything more than those words because he grabbed the base of his shaft and lined it up with my entrance, pushing inside of me like he was answering a question I'd never asked. He was hot and hard and every inch of access he gained made me only want more of him.

All of him.

When Bear met resistance, it was like all of his resistance fell apart. He groaned. "I love how fucking tight you are. I love how I have to fight your fucking pussy to push my cock all the way inside you."

He pushed in again and again until he was so far inside of me, body, heart, and soul, that I was almost afraid of how deep our connection was. It was about more than sex. It was about us, and we were a lot like our sex in a way. It hurt. It felt amazing.

I never wanted it to end.

Bear pushed my knees apart, spreading me as far as I could go, opening me up as much as I could give him. He thrust wildly. "Look at me, baby. I want you to look at me when you fucking come," he ordered. His voice was strained, his hair falling into his face all over again. The muscles in his forearms and shoulders flexing as he held himself over me, bracing himself on the mattress with both elbows beside my head.

I glanced over his shoulder as the pressure started to build, catching our reflection in the mirror above the dresser. Bear's body blocked most of mine except my legs, which I lifted up and wrapped around his waist. The muscles in his back were taut and straining. His colorful tattoos looked as if they were dancing as he fucked and fucked me.

And fucked me some more.

I watched us in the mirror as the pressure in my lower stomach tightened. With each push in and pull out, Bear touched a spot inside of me that had my mouth falling open and my entire body clenching around his relentless and massive cock.

Faster and faster.

Harder and harder.

Oh my god and holy shit.

My pussy clenched around him. I was close. So very close. I lifted my hips to grant him as much access as possible. "Aaaahhhh," he groaned, "I fucking love it when you do that," he said, his forehead beading with sweat. I lifted my head off the mattress and lightly bit his nipple. My neck injury, although still there, temporarily forgotten as the pleasure portion of my brain temporarily sent the pain portion packing.

"Fuck, Ti." Bear thrust harder, angling himself so that his shaft rubbed against my clit with every stroke of his cock. I closed my eyes, about to be taken over the edge. About to come.

"OPEN," Bear ordered again. He grabbed my face, forcing me to look into the deep dark pools of blue.

He thrust once, twice, three more times until I was coming so hard, I felt it all the way in my toes. Over and over again I pulsed around him in waves of pure pleasure, which set him off because he gripped the backs of my thighs, and with our eyes open, his nose touching mine, staring into each others souls, Bear came.

Hard.

A guttural roar tore from his throat as he spilled himself inside me. I'd never heard anything so beautiful.

His warmth spread inside me and I moaned because nothing felt better than how it felt to be fully consumed by the man inside me.

On top of me.

In my heart.

By Bear.

He fell onto my chest, and with his lips against my skin, before his orgasm had fully subsided, his cock still twitching with his release, he whispered two words that stopped my heart, "Marry me."

I paused, unsure if he was serious. My stomach knotted with nerves. My pulse still pounding from the mind-blowing orgasm was now beating so hard, I was a few seconds away from a stroke. "Is that the after sex high talking?" I asked with a small laugh.

Bear looked at me, holding my face in his hands. When I tried to turn away from the power of his unrelenting glare, he didn't let me. "Ti, I fucking love you," Bear said, dipping his head, kissing me long and hard. When he pulled back and saw that I was still confused, he asked, "Do I fucking look like I'm joking?"

No. No he didn't.

Holy shit.

Bear buried his face in my neck and inhaled, breathing me in. I could never get enough of knowing he wanted me as much as I wanted him. "Seriously though," I started, needing to clarify something that had been nagging me over the last twenty-four hours. "I know you want your club. And if not the Bastards, then a new club. A better one. You don't have to give that up for me. I need you to know that."

Bear lifted his head and narrowed his eyebrows, a worried expression crossing over his beautiful face. He ran his thumb over my lips, still swollen from our kisses. "So what does that mean?" he asked, and I knew he was wondering where I was going with all this.

"I don't know," I said, taking a moment to pause for dramatic effect. "You really think I'm old lady material?" I joked, jabbing my fingers into his ribs.

Bear laughed and it sent a wave of tingles over my skin. I made a note to myself to make him laugh more. He grabbed hold of my wrists and held my arms down above my head. "Babe, we just fucked, the best fuck of my entire life, with a dead body less than three feet away, if that doesn't make you old lady material, I don't know what the fuck does."

It was my turn to laugh.

"So say you'll marry me already and stop fucking stalling," Bear said, looking down to me with a big boyish grin on his face.

"Yes," I said, because there was no other answer. There never was.

Just yes.

Just Bear.

Just me.

Just Forever.

In that rickety old farmhouse, in my parents' old bedroom, with my father's dried blood staining the floor and an open-eyed corpse looking on, Bear had proposed.

I wouldn't have had it any other way.

'Cause life is just fucked up like that.

I realized that all my past worrying had been pointless, because not only did I fit into Bear's world.

He kissed my temple and dragged me against his chest.

I WAS his world.

CHAPTER TWENTY-ONE

BEAR

"How come I'm not dead?" Thia asked, lifting her sleepy head from my chest.

"'Cause you're not fucking supposed to be," I said with more bite than necessary. My girl was very much alive, in my arms, and full of my cum. Which was exactly where she was supposed to be.

When I came into the room and saw Ti's lifeless body on the floor, it was like a switch turned on in my mind. A kill switch. I thought she was dead but I wasn't going to tell her that. It wasn't until I saw her peek out from behind the bed when I felt as if I could breath again.

The second I knew she was alive, I knew that after I put Tretch down that I was going to fuck her. It was a messed up part of me that needed a reminder that we were both alive.

I meant it when I'd told her it was the best fuck of my life. I'd came harder and longer than I ever had before, and from the way Ti was moving underneath me when she came, the way she tightened around me, I'm pretty sure she didn't have any complaints either.

"You know what I mean," she said, elbowing me in the ribs.

Besides the body on the floor, you would have thought we were any other normal couple, laying in bed recovering from intense orgasms.

But we weren't normal.

I fucking loved that about us.

"Pancakes," I told her, watching with amusement as her face scrunch up in confusion like I knew it would.

"Huh?"

"It seems that your non-dog decided to act like the coyote he is. He tore that massive hole Tretch's arm before I'd even got here."

"My Pancakes?" she asked. I knew she was having a hard time imagining the coyote she thought was a dog, who licked toes and liked to watch us fuck was capable of that kind of violence, but it was true.

That coyote was the perfect dog for us.

"Yes, your Pancakes. Unless you know of some other non-dog coyote named Pancakes, hell bent on defending you." I laughed. "Also, I need to warn you not to freak out when you go into the other room, 'cause our non-dog has blood all over his face and fur, and right now he looks a lot less like a regular dog or a coyote, and more like motherfucking Kujo."

"He's the best dog," she said sleepily, her eyelashes fluttering against my skin.

"He's a coyote," I corrected softly.

"He's the best coyote," she muttered.

"He sure is," I said, kissing her softly on the lips. She moaned and I could tell by the way she was tossing her head around that she was trying to fight off sleep.

"Did you find her? Your mom?" Ti asked through a yawn.

"No," I answered. "We looked in every shelter up and down

the coast but there was no sign of her. Stone's lead turned out to be a dud. We have time to figure out another plan though. Chop and the MC are out on a ride. Looks like they won't be back for a couple of weeks or so."

She opened her eyes, although barely, glancing up at me through little slits. "This was kind of fucked up."

"Nah, this was nothing," I said, waving her off. "If you want to know what fucked up is, you need to meet Jake."

"Who's Jake? Is he a friend of yours?" she asked.

I shook my head. "Jake is… Jake helped us when Ray was in trouble."

"That doesn't sound so fucked up," she said, trailing soft lazy kisses all around my chest.

"No, but that's why he's the most fucked up person I know. You never know what side he's on. Also, it doesn't help that he looks like sunshine. Blond hair and blue eyes. The kind of looks you'd see on one of them TV shows all the teenagers like these days. But that kid's got the devil in him. Only human lives he values are his wife Abby's and now his kid. Jake's the only person in the world who scares the shit out of me. You know, besides you."

"Sounds a little like Rage," Ti said. "And if he saved Ray, then Jake's okay by me." Ti linked her leg over mine, her little thigh resting over mine, her knee grazed my cock which should be as exhausted as Ti but was seriously thinking of how hot another go-round would be.

I mouthed a silent "Thank you" to Tretch as I stroked Ti's wild hair. After all, it was because of him my girl realized what I'd known all along.

How strong she was.

How resilient she was.

She was going to be a great old lady.

Ti's eyes danced behind her eyelids like she was watching a dream unfold.

In the stifling Florida heat, we only had a few hours before Tretch started to smell, but cleanup could wait for a little bit, while Ti napped.

I wasn't anywhere near tired.

Besides, I had no use for dreams when mine was already lying on top of me, fast asleep.

CHAPTER TWENTY-TWO

THIA

RAGE SHOWED UP to grab some of her things and when I said good-bye to her she just shrugged and walked off into the grove. "Where is she going?" I asked Bear. Who ended his call to Wolf and shoved his phone in his pocket. Wolf was going to be the one who was going to be running 'cleanup' on Tretch's body.

Bear shrugged. "Don't know. Never do when it comes to her."

I followed him over to the truck, "Can I ask you something?"

"Shoot," Bear said, hopping in. I got in the passenger side and slammed the door. Pancakes, without having to be told, hopped in the bed.

"Why her? Why Rage? Why not have some big security dude or big bouncer guy look after me while you were away?" I asked the question that had been nagging at me since the day I'd met Rage.

Bear started the engine and we pulled out onto the road.

"Rage doesn't care about anything but the job. Things, places, people. She'd done a lot of tracking for the club and I thought she'd be the one to best protect you if it came down to it because unlike a bouncer or security guard, Rage wouldn't hesitate to pull the trigger."

"That makes sense," I said, finally having my answer, but for some reason I'd thought there would be more to it than that.

A muscle under Bear's eye twitched.

"What?" I asked. He waved me off.

"What?" I repeated, demanding to know what had his face contorted in a way that made me think he was trying not to laugh.

Unable to contain himself any longer, Bear burst out into laughter.

"What the hell is so funny?" I asked, growing annoyed as he leaned over the steering wheel, holding onto his stomach with one arm.

Bear set his hand on my thigh and gave it a squeeze. "Ti, do you really think I'd let a dude stay in the same house with you for one fucking second, never mind six fucking months?"

And there I had it. The truth behind the truth. Which when it came to Bear, made the second truth make a whole lot more sense.

We were still laughing as Bear pulled us onto the highway and we headed back to the place where it all started.

Back to Logan's Beach. Back to Ray, King, the kids, and back to the apartment I'd grown to love.

Nobody was home when we arrived and we hadn't been back for more than a few minutes before Bear had already stripped me naked and was on his knees in front of me, worshiping between my legs with my his talented tongue and mouth.

It must have been the week for people to walk in on us because right after I'd come down from yet another mind-blowing orgasm, I opened my eyes to find King and Ray standing in the living room on the other side of the coffee table. Bear stood up, completely at ease with the fact that he was still naked, although he wasn't JUST naked. He was naked and very, *very* hard. His mouth still glistening from lapping up every last bit of my orgasm.

The solemn look on both their faces made me realize they were there for a much bigger and more serious reason than trying to catch us in the act.

"You might want to put some clothes on for this," King said, and suddenly I was all too aware of my nakedness. Bear led me into the bedroom and I was still getting dressed when he left the room after throwing on a pair of boxers, leaving the door open on the way out.

"What the fuck is going on?" he asked. I looked out and spotted the worried expression on his face and suddenly I was as worried as he looked.

"It's Grace," Ray said, choking out a sob and burying her face into King's shirt. He held her close by the back of the head and stroked her long icy blonde hair.

"What the fuck is wrong with Grace?" Bear barked, an angry burst of yelling that I felt deep in my chest.

King reached out and placed his other hand on Bear's shoulder, but Bear jumped back like King was trying to stab him instead of comfort him. "Tell me," Bear demanded.

I stepped out into the living room just in time to see King kiss Ray on top of the head. He looked back up to Bear when he spoke again. "She's in bad shape, man."

"How bad?" Bear asked, grabbing a pack of cigarettes from the table. He put one in his mouth, it dangled from his lips as he scurried around, searching under couch cushions for a lighter.

"The kind you don't come back from."

Bear's cigarette fell from his mouth.

CHAPTER TWENTY-THREE

BEAR

I FUCKING HATE hospitals.
Always have.

For good reason, too. Ain't nothing good ever has come from stepping foot in one of them. Not for me anyway. Actually, the fucking worst always happened. A wave of bad shit, along with the smell of antiseptic and disappointment, hit me in the fucking face every single time those automatic glass doors opened, followed by me frantically asking a million white-coated fuckers where the brother I was looking for was.

Usually, they were dead.

It was at that very hospital where we'd come to see Grace, through those very same fucking doors where a white-coated cocksucker came out and officially told us that Preppy was a goner.

I'm sorry. There was nothing we more we could do.

I remember everything about that night, down to the pussy-ass yellow smiley face tattoo the doc had on the outside of his hand.

The last time I was there was when I drove Ray, who was in pretty bad shape after being beat to shit by her fucking ex husband douche-bag, and King, who was all shot up, to the emergency room that smelled of unhealed wounds and misery. My immediate reaction whenever I went to a hospital has been to get on my bike and drive as far away as I possibly could.

Which sounded pretty fucking good to me as we walked down a sea foam colored hallway, the wallpaper peeling at the seams.

King and Ray were ahead of us with Thia and I staying back a few steps.

The last time I saw Grace, she was in better shape than I was. Where I had been wrestling with every demon I'd ever come across, hopped up on so much booze and blow it was a wonder I was even alive, she'd looked as if she could place in a marathon or give that juice guy on late-night TV a run for his money.

We knew Grace had cancer. She'd had it for years. More than a decade, I think. At one point, her pain got real bad and King gave her some weed and showed her how to smoke it so she could manage it better. For a while that seemed to work. After that she told us that the cancer couldn't keep her down and that she decided she wasn't going to die.

Crazy thing about Grace was that we all believed her. When she said she was going to do something, she did it.

Why did beating cancer have to be any different?

But in walking down that depressing ass hallway, looking into the rooms where countless other patience were hooked to tubes and machines of all kinds, I realized that this was different.

Very different.

Which was why seeing her in that hospital room with tubes coming out of her arms and a breathing mask over her face, looking every bit the frail woman she never wanted to be with sunken cheeks and deep circles under her eyes, caused me to stop in the doorway.

The woman lying on the bed didn't even look like her. The woman I'd known for fifteen years had a fire around her that could make the biggest, baddest motherfucker out there say thank you, ma'am, and wipe his boots at the door.

"There you are," Grace said with a low scratchy voice, her chest contracted and she gasped. "I've been waiting for my boys. Where is my Abel?" she asked, taking King's hand.

"I'm right here," I said, tugging Ti in behind me.

"Maybe you should take turns speaking with her," the doctor stated, without taking his eyes off of his clipboard. "We don't want to overwhelm her."

"Who the fuck are you?" King asked, a vein in his neck pulsed and whatever the doctor said next would determine if he'd still end up a doctor at the end of the day, or a patient. The doc opened his mouth but he quickly shut it. Smart man. He scanned the barcode bracelet on Grace's wrist with a tool connected to an iPad and made himself busy by checking numbers on the numerous machines and entering them into his tablet.

"Brantley my dear. It's fine," Grace said, tugging on King's hand to bring his attention away from the doctor and back to her. Ray kept her hand on the small of his back, using her own method of calming him down.

"You guys go first," I said, tugging Ti back out of the room without waiting for King to respond. "Doc, can I see you for a sec?"

I needed a minute to think, plus the last thing Grace needed was to witness King beating the life out of her doctor, if that's the route he decided to take. Ti and I sat in two lone chairs in the middle of the empty hallway. I don't mean there weren't people in it. I meant that besides the two chairs, there wasn't a single picture or painting anywhere I could see.

The doc followed us out, still punching the screen on his tablet. His sneakers squeaked against the dull linoleum.

Ti squeezed my hand, reminding me that I wasn't alone in this. "How long does she have?" she asked, and I'm glad she did, because although that was my question I don't know if I would have been able to say the words. Also, there was a part of me. A big part. Who just didn't want to know the answer.

Actually, none of me really wanted to know.

"Are you family?" the doc asked skeptically, pushing his glasses up his nose seeking answers from his tablet. His fingers flew over the screen. When he came to a stop he squinted down, his mouth moving as he read.

I stood up and crossed my arms over my chest. I towered over the little pale-faced doctor and stepped close enough to him to make him feel how incredibly inadequate he would be in this fight not worth starting.

Because if he didn't stop looking down at that fucking thing and answer my girl's question, there would be a fight.

"We are as much family as she's got," I said. "You gonna fucking tell me what me and my girl need to know or what?"

The doc cleared his throat, his face paled. He looked down at his tablet one more time. "Um... Actually, are you by chance either Mr. Abel McAdams or Mr. Brantley King?" he asked, pushing his glasses up his nose for the millionth time.

"He's Abel," Ti chimed in. She stood beside me, and again I reached for her hand and was glad when I felt hers slip into mine.

"Well then, you are her next of kin, according to her paperwork, so I can certainly share her status with you. Is Mrs. Jeffries your mother by chance?"

"Yes," I said, without hesitation. She was the closest fucking thing I'd ever had and if this motherfucker delayed one more second, me kicking his ass would wind up being my first positive hospital story.

"Well, Mrs. Jeffries cancer has spread, as you probably know. Brain. Lungs. It's terminal. It's *been* terminal. Last year we'd told her she only had weeks left, if not days, but she defied us all by lasting a heck of a lot longer. You should be proud of her. I'd never seen anything like it," the doc said that like that bit of information was supposed to somehow make me feel like she wasn't laying dying less than twenty feet away.

"Doctor…" Ti said politely.

"Reynolds" he finished. "Dr. Reynolds."

"Dr. Reynolds," I said, rolling my eyes. "You didn't answer the question. How long does she have now? And don't bullshit me." Ti squeezed my hand. I gave Ti's hand a squeeze back, looked over at Doogie Howser, Asian MD and said the one word I rarely used, "Please."

"Not long. Due to her current condition, I would normally say only hours. But honestly, in my professional opinion, due to her rate of deterioration, it's probably less than that. All of her major organs are shutting down." He looked like he wanted to run as far away as possible and honestly I didn't blame the little cocksucker.

"Thank you," Ti said. The doctor nodded and scurried off down the hall, clutching his stupid tablet, like a mouse released from a trap.

We sat down again in the same two chairs, only to stand back up a few seconds later when King and Ray emerged from the room. For most people, I could see how King was hard to read. Especially because he never felt the need to fill the silence with words like Preppy always had. Seeing the solemn look on his face made me feel like I didn't need to talk. Maybe a little bit of King had rubbed off on me.

Ti embraced a crying Ray. King came up to me and lowered his voice. "She keeps passing out. Her breathing sounds like she's been smoking a carton a day for the last fifty years." He paused, running his hand over his face. "This is it, man. You need to get in there."

King and I had been friends since we were fifteen years old. That was the first time he'd ever reached out and embraced me in more than a pat on the shoulder, but an actual hug. It was brief, but he was my brother. Blood or not, he had my back and I had his. Even in the hospital while our pseudo mother lay dying on the other side of the wall. "She really wants to talk to you," he added.

I nodded and reached my hand out for Ti who had her hands full with a weeping Ray against her chest. "You go first," Ti said, "I'll join you in just a minute." I didn't want to go in alone, but at the same time, I felt like I had to. There was so much to say to Grace, but where the hell would I even start?

"Abel," Grace said, again lowering her mask and stretching out her fingers for me. I sat beside her on the chair and took her hand in both of mine.

"I'm here," I reassured her, giving her hand a quick kiss. Her skin was ice cold.

"I knew you would be. Even though I know you hate hospitals. Are you all right?" she asked.

I laughed because Grace knew me better than anyone. She was knocking on death's door yet she wanted to make sure I was okay because I hated hospitals. "I don't think okay is really the word I'd use," I said.

She smiled at me. The same sympathetic smile that got me through a lot of hard times during my teenage years. "I know what happened to Samuel felt like the end of your life too, my son." Grace drew in a shaky labored breath. "But it wasn't. And when I get to the other side, I know for a fact the both of us are going to have a good long laugh at your expense." She coughed and I lunged forward to place the mask back over her face.

She took slow deep breaths, her chest lurching on every intake. When she'd calmed, I said, "I wouldn't put it past either one of you." She waved away my hand and looked at me with unfocused bloodshot eyes. Her lips were a light shade of blue. Her hair was covered with a light purple bandana.

"I am dying, Abel. But I swear to fucking Christ that I'm not leaving you. You need to know I wouldn't do that. When you make Thia your wife, which I know you'll do just from the way you both look when you talk about one another, I'll be here with you." She patted my hand, again comforting me when she was the one in the hospital bed. "When you welcome your first, second, third child into this world, I'll be here. When you don't know what to do or you don't know where to turn, I'll whisper in your ear until you make up your mind. Just promise me one thing."

My heart was hammering in my chest. Tears I didn't know I possessed leaked from the corners of my eyes and trailed their heat down my cheeks, wetting my beard. "What's that?" I asked. My voice cracked.

Grace flashed me a weak smile, her chest rose and fell rapidly. The machines beeping and blinking with each intake of final breath. "When it comes to the girl out there."

"Yeah?"

"Don't fuck it up." Grace gasped.

I held her hand up to my lips. "I'll try my hardest not to. I promise." I chuckled, tasting the salt of my tears. My shoulders shook, and for a small moment I allowed myself to wallow in my grief.

"Thank you, sweet boy," Grace said, bringing my hands to her mouth and giving them a dry-lipped kiss.

"For what?" I asked, wiping my cheek on the shoulder of the shirt I'd put on as we were walking up to the doors.

"For being the son I always wished for. You, Samuel, and Brantley. I prayed for sons every single day since the day I married Edmond, and it took long enough, and you boys didn't come to me in a way I ever expected, but suddenly you were there, and you made me the mama I'd always wanted to be."

Machines beeped and blinked again. Some sort of alarm went off on the far wall. The room flashed in red light.

"There is so much I need to tell you," I said, holding on to her more tightly as if she was going to slip out of my grasp at any second and physically fall to her death.

"I know, and there is so much I need to tell you." Grace looked to the ceiling and then back to me. "I need to apologize."

"For what? Dying?" I asked, the word coming out broken.

"No. For lying. I lied to you Abel, and I'm so sorry. I really hope you can find a way to forgive me some day. I thought it was for the best, but looking back, I think I should have fought harder. Come up with another plan. I…"

"It doesn't matter. Nothing matters," I said just as Grace started to choke. She cleared her throat several times before she could speak again.

"It's all there for you to find out," she said, and I didn't know if she was still talking about the same thing, or if she was on any pain medication that might have just kicked in. "As I said, I'm dying, but I'm not going anywhere. Even death couldn't keep me from my boys."

"Kind of like Preppy," I said, forgetting that I'd never told Grace about hearing his voice.

Grace flashed me a tight, blue-lipped smile. "You hear him too."

"Sometimes," I admitted, "Although, not as much anymore."

"He was a good boy, my Samuel. Never could let anyone get a word in when he could say it louder, ruder, and a lot more inappropriately." Grace chuckled and then coughed. I reached over and sat her up, feeling the outline of the bones in her spine and the outline of her ribs as I did.

When the fuck did she get so skinny?

"Thank you," she said, after the coughing fit subsided. "Dying hurts."

"Not funny," I said.

"I didn't mean for it to be. It's just the truth."

"I should have been there more. I should have—"

"No," Grace said, effectively shutting me down. "Stop with that 'should have' shit. I have no regrets and you shouldn't have them either. I love you. No matter what. For as long as I'm in this life and for as long as the next will have me."

Grace's eyes darted over my shoulder toward the door.

"There you are," she said, holding out her other hand. Ti stepped up and took it in hers, going to stand on the other side of Grace's bed.

"What's going on with the alarms?" Ti asked.

"It's nothing," Grace said, "I'm just dying and they know it, but the machines don't have human brains so they seem to think I'm salvageable. They'll stop in a second."

Sure enough in another three seconds, the room calmed and returned to the sickening halogen green glow it was cast in when I first came in.

"Thia, my dear, remember what I told you," Grace said, without letting go of my hands. Thia leaned over and held on to Grace's forearm. "Be good to my boy."

"I will. I promise," Ti said, wiping her own tears. "Always."

"That's my girl," Grace said, followed by another coughing fit, this one twice as long as the last. More alarms buzzed and sounded, yet not a single nurse or doctor came bursting into the room.

"Is there any music around?" Grace asked, again moving the mask away from her mouth. "I don't want to die in a room full of alarms, silence, or sobs. I want to go into my Edmond's arms surrounded by beautiful music." I was about to get up and go ask the nurse's station if they had a radio when Thia chimed in.

"What do you want to hear?" she asked.

"I want to meet my dear husband surrounded by Sinatra," Grace said, with a smile. "It was his favorite. We danced to every Sinatra song there was in our living room."

Ti nodded. "Any particular song?"

Grace shook her head and covered her mouth again with the oxygen mask. She then took my hand and laid it on her chest and did the same with Ti's. Grace held on to the both of us when, much to my surprise, my girl cleared her throat and started to sing. "Fly me to the moon and let me play among the stars…" her voice was throaty and raspy, yet clear and perfect. Grace relaxed into her pillows and held our hands tight as the machines went haywire once again.

This time they didn't stop.

Just as Ti started the third chorus, Grace's grip on our hands started to loosen. "I see Edmund," she whispered, staring off into the far corner of the room with a big smile on her face. "Edmund, my darling." She paused for a moment. "Where is my girl? Where is she? And my Samuel? I want to see my..." Grace's sentence faded away just as she did.

Grace slipped quietly and peacefully into her death surrounded by love, music, and the threat of eternal haunting.

CHAPTER TWENTY-FOUR

THIA

"I STILL CAN'T believe she's gone," Bear said, removing the black button-down shirt he'd worn for the funeral and tossing it onto the bed. I picked it up and folded the collar in a way that would keep its shape, the same way my mother used to do with my father's church shirts.

I followed Bear out to the living room and sat on the couch as I watched him sift through the kitchen cabinets on the far wall, searching until he found what he wanted. He unscrewed the cap on the bottle of whiskey and took a swig from the bottle.

"I know you're hurting, but you heard her. Grace made it *very* clear that you and King were the most important people in her life." I stood up and walked over to him, wrapping my arms around him from behind and resting my cheek on his back as he leaned against the counter. "She loved you. She wanted the best for you. You're hurting and that's normal, but when it hurts the worst remember all the good she brought into your life."

"Is that what you do?" Bear asked, clearing his throat as if the words were stuck there.

"What do you mean?"

"With your parents. Do you remember the good when it all

gets to be too much?"

"I don't remember much good. A few movie nights with my mom. A dad who was the best dad in the world, until he let her bullshit take him down with her. A brother who was amazing and who I loved very much, but was only in my life for a very short period of time, so I don't remember all that much about him. They're all gone and yes it hurts to remember, but the good isn't easy to come by when it's in a big cloud of bad," I said, wrapping my arms around my mid section and rocking back on my heels. "But I know it wasn't like that with you and Grace. I know there was a lot of good."

"It was all good," Bear confirmed. "Even when she was mad at us. Even when she was disappointed with us. It was still good because she actually fucking cared when no one else did. My old man wanted a soldier, not a son. Grace wanted sons, so it didn't matter what we did or how bad we were or what decisions we made. She loved us. First person in my life who ever said that to me, who I actually believed." His eyes met mine. "Until you."

"Tell me more about her," I said. We walked over to the couch and he pulled me onto his lap, resting his head on my shoulder. He took another swig and passed the bottle to me.

"She bought me condoms once," Bear said with a chuckle.

"What?" I asked, trying to keep the whiskey from flying out of my nose. I was relieved to see the small smile that appeared on his face. The sound of his brief laugh warming my insides just as much, if not more than the whiskey.

He pulled me back in close and continued, "I went over to her place one day. She was always asking us to help her out with the garden and the trash and fixing light bulbs and shit, and honestly, I didn't mind. I felt like I mattered when she told me to cut my nails or showed me the proper way to place a napkin on my lap when I ate, or rolled her eyes when I belched at the table." His smile reached his eyes as he recalled that day. "On this one day, I went into her kitchen and there was an industrial-sized box of condoms on the table. Grace was sitting there with one of those green label makers in her hand, turning the dial and humming to herself. When she was done, she peeled off the label and slapped it on the box and handed it over to me."

"What did it say?"

Bear laughed. "It was my name in big bold letters and under it she'd written BECAUSE MAMA GRACE CAN WAIT FOR GRANDKIDS A WHILE LONGER."

It was my turn to laugh.

"She told me that she wasn't a spring chicken, but that she was a pistol back in her day and that she knew what went on out there in 'that club of yours,'" Bear said, attempting to mimic Grace's voice and failing miserably. I passed the bottle back to him.

"She sounds amazing," I said, trying not to engage the tear threatening to spill from the corner of my eye.

"She was amazing," Bear said softly, staring at the dead TV screen across the room.

"Too bad you lied to her about the condom thing," I said, feeling his smile against my hair.

"I never lied to Grace about that. Or about anything. I always wrapped up, every single time." I couldn't help but roll my eyes and pull back to look at Bear's face, who I'd have sworn would be laughing hysterically at his lie, but instead, he was sitting there straight faced. "I mean it, Ti. Never forgot a single time until you, and honestly, it wasn't about forgetting. I needed to be as close as possible to you. I needed you to feel every single inch of what I was giving you," he said, his voice dropping a couple octaves, making my skin come alive with awareness. "Still need to."

"We should probably talk about what would happen if—" I started, but Bear cut me off.

"Ain't nothing to talk about. Shit sucks right now because things are so uncertain with the Bastards, but Ti you gotta know that you carrying my kid ain't gonna make me run. I'm a grown man. It's not like I don't know what can happen. What *will* happen if we keep going like this." He tipped my chin up to him. "I want to keep going like this. I like the idea of you all fat with my kid."

I playfully pushed on his chest. "She threatened me," I announced, trying to change the subject and trying to get the hammering of my heart under control. The smirk on his face told me that he saw right through me, but he humored me anyway.

"What?" he asked, not sounding the least bit surprised.

I pushed my hair behind my ear. "Yeah, it was the first time I met her actually. We weren't even an *us* then."

"She threatened Ray too, back in the day. It's a good thing. It means she liked you," Bear said. He closed his eyes and sighed.

"Grace said if I hurt you she'd come after me," I told him, "The way she said it, it still scares me." The hair on the back of my neck stood on end.

"Yeah, but babe we just came back from her funeral," Bear reminded me. "No reason to be scared now."

I shook my head. "No, you heard her in the hospital. There was something in the way she said it that made me think that even death couldn't stop her from making good on her threat."

"I think you might be right on that one," Bear said, planting a kiss on my jaw.

"I think so too," I said. The lamp on the end table flickered.

"Promise me you're not going anywhere. It sucks that Grace is gone, but I can handle it, or I *will* be able to handle it, because I knew it would happen someday. But if something happened to you..." Bear paused. "I don't know if I could...no, I know that I couldn't."

"You won't have to. I'm not going anywhere," I reassured him.

I made a promise and I'll keep it. I will take care of him, I silently vowed to Grace.

I snuggled in closer to Bear who kissed me again, this time on my temple. I'd meant it. I'd take care of him with everything I had...or I'd die trying.

CHAPTER TWENTY-FIVE

THIA

SILVER COLORED CLOUDS interfered with the normally unrelenting rays of the sun. With the clouds came a few moments of relief from the constant sweltering heat. A light breeze flowed in through the open windows of King's truck as Ray and I made our way to Grace's house to pack her entire life into boxes we'd gotten from the back alley of the Quick Stop. "What the hell are they even doing in there?" I asked Ray. It'd been almost twenty-four hours since King and Bear locked themselves in his tattoo shop. Rumbles of laughter, crashing, banging, breaking, and all sorts of loud music could all be heard from the room. The smell of weed and liquor permeated from underneath the door.

"Nothing good for them. I'm pretty sure they have enough booze and other shit in there to last them a week."

"A week?" I asked.

"Yeah, but they obviously don't have a week." Ray was right. Chop and the Bastards would be back in just a couple of days. Gus had called to let us know the MC had started their trek back from the Carolinas. The war was on its way. "At least they have each other."

"Yeah, that's why even though you showed up in bad shape, I'm glad you came because if you didn't, Bear would still be out there somewhere when he belongs here, at home. With family. You brought him home," Ray said. "And you should have seen those two when Preppy died. They locked themselves away for what seemed like forever. But in the end, they came out better for it. Not healed. Not whole. Just…better." Ray paused. "I told the kids about Grace," Ray added, taking a sharp corner without bothering to use the breaks. I held on to the handle on the headliner above the window in fear that I might fall out, suddenly very glad I remembered to wear my seatbelt. "Sorry," she said after noticing either my white knuckles or the look of fear in my eyes. "I just recently got my license."

"You're doing so good," I lied, releasing my death grip on the handle and dropping back into my seat after we settled onto a straight patch of road. "How did they take it? The kids?" I asked, as I looked in the rearview mirror to make sure Wolf and Munch were still behind us. Bear may have been having his moment with King, but he didn't like the idea of us going over to Grace's unprotected, especially after what had happened with Tretch.

"King and I talked to them for a while," Ray said, keeping her hands at ten and two. "But all they got out of it was that Grandma Grace won't be around to play with them anymore." Her eyes never left the road. "That alone was enough to set them both to tears. Took us three hours to get Max to settle down. Both her and Sammy wound up sleeping in bed with us."

"I'm so sorry," I said, knowing there wasn't much else I could say that would make the situation any better for her. "I don't know how you do it. Managing three kids. It's like you're not even human."

Ray flashed me a brief smile and parked the truck in front of a small white house that looked more like a little cottage with its little picket fence and white siding. "I'm not human," she said, hopping out of the truck. "I'm a mom."

We spent all afternoon at Grace's house going through a lifetime of her things and packing them into boxes to either keep in storage or donate. I'd never been to her house before, so seeing thousands and thousands of rabbits stacked on every shelf and surface was quite a shock. "They were from her husband," Ray explained, which was the least crazy explanation for having so many little glass eyes staring at you all day.

I was on a ladder, going through the higher kitchen cabinets and I was packing away Grace's wedding china, which I knew was her wedding china because when I opened the cabinet door I was greeted with a label that said WEDDING CHINA.

I wrapped the long stemmed glasses and gold-rimmed plates in newspaper before placing them in boxes and filling the empty spaces and crevices with bubble wrap.

When I pulled the very last plate from the back of the cabinet, something taped to it caught my attention. I turned the plate around and found that it was a picture of a baby boy.

When I read the caption on the back I dropped the plate and it shattered into a million pieces, scattering all around the kitchen in a symphony of delicate porcelain bits. "Shit," I said, hopping down from the ladder.

"You okay?" Ray shouted out from a back bedroom.

"Yeah, I'm fine." I grabbed the broom that had been leaning up against the wall in the hallway and swept the broken pieces of china into a dustpan. I set the dustpan down and sat down at the table. I sorted through and picked up the piece that still had the photo taped to the back and shook off the dust. Maybe I'd gotten it all wrong. Maybe it hadn't said what I'd thought it had said.

But I wasn't wrong. The caption underneath the picture was clear.

"Ray?" I called out, confused by what I'd stumbled upon. Maybe I'd misunderstood the story of how Grace and Bear met when Bear had originally told it to me. He could be very distracting. I wouldn't be surprised if I'd gotten the details wrong.

The little boy in the picture was still in diapers though, and I could have sworn that Bear had said—

"Yeah?" Ray shouted back from the end of the hallway where she was sorting out a linen closet.

"Do you know when Bear and Grace met? Like how old he was?" I asked.

"He was a teenager," she said, coming into the kitchen with another box in her arms. She set it down on the kitchen table and grabbed the fat black marker from the counter. Ray labeled the box RABBITS PART-SEVEN and set it on top of the other rabbit numbered boxes already stacked in front of the refrigerator. "King and Preppy met Bear when they were fighting about stupid kid shit. They all got into some sort of brawl or something and then shortly after King introduced Bear to Grace. Preppy told me the story, although I'm pretty sure he embellished a bit because the way he told it to me was that after he kicked their asses, he made them apologize to him and buy him new pants. I don't know about you but I don't think Bear or King were much of the apologizing type."

"Ain't that the truth," I agreed.

Ray leaned on the back of the chair and set a hand on her hip, cocking her head to the side. "Why?"

I held up the picture that was clearly marked ABEL. "If Grace met Bear when he was a teenager then why does she have a picture of him as a baby?" Ray snatched the photograph from my hands, knocking over a ceramic glass ballerina rabbit from the corner of the table. It shattered on the linoleum but neither one of us reacted to the sound of the second piece of Grace's life that we'd broken.

"Maybe it's not really him or something?" I asked, hesitantly. Ray pulled out a chair and took a seat next to me at the table, her mouth agape as she stared down at the smiling boy who was sitting on a checkered beach blanket under the shade of a blue umbrella. "Maybe it's another Abel?"

Ray rolled her eyes. "Another Abel, with sandy blond hair and blue eyes that just *happened* to be lying around in Grace's house?"

"Maybe?" Unsure of what other logical explanation there could be.

"Ti, what do you think this could mean?" Ray asked. She'd been using Bear's nick name for me a lot lately, and despite the fact that when I was a kid every nickname I ever had made me twitchy, it didn't bother me at all coming from her or Bear.

"Maybe Bear gave it to her, but then why would it be in her cabinet taped to the back of a dish?" I asked.

"There is no way. Grace would have no reason to hide that. She loved pictures almost as much as she loved rabbits. If this was a picture he'd given to her it would have been in a frame displayed next to a rabbit somewhere," Ray said, turning the picture over in her hands.

"But then why?"

Ray shook her head. "I have no idea, but whatever it is it's making my brain hurt," she said, rubbing her temples. She reached into the back pocket of her shorts and pulled out her phone, snapping a picture of the Polaroid. "Put this in your pocket," she said, handing the photo back to me. "I have a feeling that the boys don't know anything about it either. I'm not going to call now and take them out of their pow-wow, so we will have to wait until tonight to show it to them. Grace wasn't one to keep secrets. Her policy was always about honesty, which is why this is all so confusing."

"Yeah, I didn't think so either, but it pains me to have to wait until later. My curiosity is on a level ten right now," I admitted. Patience was never a strong suit of mine. Six months waiting for Bear didn't help that.

"Mine too." Ray stood up again, grabbing another empty box from the pile by the front door. "Although I think I may have to wait even longer to talk to King because lately he won't let me get a word out before trying to impregnate me again. Chances are slim to none for meaningful conversation before he accomplishes that mission. He's been knee deep in baby fever ever since Nicole-Grace was born." There was a slight annoyance in her tone, but it sounded forced. "It's like he's not going to be happy until we have to build another house for all these kids, and I'd really like to at least have a wedding before he goes through with his plan of using my uterus as a clown car. Or better yet, turn twenty-one. That would be cool."

I wagged my eyebrows. "Yet, I get the sense that you don't really mind his methods all that much," I said, pressing my lips together and trying not to laugh.

"No. His *methods*." She sighed dreamily. "His methods are *goooooood*." Ray looked at me straight faced before bursting out into laughter. "He has this way of making me give in to him, no matter what. He could ask me to do anything short of nuking a third world country and I'd be all, 'mmmmm-kay.' Makes me feel like an idiot." Ray shook her head and used the corner of the box in her arms to point at me. "But hey! At least King wears shirts! I don't know how you ever get anything accomplished around Bear. If King never wore a shirt, I'd stand less of a chance than I already do. I'd be in that house giving birth like the old lady who lived in a shoe," she said, fanning herself with her hand. "On that note, I think I'll go back and pack another box of bunnies." She disappeared down the hall.

I took one last look at the baby in the picture before putting it in my pocket. I went back to the business of packing away Grace's life. For the rest of the day, I couldn't keep my mind off the photo or what it meant.

Grace may have kept a lot of rabbits in her house, but that day I found out that she was also keeping something else.

Secrets.

CHAPTER TWENTY-SIX

BEAR

THE LAST TIME King and I locked ourselves in a room and got fucked up for days was when Preppy died.

This time may have been for Grace but we had every intention of following through with the fucked-up part again.

"I don't know how the fuck you expect me to cover that entire thing," King said, blowing out the smoke he was holding and passing me the joint. He ran his fingertips over my biggest Bastard tattoo on my shoulder and scratched his head.

I rolled my eyes. "You're good at this shit. You covered up Ray's scar and you did that piece on Abby's back. Get on it man. Don't let me down," I said, taking a hit.

"Do you even know what you're gonna wanna cover it up with?" King asked, pulling at the skin on my shoulder like it would somehow change the tattoo into something he could work with.

"No and I don't care. Fucking surprise me. Anything but a big dildo or a portrait of the fucking queen of England would be fine with me as long as this bullshit is gone," I said.

King nodded, leaning in closer to again examine the largest of my Beach Bastards tattoos on my shoulder.

"All right, fucker" he said, leaning back. "I'll come up with something."

"Good, now do this." I pointed to the much smaller sketch I'd just had him draw.

"Do I look like your bitch?"

I shrugged. "No, but you're my tattoo bitch."

"Call me that again and you might get that dildo after all." King opened drawers in his toolbox and started pulling out his gloves, ink, and other equipment.

"Bad Habit," by The Offspring was blaring through the speakers in the ceiling. As I waited for King to start, my eyes landed on something I hadn't seen in a long time. "Fuck, I can't believe you still fucking have that," I said, pointing to the plastic hog head on the wall. "And I can't believe you actually hung it up."

King looked to where I was pointing and laughed, taking a long pull from the bottle of whiskey before setting it on the floor snapping on his black gloves. "I found it in the attic. Ray begged me not to hang it up until I told her the story behind it. Now it's her favorite thing in here." King adjusted the height of his stool and rolled back over to the table I was sitting on. "They say you have to pick your battles," he said, looking back up at the hog's head. I'm glad I actually won one for a change.

I laughed but talk of a battle had my mind going somewhere else. Somewhere not too far off. "We got three days before the war. A fourth of the soldiers that they have. You think we stand a shot?" I asked King, knowing he'd give it to me straight.

"I don't know," King said, tapping his gun into a small plastic container of black ink. "But if we don't do something, the threat never goes away."

"Ain't that the fucking truth," I agreed. "I don't wanna be

looking over my shoulder, or Ti's shoulder, for the rest of my fucking life." I paused, taking another hit. I held it in as long as I could and released it with a small cough as my lungs fought to push the smoke back out. "You gotta do me a favor though, brother," I said. "If nothing else, you gotta do this one fucking thing for me."

"Anything," King said, pressing on the foot peddle that brought his gun to life, buzzing louder and louder as he brought it to the spot behind my right ear.

"If I lose. If I... if he wins," I said. I dug out the cash I had buried on the island. "I need you to use it to make sure Ti is taken care of."

"Ain't nothing gonna happen," King said, pushing the ink into my skin.

"I hope not, but you gotta promise me," I insisted, King needed to know how serious I was about this. If something did happen to me I needed to know that my girl was still be okay.

"I promise. She'll be taken care of," King said, "but you talk like I'm not going in with you."

"You're not," I spat.

"Like fuck I'm not," King argued, pressing the needle in harder to punctuate his point.

"Fucker," I said. "I just mean that I need you to hang back a bit. We can't both be six feet under."

King dipped the gun back into the ink and wiped at the spot he'd just finished with a paper towel. "Ray knows everything. We have a contingency plan if something happens to me. Shit's in place. Don't worry about me or Ray or the kids or even Thia. Do you, man, and I'll be there to watch your fucking back." He held the side of my head down with his forearm. "Now sit fucking still or your girl is going to think I'm shit at this."

"Yes, sir," I said, mockingly, staring back up at the plastic hog's head. I let the pain from the sting of the needle envelope me as I remembered a better time. Less threats. More fun.

More plastic hog's heads.

"I still can't believe she's fucking gone," I said, saying the same thing to King that I'd said to Ti after the funeral.

"I can't either," King said. "But what I really can't believe is that she put up with shits like us."

"Aint' that the fucking truth. There was this one time, when I got suspended from school, just shortly before I dropped out entirely, the guidance counselor scheduled all the parent teacher conferences. When my time slot came up I knew it would be just me and the guidance counselor because I hadn't even told my old man about it, not like he'd fucking show up if I had. But the second my ass hit the seat in his office, Grace burst through the door wearing her church clothes."

"I didn't know that," King said, concentrating on my new ink.

I smiled, recalling the memory. "Yeah, and the cool part was that when he asked her who she was she looked at him like he should've already known. 'I'm Mama Grace, of course,'" I said, mimicking Grace's voice. "The thing about her that I always liked was that no one questioned her. She really hadn't told the counselor shit, but he told her to take a seat anyways and off they went, talking about my fucking grades and shit like she was always meant to be the one there."

King paused his gun. "Probably because she was."

"Yeah man. She was."

CHAPTER TWENTY-SEVEN

BEAR

EIGHTEEN YEARS OLD...

"YOU KNOW, YOU should just give back your name now. Just hand it over. 'Cause with a name like Bear, you should be fucking happy to be in the woods. You should be rubbing your cock up against a fucking tree or something. Humping the dirt. Getting off on the wilderness or some shit, not moping around like I just fucked your golden retriever. So change your name to like...Ralph or something, and just be done with it. Embrace your inner vagina," Preppy said, waving his hand around dismissively before laying on the ground with his ear to the dirt like he probably saw someone do in a movie.

Or YouTube.

That's it. I made up my mind right then to destroy his fucking computer when the day was over. Sleep first. Destroy computer second. Then maybe he won't be able to search for new ways to torment us and besides, a little less porn wouldn't hurt the kid.

"It's not the outdoors that's pissing me off. It's the fucking cunt of an hour," I muttered, running my hand through my hair. Preppy rolled his eyes and parted the leaves of a tree that didn't need to be parted with the machete he insisted on bringing.

"So why *do* they call you Bear?" Preppy asked. Grabbing a handful of dirt, he tossed it into the breeze and sniffed it before the wind blew it right in King's face.

I was also canceling the Discovery Channel.

"Do *you* know?" Preppy asked King who ignored his question and growled while shaking the dirt from his shirt.

"You don't want to know," I said with a sigh, making it sound like the reason behind my name was a lot more sinister than the real story, which was as simple as the cleaning lady at the club calling me Abel Bear every time she visited, which turned into everyone calling me Bear. Thank God she didn't call me Abel Lovey or Abel Babydoll.

I'd be fucked.

"Whatever, RALPH," Preppy said, and on any other day I would bitch slap him into tomorrow.

But not today.

Today I was under strict orders from King that there would be no bitch slapping of any kind.

How many hours until tomorrow?

The sun finally started to make an appearance, shooting soft rays of pink through the tops of the trees, reminding me of the hours we'd already been awake thanks to Preppy's 4:30am wake up call where he'd jumped on my bed like it was Christmas morning and Santa had just delivered a shit load of blow and porn.

Preppy was so amped up that for a minute I thought his excitement was going to burst right through his skin. Unfortunately, at that hour, his excitement was not contagious.

We'd driven an hour in the dark to a plot of land near

Charles Harbor where Preppy was convinced we'd find the biggest and baddest wild boar, just begging to be hunted down. The way he pitched the idea made it seem like the pigs would come out of the brush waving a white flag before putting our guns to their own heads and finishing the job for us.

A sharp poke drew my attention down to where yet another bunch of sandspurs had attached themselves to the bottom of my jeans. I plucked them off and tossed them into a nearby bush, hissing through my teeth as one of the sharp-ass seedpods pricked me. A drop of blood pooled on the pad of my index finger. "Fuck," I muttered, sucking the coppery red from my skin then waving it into the air to dry it off.

"Tell me why the fuck we're out here again?" King asked on a yawn as Preppy led us through the tall grass and deeper into the woods. In Logan's Beach, the woods were wet and swampy with dark green foliage and soft mud, where as the area around Charles Harbor was dry with brittle grass and hard packed dirt that cracked into pieces under the weight of our boots.

In our part of Florida, hunting after school or on weekends for guys our age was as commonplace as getting your driver's license or feeling up your date after prom. It was what the normal guys did.

We weren't the normal guys.

Never were.

Never wanted to be.

Some of my brothers in the club were avid hunters. I'd even gone out with them on one occasion. But in my eighteen years I'd already shed enough blood of the human variety to not really give a shit about the pointless killing of a dirty animal that, when sliced open, the inside of it's belly smelled worse than a fucking rotting corpse.

"Well, my friends, we're out here because I'm a man now. And this is the kind of shit that real men do. So come on, little girls, pick up your panties and grab your balls because we are gonna kill us some fucking wild piggies," Preppy said, before giving us his best nasally impression of a wild hog oink.

"What the fuck was that?" I asked, rubbing my eyes. I reached into my cut for my smokes. Unlike Preppy, who was dressed for the occasion with his cargo pants, bright orange vest, and a camo hat that read PUSSY HUNTER in neon green lettering, I opted for my usual uniform of my cut, no shirt, and dark jeans. I held my shotgun in the crook of my arm with my chin across the barrel while I fished a lighter out of my back pocket. I wasn't exactly following proper gun holding etiquette. Hell, I didn't care if I blew half my face off in the process, because nicotine was going to be the only thing able to keep me from jumping into the harbor and swimming back to Logan's Beach.

"I've been practicing my feral hog mating call so that the biggest and baddest alpha motherfucker comes out to play 'catch a bullet' with us. And what the fuck are you doing smoking, Ralph? Put it out! They will smell it or see the smoke and they'll spook and run the fuck off!" Preppy scolded. Turning back around, he crouched down and scanned the foliage around us for any sign of his feral fucking pigs.

I stayed upright and so did King. I rested my gun against my shoulder in a very not-ready-for-this-shit kind of way. I had no intentions of putting my smoke out, but out of the corner of my eye I caught a glimpse of the look King was flashing me, a reminder of the reason why we were there in the first place, and, reluctantly, I put out my smoke on my boot and flashed King an exaggerated "You happy now?" smile.

There was only one reason on fucking earth why either King

or myself would be up before the sun and in the middle of the fucking woods, and thank fuck that reason only came around once a year.

Preppy's birthday.

In the three years or so since I'd met King and Prep, I'd been roped into their unspoken tradition, where for one day, Preppy calls the shots. "I should have skipped town when I saw you looking up these beasts on my computer" I said, stepping over a downed pine tree.

"You were just shocked he wasn't looking at porn for once," King quipped, and he was right. It may have been the one time I would have preferred to open my screen to find some of the sick shit Preppy liked to occupy his time with, rather than what he had in store for us on his birthday.

"Actually, if you motherfuckers must know, I *was* looking up porn," Preppy said with a shrug of his shoulders. There was a rustling in the brush up ahead. A huge brown hog with wiry hair and a broken tusk darted out from its hiding place and into the clearing, making a run for his life through the trees. Preppy lifted his gun and pulled the trigger. He missed the fast moving pig and the bullet blew a huge hole into a tree stump. "But you'd be surprised how one little misspelling of the word BEASTIALITY can change the entire fucking nature of a search." King and I looked at one another and followed Preppy, who started reciting lines from *Braveheart* as he ran full speed after the hog there was no way he was ever going to catch.

After an hour of chasing Preppy through the trees and almost accidentally shooting one another a few times, Preppy finally gave up and we headed back out to the truck. "Fuck this. I'm just going to get one of those plastic pig heads they sell at the gas station and mount it in my room."

"Could have decided that a lot fucking earlier," King muttered.

Preppy cracked his knuckles. "And now for the business portion of the day," he said, grabbing two shovels from the bed of the truck which were laying over a blue tarp. He tossed us each one and pulled off the tarp, revealing the tied up body of a man underneath.

"Who the fuck is this?" King asked.

"This *was* the motherfucker who pulled a gun on me last night when I was out running collection," Preppy announced, poking the corpse with the handle of his shovel.

"Ugh, why are you guys dragging me into this. This is your shit," I huffed.

"Bear you can't fucking complain," Preppy snapped, grabbing a hold of the man's ankles.

"Why the fuck not?" I asked.

"'Cause, bitch," he said, flashing me a big white-toothed grin as he slid the body from the truck bed until it was about halfway and then he let it fall to the ground with a dull thud. "It's my motherfucking birthday."

CHAPTER TWENTY-EIGHT

THIA

I WRAPPED MY arms around my legs and held them close to my chest, resting my chin on the tops of my knees. I closed my eyes and slowly inhaled through my nose, breathing in the wet air and the smell of Grace's roses.

We'd finished with all the boxes just as the sun set. Ray was inside making a call to the babysitter to check on the kids while I sat outside on the deck in Grace's backyard and wondered what the hell the future had in store.

For Bear. For me. For us.

Only time would tell, but the time I was most concerned about was the next few days, and whether Bear would come out of them alive.

I tried my best to steady my erratic beating heart, but I felt helpless—a feeling I hated more than anything.

Crickets chirped loudly from out beyond the fence. I rubbed the heels of my bare feet over the warmed fabric of the chair. There were so many questions in my head that I just wanted to do a hand stand and shake them out of my ear.

He could be hurt. He could die.

My stomach twisted as I forced myself away from that

thought.

He could also succeed.

Then what?

I didn't hear Ray approaching until she sat down next to me, her shoulder bumping mine. "In my life, everyone close to me has died," Ray started with a sigh, looking out over the backyard as if she were wrestling with something in her head too. "My best friend from when I was a kid. Well, I guess my two best friends, although one was kind of my husband for a minute. A woman who was more like a mother to me than my actual mother, and someone I knew for only a short period of time, but was more connected to than anyone else, besides King." Her eyes flickered from the house to the trees and finally back to me.

"Preppy," I said, wishing I'd had a chance to meet the guy that King, Ray, and Bear had all cared for so deeply. Ray nodded and attempted a small smile that did nothing to mask her hurt.

"Yes, Preppy. I was in love with him you know," she said with a sniffle.

"You were?" For a second I thought that Bear hadn't told me the entire story.

"Yeah, not in the way I'm in love with King, but I was...or I *am*," Ray corrected, "as in love with Preppy as I could be without it being a romantic kind of love. I loved him deep, and so it hurts deep. That's just the way love works, I guess."

"Aren't you afraid something will happen to King?" I asked, needing to know if I was alone in the anguish I felt over them going to war against Chop. "If he goes to bat for Bear, he's putting his life on the line. It's not even his fight. Even Bear has tried to talk him out of it." I was grateful that Bear had King in his life and that King was so willing to step up for Bear, but being no stranger to loss myself it was easy to put myself in her shoes.

If something happened to King, it would leave their three kids without their father, and she would lose yet another person she loved. "I know how it feels," I added, reminding her that she wasn't alone.

Ray shook her head. "No, I'm not afraid. If I've learned anything over the past year, it's that going to bat for one another is what family does, regardless of the cause. This *is* King's battle because it's Bear's battle." Ray absentmindedly picked at the threads of the fraying chair cushion. "I grew up in a house with two parents and it still took me coming here to learn that myself. Besides, it wasn't like when I met King he was an accountant or something who suddenly decided to venture into another questionable and dangerous line of work. I knew what I was getting into from day one." Ray let out a quick burst of laughter. "Did. I. Ever."

I laughed with her as she disappeared for a moment into some memory she'd been recalling. When she came back she said, "King isn't the kind of man you change, and I never went into this thinking I could change him. I went into this loving him. That's all."

"I know exactly how that feels," I admitted.

Ray nudged my shoulder again. "The Bear I first met was a little bit different than the Bear you know now," she said, looking out over the water. "I met him at a party, right before I met King. Such a smooth talker with his crazy deep voice. He was strong then. Confident. Then after Preppy died that all changed. He turned into a shell, then he just up and left." The smile briefly left her face but returned when she added, "But he's Bear 3.0, better than before…and it's all because of you."

"I can't take all the credit. There was this guy who gave me a ring once," I said, rubbing Bear's ring between my fingers. "He made me better, too."

I couldn't help but think that even though Ray and I took very different paths to get to the same place, that our stories were a lot more similar than I'd initially realized. I too was learning more about family than I ever had before. "So you're really not afraid? Because honestly," I said, a lump forming in my throat. "I don't know what I would do if something happened to B..." I stopped and squeezed my eyes shut, willing away the unwanted thought.

Ray put her hand on my shoulder and I opened my eyes, peering into her doll-like icy blue's that projected nothing but sincerity and sympathy. "No," Ray said. "I'm not."

"You're crazy," I said. She'd lost so many people she'd loved, so why wasn't she afraid of losing King too? "Why?" I asked again.

"King promised me he would be okay," Ray said, "and he always keeps his promises."

I wanted the same to be true for Bear, for him to promise me he'd be okay and swear to me that he'd come out of all this alive. As much as I loved the broken promise that had brought us together to begin with, it was one I really wanted him to keep.

"I just wish there was something I could do to help," I admitted.

Ray nodded. "I feel exactly the same way, but aside from grabbing a gun and storming the compound we are S.O.L," Ray said with a laugh, "or unless you have an army laying around they could borrow."

I jolted upright as an idea went off in my head like I'd been struck by lightning. Circuits were connecting. An idea was taking shape. I turned to Ray. "What if I did have one?"

"One what?" Ray asked. Her lips turned to the side in confusion. I leapt to my feet.

"Stay here, I'm going to grab my phone. I'll be right back!" I yelled.

"But one what?" she asked again. I turned around before going into the house and smiled wickedly.

"An army."

I disappeared inside and ran to the kitchen table when I remembered that the phone was in the truck. I jogged out the front door and stuck my hand through the window, grabbing the phone off the seat. I dialed and waited but there was no answer. "Crap," I said as I typed out a text and hoped to God he would get it and know what it meant.

I jogged back up to the house, still looking down at the phone, waiting for a reply, when I ran into something hard.

Someone.

I didn't get a chance to see who that someone was before I was zapped by a bolt of blue lighting. Hovering somewhere between consciousness and unconsciousness, I could still hear the crickets chirping and Ray calling out for me as I was carried away, bombarded by the sensations of both familiarity, and dread.

CHAPTER TWENTY-NINE

BEAR

THE ONLY THING my old man ever gave me was the promise of the gavel and his fucking temper.

Cocksucker.

With Preppy's death, I reached an entirely new level of anger, a feeling so far beyond anything I'd ever experienced before, I never thought I'd be able to unclench my fists or take a deep breath again.

For a while I let it destroy me from the inside, like the cancer that took Grace, tearing apart the very foundation of who I thought I was, and leaving a fraction of the old me in its place.

By comparison, the anger I felt when Prep died was a mere blip on the fucking radar compared to the out of body rage I experienced when Ray called to say my girl had been taken.

Ray hadn't seen who it was, neither did Wolf or Munch who were in the back yard watching the girls. When Munch saw Ti duck inside he didn't know she was going out the front of the house. They ran out just in time to see a van driving away.

They may not have seen who took her, but they didn't have to see it for me to know who was behind it. If he thought for even one fucking second that taking my girl would in any way give him the upper hand that fucker was *dead* wrong. All it did was move up the war, his imminent death, and the probability of torture unlike he'd ever known before.

Go get her, Bear.

Preppy's ghost voice was the most serious I'd ever heard him, and that filled me with even more rage, and something else I wasn't familiar with ever feeling.

Terror.

The plan had always been to storm the MC. Take back what Chop had taken from us. Take back the club. Not once while making those plans had I feared for my own life, but now that Ti's life was in the hands of the man who'd already caused her so much damage, and was capable of inflicting so much more, the fear within me was damn near overwhelming.

Life and death had always been very factual for me. We all lived, and we all died, and I was fully prepared to take a bullet when my time was up. I was okay with *my* death, regardless of when it came.

I wasn't okay with the death of Preppy.

In thirty years, if I'm still walking the earth, I still won't be.

If something happened to Ti, the pain I would inflict would be endless because my pain would be endless.

Hurry. Ghost Preppy said.

I throttled my engine and forced my bike to breakneck speeds. I ran every red light, stop sign, and dodged every stopped car. I lead our group, which consisted of Wolf, Stone, and Munch, with King taking up the rear. Gus was meeting us there. We weren't the largest group, but we had a lot of talent between us, and it was that talent that I was relying on to get my girl back. Then and only then, when I knew she was safe, would I take my time to dispose of my old man for good.

I wasn't stupid. I knew it was all a trap to lure me in—no fucking doubt about it. I even think Gus was fed false intel on purpose about the club being out on a ride, but trap or not, Chop had brought the war to his doorstep and I was about to reign down a hell on him like he'd never imagined possible. If there was any part of my old man left who thought I might be incapable of laying him out because he was blood, he was about to learn just how wrong he was.

Dead fucking wrong.

I frantically flew into the night and used the thoughts of my girl to fuel my hatred and push me forward.

The war we had been preparing for had officially been moved up, to right fucking now.

Hang on, Ti. I'm coming.

I was going to get my girl back and I was going to bathe in the blood of any motherfucker who stood between us.

I wasn't just after revenge.

I was on a fucking hunt.

I kind of missed the psychotic part of me that had been lying dormant since Preppy died and welcomed the thought of mounting Chop's severed head on the fucking roof of the MC as a warning to any other piece of shit who thinks they can cross me and somehow get away with it.

The Beach Bastards wasn't Chop's club anymore.

He wasn't their Prez.

They didn't exist.

Or at least, they wouldn't after I was through with them.

Ti may have taught me how to be a man again, but I shoved the man to the side, because right then I needed the biker, the devil, the fucking demon who would shoot without question or hesitation. Cut without feeling. Hurt without hurting.

On my bike, with Logan's Beach blurring around me, I became the soulless monster who was willing to spill rivers full of blood for my girl.

There were a lot of motherfuckers heading to hell tonight.

After I made sure Ti was safe, I didn't care if I was one of them.

I laid down on the throttle and pushed my bike to her limits. I barreled down the road toward the compound, unsure of how the fuck I was able to see the road, because in my vision all I could see was red.

Blood. Fucking. Red.

CHAPTER THIRTY

THIA

"NO! DON'T PUT *that in my arm! I don't need it. I swear. I'll be good. I'll be calm. Just please. Don't! I promise. I'll be calm. I promise!*" *I screamed, and struggled against several men and women dressed in grey scrubs as they held my arms and legs down on a gurney. A petite woman with short black hair held up a syringe to the light and flicked it a few times before inserting it into the IV drip already in my arm. She looked down at me unapologetically before pushing down on the plunger.*

Then it all went out of focus.

Everything.

Including the room.

Suddenly, I was alone. I sat up on the gurney with ease. My wrists and ankles no longer tethered down. I was in the same room as moments before, same pale green walls, but this time it was empty.

At least I thought it was empty.

"And I used to think Bear was the smartest of us three fuckateers," *a male voice said, followed by a short burst of laughter.* *"Actually, that's not true. I've always been the smartest one, it's a scientific fact. Also, my cock's the biggest. It's important you know that."*

I lift my head to find a man leaning against the window, his arms and legs both crossed. He's just a shadow under the light of the moon until he unfolds himself and starts to walk toward me. As he moves, the shadows do too, and I can make out his features. He's tall, though not nearly as tall as Bear. He's muscular but very lean. He's wearing a short-sleeved, white shirt and khaki pants, with an orange bow-tie, and black suspenders. His arms and hands are decorated in tattoos and his sandy blond hair is tied back in a high, messy ponytail, but that is the only thing about his look that's even remotely messy. His shirt is neatly pressed and his pants have a crease on each leg that runs straight down the front. His beard is shorter than Bear's, somewhere between stubble and a beard, but immaculately groomed.

"Who are you?" I ask. "You know Bear?" The man comes up beside me to sit down on the gurney, and that's when my fuzzy brain starts to recognize him, but I can't remember how I recognize him. I try to stand up from the gurney but when I make a move to stand, I wobble. The man grabs my arm to steady me and sets me back down.

"Of course I know that fuck. He's one of my best friends," he says, like I should already know this. "You're fucking smoking hot," he says looking me up and down. "You wanna make out?"

"Huh? What?"

"But since Bear's my friend, no tongue though. Okay, maybe a little tongue, but only because you asked. No dick though. I draw the line there. Okay, only all the way in, but only for like an hour or two. Sound good?"

"What?" I ask again, rubbing my temples and trying to clear my mind so I can get a grasp on what exactly is going on here.

"Okay, okay, just until we both come. Or just me. Or whatever. Ground rules are important when starting a new relationship. I saw that on Oprah and that bitch knows her shit. If you don't follow her book club you should."

"Who are you again?" I ask and as I look at him, it finally registers how I recognize him. From the photo in Bear's apartment. He's telling the truth. He's Bear's friend.

Bear's DEAD friend.

"I'm Preppy."

"But you're..." I start but Preppy waves me off.

"That's not important," he says dismissively.

"How are you here?" I ask.

"Shit you ask more questions than Doe. I didn't think that was possible."

"Doe?"

"Ray," he says. "But if you want to sing the entire song from the Sound of Music I'll have to find a pitch pipe and I'll need to lube up my vocal cords." He looks between my legs. "I think I know how to—"

"Preppy, can you focus for one sec?"

"Mmmmmmm?" he asks finally looking at my face. He reaches out and plays with a strand of my hair.

"Please just tell me why you're here. Why I'm here."

"You're here because people suck, and I'm here for you because you need me and because I didn't know when I was going to get a chance again to introduce myself to Bear's girl."

"But you're..."

"Still not important," he says.

"Then am I in a mental hospital?" I ask.

"No, why would you think that? Are you crazy? Did Bear catch a crazy one? He's supposed to toss the crazy ones back. Didn't I teach that bitch anything?" Preppy asked with a huff.

"I don't know why I think I'm in a mental hospital, maybe because I'm sitting on a gurney talking to Bear's best friend, who's dead?"

"Awe that's cute," Preppy says, running the back of his index *finger across my cheek.* This man is a stranger to me. This gesture is an intimate one, like we know each other, so it should creep me out and make me jump back, but instead I find myself leaning into his touch, finding comfort in it.

"What's cute?" I ask.

"That you think that even death could keep me away from my family," Preppy whispers.

"I'm so confused," I admit, falling backwards onto the gurney. Preppy follows and when I look to my right, I find him lying beside me and looking right at me. I could feel his cool minty breath across my face as he spoke.

"When you see King and my girl Doe can you please tell those bitches that Preppina the Magnificent would have been a way better name than Nicole Grace? That shit sounds like she's already in line for the fucking nursing home. I'm going to have to watch over her just to make sure she doesn't get beat up on the playground and trust me that shit is no fucking fun. I used to get into fights every single day, and even though I won every single one of them with my brawn and wit, I don't want that for little Preppina."

"Okay?" I say, unsure of what I am really agreeing to or what exactly it means.

"Now sleep, baby girl. Because I have a feeling that this big bad biker I know is coming to rescue his ole lady," Preppy says. He leans forward, and for someone so harsh with words, he plants a gentle kiss on my lips.

"He's coming?" I ask as Preppy tucks me in.

"Fuck yeah, he is. He's coming to rescue your fine ass and then, if you're lucky, he's going to come everywhere else." Preppy barely takes a breath between sentences. "I love that big fucking brute. I never doubted him for even a second. Or just for a minute. Maybe it was 50/50 for a while, but the bitch is lucky he came to his senses, because I had this whole plan laid out to haunt him by starting his bike in the middle of the night. Ghost Rider style."

"I still have no idea what's going on," I admit to the confusing man.

"Shhhhhh, pretty girl. Get some rest, will ya? I'm sure Bear is gonna throw some D like a champ once you get some energy back, so you're going to need to rest up unless you want to tap out from that shit, and I've seen that fucker in action. I mean to this day he's never found that camera…" Preppy looked off into the distance. "Good times. Good times," he mutters, smiling as if recalling the memory.

Preppy brushes my hair off my forehead and again looks me up and down, his gaze lingering for a beat too long on my midsection. "But in all seriousness, there is one thing I need you to remember, Ti, baby. Promise me that when you get the chance, you'll do one thing for me and you can't forget."

"What's that?"

"Run."

With that Preppy walks back toward the window and in the time it takes me to blink, he's gone. As my eyes again grow heavy and the call of sleep becomes all too powerful to ignore, I could swear I hear him mutter, "Do any of those fucking dildos know how to use a motherfucking rubber?"

CHAPTER THIRTY-ONE

THIA

*D*RIP. *D*RIP. *D*RIP.

The sound of a pipe leaking echoed in my ears, dragging me slowly back into reality.

Handcuffs bit into my wrists. My arms strained above my head as I hung from a pipe that ran across the ceiling. When I could no longer hold myself up, my muscles gave out with a *pop* as my joints painfully dislocated. My chin fell to my chest. Wide tape covered my mouth, wrapped around the back of my head, pulling on my hair every time I turned my head. With one nostril stuffed up I felt dizzy, barley able to get enough oxygen through the other.

My vision blurred as I tried to focus on my surroundings. Grey. Concrete. An open ceiling with pipes and wires. Nothing on the bare walls. A metal cage in the far corner. In the center of the small room was a blue tarp. Next to the tarp was a red toolbox with a yellow electric drill set on top. It was all so clean.

Sterile.

I pulled on the cuffs above my head with a newfound strength I didn't have seconds earlier. My legs flailed around uselessly in mid air as I struggled against my restraints.

The door opened and Gus entered the room. When I first met him in the park he'd protected Bear and myself. I'd even thought he was cute in a chubby-cheeked best friend kind of way.

That Gus wasn't who walked into the room, though. This Gus looked up at me as I dangled from the ceiling, like I was a steak and he was a hungry lion who hadn't eaten in months.

"I really wish it could be me who gets to have all the fun with you today, but you see, little one, I have to continue playing the role of loyal soldier, so unfortunately for me, I had to call in a substitute." He stepped up to me and I braced for whatever it was he was about to do, my heart hammering in my chest.

The tape being pulled off was painful, but it passed quickly and I was finally able to take deep breaths. Gulping for air as if I'd been drowning. "Why do this at all?" I asked, after finally being able to catch my breath. "Me, Bear, the MC? Why?"

"I don't ask why. I do what I'm told. Asking why is not my job."

"Then what is your job? Who hired you?"

Gus covered my mouth with his hand and pressed his forehead to mine. My stomach rolled. "That doesn't matter. All that matters now is what's about to happen to you. My advice? Give into the pain. Enjoy it. The human body is a fascinating machine, and although I don't get to do it myself, I'll be watching the video later and I'm sure watching that machine come apart is going to be nothing short of spectacular." He let go of my mouth and set the tape back in place. "Although I'm sure Bear is not going to love it as much as I will. He doesn't appreciate the beauty in it, like I do."

He stuck out his fat tongue and licked my face from my jaw

to my eye, and my stomach rolled again and this time I tasted the bile rising in my throat.

Gus stepped back and took one last lustful look at me. "Such a shame, little one." Before he left the room, he adjusted a camera I hadn't noticed next to the door. A red light came on. "Maybe, I'll stay. Just for the first part," he said, opening the door. "We're ready," he called out, and a blond man appeared in the room, shutting the door behind him. He was shirtless, cut and muscular, black and grey tattoos covered one of his arms and all of his chest.

"I don't like cameras," the blond man said, tapping the wrench he was holding against his palm over and over again as he looked me up and down.

Gus was evil.

But this guy, with his classic good looks, was the fucking devil.

His eyes were black and glowing like a demon in a movie and I realized there was no getting out of this. My fate had been sealed. With every step the devil took toward me, the fear I felt increased higher and higher until I hoped I'd die of a heart attack before this lunatic could carry out whatever sick plan he had for me.

The devil set the wrench down by the toolbox and pulled his shoulder length hair on top of his head and tied it with an elastic. He bent his head from side to side, making a sickening cracking sound. He did the same with his knuckles.

Then, he came for me.

While Gus looked on like he was lusting after my blood, the blond devil looked natural. In his element.

Possessed.

He reached up and unhooked one of the cuffs, catching me

before I fell to the concrete floor. My arms still raised above my head as they'd become completely useless and disjointed. "Nooooooo!" I tried to scream behind the tape, tears ran out the side of my eyes. He carried me to the tarp and laid me on top of it, binding my ankles together with the tape.

"You can take the tape off. No one can hear her out here," Gus said. "Start with the teeth. They're the most painful."

"Why are you still here?" the devil asked. I was shaking so hard I could hear my jaw rattling.

"Just wanted to watch the fun start."

"I don't do audiences," the devil said adamantly.

"Come on, man, just one tooth. Then I'll leave," Gus whined.

"Do it yourself then," the devil said. Standing up, he tossed him the wrench. Gus's face lit up and he practically ran over to me. Crouching down by the toolbox he lifted out a metal contraption.

"Just one, and then I gotta go," Gus said. Ripping the tape off my mouth, he pried it apart using pressure points on the roof of my mouth to force me to comply.

It wasn't the first time he'd done this.

The blond devil stepped back and looked down at us with an annoyed look on his face. He was obviously pissed that Gus was taking his sick work away from him. "I got shit to do so hurry the fuck up," he snapped.

"I'd love to take my time, little one. But this is going to have to do." He pushed the wrench into my mouth and clasped onto one of my molars. He didn't just start to yank on it, he started pulling slowly, building the pain, setting each nerve on fire, prolonging the inevitable as he pulled harder and harder until I felt as if my entire jaw was being ripped from my skull. I screamed so loud my chest hurt. Warm copper flooded my mouth.

Gus sat back, his chest heaving up and down. My bloodied molar between the tongs of his wrench. "That was fucking fantastic."

"Great. Now get the fuck out or I'm leaving," the blond devil spat.

"Fine," Gus said, standing up and setting the wrench down on the tarp. "Just make sure she screams, she was adamant about that." The devil nodded and knelt down next to me again, picking through the toolbox. I started to choke as the blood dripped down my throat. He pushed my head to the side so the blood could run out of my mouth, the spreader bar painfully tearing into the flesh inside of my mouth.

How could someone so beautiful be so evil? I thought, but then I remembered something Bear had said.

He looks like sunshine. Blond hair and blue eyes. The kind of looks you'd see on one of them TV shows all the teenagers like these days. But that kid's got the devil in him. Only human lives he values are his wife Abby's and now his kid's. Jake's the only person in the world who scares the shit out of me. You know, besides you.

It was my only chance. It had to be him. One of the tattoos on his chest was the name Bee. *Maybe short for Abby?* "Jake," I said. But I was tired, so very tired, and with the spreader in my mouth it sounded like, "Gggggggech."

He ignored me and shuffled through his toolbox and that's when I realized it was over.

I was going to die.

I love you Bear.

CHAPTER THIRTY-TWO

THIA

When Jake turned back around he was holding a box cutter. He looked from me to the instrument in his hand. He slid his thumb up and down on the handle and watched the blade as it retracted again and again, as if he were in some sort of trance.

"Air Air!" I screamed, trying to shout Bear's name to Jake, but it was too late. There was no decision to be made. My fate had been sealed. There was no drawing him back from whatever murderous place he'd gone.

A car backfired somewhere outside, or maybe a motorcycle. Whatever it was, it got Jake's attention. The creases on his forehead relaxed, and his eyes focused. He dropped the box cutter to the floor. With an angry roar he pulled a gun from his jeans and cocked it.

"Nooooooo!" I screamed, trying to roll away from him like there was somewhere I could go. Somewhere I could hide.

There wasn't.

He fired, the sound of the shot echoing through the room like a shrill scream in a cave, ringing my ears. I waited for the pain. Or the nothingness.

It never came.

"Shut the fuck up," Jake whispered, and it was only then I realized I was still screaming. He looked over his shoulder toward the door and paused, listening for something. I noticed the camera had been the target of Jake's shot. "Fuck!" he said, running his hand through his hair.

He lowered himself next to me, his mouth close against my ear and I tried to roll away again. "Do what I say."

I stilled. Why was he whispering?

"Gus hasn't left yet," he continued. "That fucker is waiting in the other room to make sure I'm going to follow through. I am going to hurt you. Scream. It helps. I promise."

What the fuck?

"Okay?" he asked. I nodded, oddly trusting the man who was now holding the same wrench Gus had just used to pull my tooth out.

It's not like I had any other options.

"The louder you scream, the more satisfied he will be and the sooner he'll leave." Jake pushed the wrench into my mouth and clamped it around another molar. Tears ran down my face in anticipation of the pain.

"Scream as loud as you can, because if you don't he'll just stay longer and I'll have to take more teeth." He paused. "And do God only knows what the fuck else."

Screaming wouldn't be a problem.

He yanked, and I screamed as he ripped another tooth from my mouth, flooding it with more blood. But unlike Gus, it was over almost instantly, almost painlessly. "Keep screaming," he whispered, long after the tooth had been extracted, so I did, until my lungs burned. Until my vision blurred.

The door opened and Gus stepped back into the room.

"Don't you have somewhere to be?" Jake asked, picking up the drill and selecting a bit from the toolbox. Blood from my mouth dripped down his hand. I continued to scream although no sound came out.

"I was about to leave, but I wanted to make sure you were doing your job. Wanted to make sure the rumors weren't true about you going soft." Gus said, taunting Jake.

"You want to finish this? Finish it. Fuck it. I don't need this bullshit," Jake snapped. He stood, and on his way out the door, he tossed something to Gus who held up my bloody tooth with a look of approval. A phone rang and Gus answered. "Yes. He's got it all handled," he said into the phone. Jake stopped and turned back around. "I'm on my way, now," Gus said, hanging up. "She's all yours," Gus said. He was about to close the door when he spied the camera in pieces on the floor.

He looked to the camera and then Jake, narrowing his eyes. The look lingered and anyone else would have crumbled under the scrutiny, but not Jake. He just shrugged. "Told you I don't fucking like cameras."

"So much for watching the fucking replay," Gus muttered, closing the door and again leaving me alone in the room with Jake.

Jake walked over to the only window in the room, which had been painted over with black paint. He crouched down and looked out from the corner of the window where a chunk of glass was missing. "Scream," he ordered, and so I did. When he was satisfied that Gus had left, he waved me off to stop.

When he came back over to me and leaned down with the drill still in his hand, I flinched and again tried to roll away, but he held me by my chin, ripping the spreader bar from my mouth. The fresh holes in the back of my jaw throbbed. My jaw ached. I spit blood onto the tarp when he sat me up.

Jake separated the chains of my cuffs with a pair of bolt cutters. "I don't have the keys," he explained.

"I can't move my shoulders," I said. "I think they're dislocated. I don't know how long I was hanging there."

"This is going to hurt," Jake said, crouching down behind me. Without warning he pushed my arms down and back. This time I didn't need any prompting to scream. "Roll your shoulders," he ordered.

I did as he said and instantly the pain started to subside. "How—" I started, but Jake shook his head.

"No time for questions. Here," he said, handing me a bottle of vodka. "Swish this around in your mouth."

The vodka burned as it entered the new gaping holes in the back of my mouth. I don't know if he intended for me to spit it out or swallow it but I swallowed. "More," he said, pushing the bottle back into my hand. I took another long pull and swished it around. It burned less the second time around.

Jake pulled out his phone and pressed a few buttons before shoving it back in his pocket. "We have to go. Now. Can you walk?"

"I'm not sure."

"No time to figure it out," Jake said, lifting me into his arms. "Stay quiet. I mean it. Not a sound." He carried me effortlessly out the door and down a flight of steps. When he kicked open a back door, I'd never been so happy to be met with the wet heat of the stagnant night air. A black van was waiting.

A minivan.

The automatic door slid open as we approached. Jake set me across the middle row of seats. He pulled out his phone and pressed a number. "Fuck. Bear's not answering." He leaned into the van. "I'm going to the MC. Take her to King's and don't stop anywhere, you got it?"

"Who are you talking...?" I asked.

"He was talking to me," a feminine voice said. A girl turned around in the driver's seat. Long, straight, red hair framed her perfectly round, pale face. Both of her arms were heavily tattooed with colorful yet feminine colors, one arm rested over a hugely rounded pregnant belly. "I'm Abby."

I groaned as I sat up. My head spun. I looked to Jake. "But I'm going with you, Jake. And we have to go now. Bear went to the MC. It's a trap," I said as my adrenaline started to take over, muting the pain in my arms. There were more pressing matters than pain.

"No," Jake said simply, and started to walk away.

"Wait!" I said, but it didn't matter what I said because he wasn't coming back.

"Jake?" Abby called out, and immediately Jake circled back and ducked his head inside the van. "My water sort of just broke."

After those words I ceased to exist.

Jake jogged over to the driver's side and much to my surprise he lifted Abby out of the van and carried her over to his bike, setting her down on the seat and getting on behind her. "Take the van," Abby called out to me with a calm smile. Jake muffled her words by setting his helmet on her head, and she rolled her eyes and laughed. He started the engine and tossed me a gun. With one hand on the handlebars and one hand on Abby's belly, they took off.

There wasn't a second to waste. God only knew what the hell Gus was up to or why, all I knew was that I had to get to Bear before Chop or Gus did.

Our story, it wasn't over yet.

It couldn't be.

I'd come so far.

Bear had come so far.

We'd both been through so much.

Too much.

We deserved our chance at life. At love. At figuring out what any of this meant.

It was far from a romance.

But it was still a love story.

And it was *ours*.

I was going to stop at nothing until we had our happy ending.

I used the cell phone sitting in the center console to call Bear, but just like when Jake tried earlier there was no answer. I ended the call and made one more as I drove to the MC at breakneck speed. There wasn't anyone or anything in this world that was going to keep us apart, including the chained gate at the entrance of the MC, which is why I slammed my foot down on the gas pedal…and drove right through it.

I wasn't about to let Bear die.

He'd lost everything.

I wouldn't let him lose his life.

I was crazy. I was reckless.

I was free.

And I was going to get my biker…or die trying.

CHAPTER THIRTY-THREE

BEAR

THE PLAN WAS simple. We'd hop the back fence and once inside, we'd spread out and search for Ti. "If anyone tries to prevent you from getting to her, pull the fucking trigger, we don't have time for hesitation," I ordered. Munch would stand guard by the ladder while Stone and Wolf swept the first floor, leaving King and I to split the second.

I wasn't halfway up the steps when the alarm went off along with the first sounds of gunfire, but I didn't stop. There was one place I was going to search first because somehow, I knew that the motherfucker would be there, and he was there, chances were that Ti was there too.

"I wish I could say it was good to see you, son," Chop said after I kicked down the door to his office.

"Don't fucking 'son' me, you cocksucker," I warned. "Where the fuck is she?" I held my gun on him and rounded the desk, pulling out the gun he kept hidden underneath, tossing it to the couch on the far side of the room.

"You're gonna to have to be more specific than that," Chop sang, turning around in his chair to face me. It had been a long time since I'd seen him and the only thing that had changed was that his belly had grown a little larger and the bags under his eyes were so dark it looked as if he had gotten into a fight and had two black eyes. "'Cause, as you know, we've got a lot of bitches around here." He laughed. "Well, *had*."

I would of ended him right then and there if I didn't need him to tell me where Ti was. Instead I settled for hitting him on the side of the head with the butt of my gun. "You sick fuck! Don't fuck with me, old man. The only way you prolong your fucked up life is to tell me where the fuck she is right now or it's motherfucking lights out."

Chop rubbed the side of his head where a knot had already started to form. "Aaaahhh, the girl? Is that who you're looking for?" he asked. "She probably realized she's too young and pretty for you and ran away. Really, she's too fucking innocent to be all dirtied up by a son of a bitch like you." He leaned back and rested his hands behind his head, his elbows high in the air. "My time with her was short, as well. We were going to have so much fun playing together before we were so rudely interrupted by whoever you sent to bomb me the fuck out."

Gus had done that on his own but I wasn't out to correct him, there was no time. I pressed the barrel of my gun into his forehead, and growled, "Where the fuck is she?"

"Do it," Chop said, pushing his head forward against my gun. "Go ahead and do it, you ungrateful little cunt. I gave you everything. Everything I had was yours, but it wasn't enough for you, was it? Now you show up here with the other fucking traders and expect me to what? Roll over? If that's what you want then pull that fucking trigger, boy, because it's not going to fucking happen!" His face reddened, saliva flew from his mouth.

I shook my head. "What is it that you think you've given me, old man? 'Cause you haven't given me shit. Nothing. Not a childhood. Not a family. *NOTHING.*"

Chop pointed at me. "That's where you're wrong, boy. I've given you everything I ever had to give. This club? This was for you. The gavel was for you. The power was for you. You were born to be a Bastard, but it wasn't enough for you. Your brothers weren't enough for you." He pointed to himself. "*I* wasn't enough for you."

"You're right, you weren't enough for me. I needed a dad not a fucking Prez." I paused, the idea that he gave me everything was so ludicrous that I laughed. "I don't know what part of history you've decided to rewrite in that demented fucked up head of yours, Chop, but let me remind you of what you've taken from me, starting with my mother." I neglected to mention the fact that I knew she was alive.

Chops shoulders shook and I answered his laugh with a kick to his shins. He paused, his eyes narrowed. "It doesn't matter what I did to that cunt of a mother of yours. You seem to think I was so horrible to you growing up but I never had the heart to tell you who she really was." Chops jaw ticked. "She was a fucking RAT."

I rolled my eyes over whatever game he way playing at. "Bullshit. You were just pissed she was—"

"Because she was trying to take you away from me," Chop finished for me, looking amused that he knew exactly what I was going to say. "If that was the case, she would have felt my wrath. I know that killing women and kids is against code, but killing a woman who's a rat? Well, that's not exactly frowned upon," Chop said.

I scoffed. "You've probably said that same line over and over again that I really think you believe your own fucking lies, old man. But here's the problem with your lies. We both know that my mom wasn't the rat." I paused and made sure his eyes were on mine when I added. "And we both know she's alive."

"What the fuck do you know about that?" Chop said, abruptly standing up.

"Easy, old man," I said, nudging him back down into his chair with my foot on his chest. His mask temporarily fell from his face, and for a second, I could have sworn he looked, concerned? Sad? Whatever it was, it was something I'd never seen from him before. "I don't need to here more of your bullshit anyway. I didn't' come her for a fucking reunion or a nice chat with Daddy." I cocked the gun. "Just tell me where the girl is," I said through my teeth.

Chop twiddled his thumbs. "Son, if I had her, don't you think I would have delivered her fingers and ears to you in a fucking box by now?" The gunfire outside the office grew louder.

Closer.

Apparently Chop didn't get the message that it wasn't fucking story time. "You were five years old," he said, pouring himself a glass of whiskey from the bottle on his messy desk. His eyes were fixed on the glass as he spoke. "Your mom was acting fidgety. Had been for a while. Should have suspected something sooner, but believe it or not, I loved that stupid bitch. Gave her an old lady's cut. Even gave up other pussy for her." He finished his drink in one swig and set down the glass. "She was family, and almost as much of a Bastard as I was. She loved the life, or at least I thought she did." Chop looked back to me. "But then she started asking questions. Questions about meetings. Money. Where it came from, where it was going. Things old ladies didn't need to know shit about. I didn't even think anything of it for a while. She was always more involved than the other bitches who hung around. She was smart too, so I never thought she'd actually be dumb enough to cross me." I'd never heard Chop talk about my mom. Not since the night in the woods.

Not once.

Chop rested his hands on his desk and looked absently at the door. "Guys started to go down for shit we'd never had heat about before. We owned the fucking law but the county sheriff was suddenly all over our asses. I wised up. Hurt like fucking hell, but I tested her. Leaked something to her, something I made up. Told her that we were making a gun run. Told her the when and where and what route we were taking. I went with Tank and a few of the other boys who weren't on probation. When we got there, no one was there. No FBI no ATF. I was so relieved and so fucking happy. Waited a full hour just to be sure." He poured himself another glass, emptying the bottle and downing it faster than the first. "Came to the conclusion that it was all in my head. Convinced myself that we'd just been unlucky." Chop slammed his fist on the desk. "It wasn't until we were pulling out that the ATF swarmed the van."

Chop laughed, but in a way that told me he didn't find shit funny about what he was saying. He cracked his knuckles. "The only good thing about that night was the look on the ATF's faces when they opened the doors and only found a bunch of bicycles we had fixed up to donate to the Y."

I stood over him, searching his face for any traces that he could be lying. "That's not true," I said, although something deep in my gut told me it was.

Chop reached over to the shelf behind his desk and I cocked my gun. "Just getting a drink, son." He grabbed a fresh bottle of Jack and poured himself a glass. He tipped it back and downed the entire glass in one swallow. "If you're going to blow my fucking head off, I at least want a last drink." He slid a cigarette from the open pack on his desk and lit one. "And a smoke."

"You've got three fucking seconds before lights out. I'm done playing your games. We do this my way. Tell me where Thia is or I'm pulling the fucking trigger." My jaw was clenched so tight it hurt. My anger solely focused on Chop.

Chop threw his hands in the air. "You know what? I wish I had her, but I don't. I wish I could have finished what I started and show you what real hurt feels like. Betrayal. It broke my heart when I found out your mother was a rat, but not nearly as much as when I found out that you were just like her. Like mother like son. Dirty. Fucking. Rats," he hissed.

I scrunched my face. "What the fuck are you talking about, old man?"

Chops lip raised in a snarl. "You're more fucked up in the head than I am if you really thought that I wouldn't find out what you and King and that Preppy kid were up to. Well, guess again, because I have eyes and ears everywhere. We started taking more heat again, losing runs, losing work. It was like the shit with your mother all over again. It wasn't hard to put two and two together."

"I never betrayed the club. Not fucking once. Not fucking ever," I seethed.

Chop rolled his eyes. "Bullshit. But you know? I didn't believe it either at first. Don't you see what I was doing? I was giving you another chance. I was giving you one more shot to prove to me that you weren't the dirty fucking rat I thought you were, and just like your mother, you disappointed me. You chose them over us. You chose going off on your own over your club and turned your back on me." He finished his glass again and slammed it down on the table, the bottom of the glass cracked, a crooked line snaked up the side. "If Gus hadn't told me what he saw? What he'd heard? What you had confided in him? I would have never believed it. I'd still be searching for the rat to this day. But lookey here," he said, staring up at me. "I don't have to search anymore. 'Cause the rat is right in fucking front of me."

"What the fuck did you say?" I asked, his words still ringing in my brain. It didn't make sense, but it wasn't until he mentioned Gus that I started to piece it together. "Who told you I was a rat?"

He raised his eyebrows. I stayed still as stone, fearful that if I moved it would be my trigger finger first. "Gus. Surprised, eh? Thought he was loyal to you because you didn't pop him in the head when you had a chance? Guess again. That little fucker was more loyal to me than you would ever be, and you think that—"

"Chop!" I shouted, but he wasn't listening.

"You are owed everything you selfish—"

"Chop!" I shouted again, getting his attention. He finally paused long enough for me to get a word in. "Gus. When the shit went down with Isaac here, when he killed Preppy, I knew someone on the inside had to have leaked that information."

Chop shrugged like what I was telling him wasn't new information. "It was me. I didn't want the brothers to know outright that I was taking you out. Thought I'd kill three birds with one stone." He smiled. "Literally."

Hearing him admit to what I already knew didn't make me any less pissed about it. "I already knew it was you because—" I started, with Chop finally cluing in.

"Gus," he said, sitting straight up as the realization hit him that we'd both been crossed by the same brother.

A voice boomed from the doorway. "It's so nice that you two are talking about me." He looked at me, his semi-automatic at my head. "Put your fucking gun down." I reluctantly tossed my gun to the floor, half hoping it would go off and kill the motherfucker, but no such luck.

"Glad to hear you two fucking idiots finally figured it out." He looked right at me when he said, "I was kind of hoping you'd kill your old man before you put it all together. But, oh well. That can be fixed."

"You little shit," Chop said, standing up from his chair.

Gus gritted his teeth and switched his aim from me to Chop. "I really fucking hate it when you call me that!" Gus roared, tapping the barrel of his gun on top of his head before pointing it back toward us. "And I've been good. So, so good. But I'm done being good. I'm done being your bitch. I can't wait to take you apart piece by piece, just like she said I could. I can do whatever I want, because you're mine. You both are. You're my gifts from her." Gus said, with a huge manic smile on his face.

I couldn't believe what I was hearing. "I spared your life and took you in, and this is how you fucking thank me?" I asked my one-time protégé. "I should have pulled the fucking trigger when I had the chance."

Gus took another step into the room. "Yeah, but you didn't."

"Who the fuck are you talking about, boy?" Chop chimed in. "Who the fuck is she?" I already knew who he was talking about and I had a feeling Chop did too.

"He's talking about me," said a feminine voice. The clank of heels against the concrete echoed in the hall until she appeared in the doorway.

My mother.

"Sadie," Chop said, dropping his already broken glass. It shattered on the floor, cutting through the momentary silence as Chop and I both glared at the woman in the doorway. "You evil fucking bitch."

She rolled her eyes and waved Chop off dismissively. A curt smile on her once again red lips. "Here," she said, tossing a pair of handcuffs on the floor and kicking them over to us. "Cuff yourselves together."

"Fuck you," I spat.

Her voice was sweet and high, like she was practically singing when she said, "Cuff yourselves together or I will make a call right now that ends with your darling Thia being dumped off the causeway within ten minutes."

"If you so much as fucking—" I started, taking a step toward her. Gus held out his gun and Sadie held up a phone.

"Save it, Abel. Cuffs. Now. Or the girl dies."

I picked the cuffs up off the floor and did as she asked, cuffing my hand to my old man's whose gaze was still fixed on Sadie.

"Can I kill him now?" Gus asked, shifting from foot to foot. "Is it playtime yet?"

"No, sweetheart," Sadie said, like he was a toddler that needed to be taught a lesson. She sauntered over to Gus and planted a kiss on his lips. He closed his eyes while she kept hers open, tugging the gun from his hands. "You've been a very, very good boy to me all these years. You took very good care of me while I was that pig's captive, and I thank you for that." She patted him on the top of his head and raised the gun. Gus opened his eyes just long enough for the shock to register. "But I'll take it from here, baby." She pulled the trigger, firing off multiple rounds, sending Gus's brains splattering against Chop's old trophy case in a mist of pink and red.

★ ★ ★

"WHAT THE FUCK?" I asked as Gus's brains slid down the glass and fell on top of what was left of his forehead. Sadie pulled her own gun from a holster on her thigh and held one on each of us.

Sadie not only acted very different from the woman who visited me in County, she looked different too. She wore a high-waisted red skirt with a tight black blouse and shiny black pumps. Her long hair was now an auburn color, void of silver streaks. Instead of flowing down her back it had been cut short to her chin. She looked easily fifteen years younger than she did only months before.

"So what? You're here to seek revenge?" Chop asked, and I wondered if she would really shoot if I took a run at her. I glanced down to Gus's bloodied corpse and decided that it was highly likely she would.

"Something like that," she purred, perching herself on the edge of the couch.

"You should be thanking me for not killing you," Chop said flatly. He hadn't once taken his eyes from her since she'd stepped into the room. Not even when she blew Gus's head clean off. He barely even blinked.

She moved back a few inches, physically putting more distance between herself and Chops statement. "Thanking you? I should be thanking you?" she yelled, getting up from the couch and pointing the gun at Chop's head. "You hunted me down and shot me!" Sadie screamed, pointing to the faded scar on the side of her forehead. "You left me on the side of the fucking road for hours before you came back for me, but only so you could keep me prisoner you sick, SICK FUCK!" Her hands visibly trembled. So did her lower lip. "The humane thing would have been to kill me! The only human interaction I'd had in decades was *that* piece of shit," she said, pointing the toe of her heel at Gus, the pool of blood growing beneath his body. "And the wails of whoever else you decided to torture."

The bigger picture was coming together, but not fast enough. "Why Gus? How?" I asked, and when I raised my hand, I raised Chop's as well, reminding me that I was still cuffed to the cocksucker.

Chop spoke up. "Because he was the one who fed her," he muttered. "I thought he was the only one I could trust with that type of thing. Given his…oddities and all."

I looked at Sadie as it all fell into place. "Chop was right. It was you. You were the rat," I said, pausing only to watch as Gus's blood reached the toe of my boot. My eyes darted back to her. "Well, you and that fuck," I said. "It was you all along." Still not quite believing what I knew then to be true.

Sadie nodded and her hands stopped shaking as she switched her attentions from Chop to me. "Yes. I've spent every day of my long captivity, when I wasn't being raped by your father, or beaten, or *tortured*," she said, slowly emphasizing the word TORTURE. "I was trying my damnedest to bring this club down." She smiled like she'd just remembered something funny, or at least, funny to her. "The cartel pulling out? That was me," she said proudly. "The deal with the Miami mob falling through? That was me. The fucking ATF at your door? THAT. WAS. ME!" she screamed, jabbing her gun in the air at us. "And I regret none of it. I've been putting the two of you against one another since the first day I met Gus, and it looks like it worked." She looked to me. "You thought Chop was the rat, and Chop…" she said, turning to my old man. "…thought it was you. It was brilliant, really."

"If Gus was your little bitch boy then why didn't you just have him kill Chop?" I asked. "Why go through all this trouble? Why try and kill me too?" I stared her down, daring her to answer my questions. "What the fuck did I ever do to you?" I wanted nothing more than to snap the neck of the tiny woman holding the big gun.

"Because," Sadie said, her eyes glassy. "You were my little boy. My Abel. I couldn't let you be just like him. I wouldn't, and when Gus told me how much you really were like him, the things you did. I knew I had to end it."

"So you would rather Isaac or Eli kill me?" I asked, feeling sick. "You wanted them to kill me so I wouldn't end up like Chop? Do you even know what those sick fucks did to me?"

She didn't answer. Stepping over Gus she briefly peered out the window to the soldiers below, oblivious that the person they really needed to kill was one floor above them and wearing a fucking skirt. "Yes. I failed you, and I'm sorry, but it's too late now. It's all too late to change it now."

A realization hit me. "You're the reason Preppy's dead. I should fucking end you right fucking now you fucking cunt!" I said, pushing the desk aside and almost knocking over Chop, who I was inadvertently dragging with me.

Sadie aimed her gun at my chest, and if I didn't care about ever seeing Ti again, I would have ran right through a spray of bullets to rip my mothers head off. "See?" Sadie asked, pointing at me. "Just like him." She sighed. "All I ever did was love you and try to give you a better life, and then he took it all from me!" Sadie paused, her eyes glassed over. "I loved you!" she cried, her hands again shaking. To my surprise she wasn't looking at me when she said it this time. She was looking at Chop. "I love you and I gave you a son and you ruined it. You ruined everything! All I wanted was for you to leave the club, the life. I wanted us to be a family. To be together."

"So that's why you turned rat in the first place."

Chop cleared his throat but didn't say anything. I took Sadie's temporary silence as an admission.

"I love you, too, you know," she said, this time to me. "I—"

I cut her off. I'd already heard more than fucking enough. "YOU are NOTHING to me!" I roared, pulling at my own hair in frustration. "I don't give a fuck where you've been or for how long or what the fuck Chop did to you. There's only one fucking thing I care about right now." I narrowed my eyes and gave her one last warning. "You better tell me where the fuck she is, and if you so much as laid one fucking finger on her—" The sound of bullets grew even louder, but I didn't care. They could be sailing through the room and I still wouldn't have taken my eyes off of the bitch who had my girl.

Sadie's shoulders fell, but it was like I wasn't in the room. The conversation she was having was entirely one sided. I didn't know what I needed to do to get her so she could tell me where the fuck my girl was. "I came back for you once, you know," she said. "Escaped all on my own." Chops eyes widened like he hadn't known that. "I disguised myself. At first I was going to take you away with me, that time for good. You were sixteen at the time and when I finally found you, you were at some biker bar. Some whore was sitting on your lap. You were snorting that shit up your nose off of her legs. That's the very moment I knew it was too late." She searched my face, "You looked just like him sitting there. A spitting image. I knew then there was no saving you. I could have just left then. Disappeared. But I didn't. I had to make sure that the two of you were put down and the best way to do that was from the inside. So I went back down into my hole before Chop even realized I was gone and I put up with his abuse every single day knowing that I wouldn't stop until I took every last one of you leather-wearing psychopaths down."

She turned her nose up at us. "Especially the two of you."

I rolled my eyes. "Great speech. Now, where the fuck is my girl!"

Sadie laughed and stepped to the side of the door. "I'll tell you. But you need to move, outside. NOW!" she ordered, and when neither of us budged she fired at the light fixture, sending glass raining down around us.

Chop moved first, and I followed. Sadie stayed out of arm's reach, as we stepped through what was left of Gus and made our way out to the balcony of the second floor, which overlooked the courtyard where sporadic gunfire was being exchanged.

A monster of a man wearing overalls with no shirt underneath walked casually beside the pool on the floor below, holding a semi-automatic in each hand, and I could have sworn I heard him whistling, but when I looked down again, he was gone.

"On your knees," Sadie ordered. I lowered myself to the ground but only because she still hadn't answered my question about Ti, and Chop did the same, because we were cuffed and he didn't have a fucking choice. "I'm on my fucking knees, bitch, now tell me where the fuck my girl is."

Sadie clucked her tongue and moved to stand beside us. "Unfortunately for you, I needed the girl in order to get you here, and since Gus was so insistent on joining me here tonight, he hired outside help to do the sick shit he wanted to do her and tape it. I'd show you the tape, but something tells me you won't be around long enough to watch it."

"I'll fucking kill you!" I shouted, rising off my knees. She fired, sending a bullet straight through my thigh and sending me crashing back down to the floor.

Chop remained silent, only watching as I flailed around on

the floor, clenching my teeth together, warring against the agony tearing through my leg. "Where was this girl when I needed her?" Chop suddenly asked, drawing my attention away from the pain. I managed to sit up on my good knee and with my free hand I pushed against the wound to slow down the blood loss. "Where was this girl twenty-five years ago?" he asked. "Why, my Sadie girl? Why did you turn on me? You could have come to me. You could have told me what was going on. What you wanted to do. You had a choice, and you made the wrong fucking one. It's your fault. You made me pull that fucking trigger!"

Sadie turned to him, her eyes rimmed with red like she was on the verge of tears. "I did what I thought could get us out from under your shit," she spat.

"But don't you see?" he asked. "I couldn't do it. I couldn't kill you even when I should have after what you did. So I kept you. I kept you all to myself because you were mine." Chop shook his head. His face reddened. "You were a rat who deserved to fucking die but I didn't kill you!" he said, raising his voice to a scream. "You claimed to have loved your kid, but I can see right fucking through you. You never once asked to see him in all the years I had you. You didn't love him, you were jealous of him. Of the club. Of anywhere else my attention was besides you, and you couldn't fucking handle that, so you ran to the law with your tail between your fucking cunt like the bitch you are."

"You still don't get it do you Chop-Chop?" she asked. "None of that matters now." Sadie stood behind me and pressed the gun to the back of my head. "I'll kill your precious son first, so you can watch him die. Then it's your turn, baby." She blew him a kiss.

She leaned in and whispered in my ear. "I may not have had

the chance to raise you up, baby boy, but I'm not going to pass up the chance now to put you down."

"Let me do it," Chop said. "Give me a gun. You can still kill me after. Just let me do this one thing right for you."

"Fucking pussy," I muttered.

Sadie was quiet and my head wasn't blown off, but I couldn't believe she was even considering what he was offering, and even after all the shit Chop had done, I was mad at myself for being surprised at the offer.

I couldn't believe it even more when Chop raised up to his feet and was suddenly the one standing behind me with a gun, my arm that was cuffed to his was pulled backward at an awkward angle. "This is for you, baby," Chop said with a sadness in his voice I'd never heard before.

Chop pulled the trigger.

The sound of the gun shot was fucking deafening.

CHAPTER THIRTY-FOUR

BEAR

THE ENTIRE COURTYARD rattled like a cannon had been fired. So did the inside of my head. Wet and warm liquid poured thickly over my head and shoulders. The heaviness that was Chop's lifeless body descended over me, forcing my face against the rusted railing.

I pushed Chop off of me, his body falling through the broken railing. If King hadn't appeared and grabbed on to my legs I would have went over with him. "Thia, keep the gun on her," King ordered, and at the mere mention of her name, I found the strength to hang on. King laid next to me on his stomach leaning out over the balcony under the railing as far as he could stretch. "Pull up as much as you can," he said. I felt my arm separating from the joint. I pulled up as hard as I could, straining with everything I had in me until King could reach Chop. With a guttural roar he pulled his fat corpse back onto the balcony. My arm and shoulder felt instant relief.

King pulled a machete style knife from his boot and hacked away at Chop's wrist, blood spurting into the air and all over his face and shirt, until it was severed, and King and I were so covered in blood it looked as if he just starred in a horror movie.

Our horror happened to be very real.

"Noooooooo!" Sadie screamed, and while she was momentarily distracted, I grabbed the gun Chop had dropped and turned it on her. Sadie's mouth was wide open as she looked from the railing to the pink-haired girl holding the gun.

Ti.

"Thank fucking Christ," I muttered.

"You bitch!" Sadie screamed at Ti, "What did you do?"

"Same thing I'm about to do to you if you don't put that fucking gun down."

I'd thought King had fired the bullet at Chop, but I'd been wrong. It was my girl who'd saved me.

"You leave her the fuck alone," I said, standing between my mom and my girl. "Put your fucking gun down."

"Abel," she pleaded, taking a step toward me.

"Stop," I warned. "Don't fucking call me that. You don't get to call me that." Without turning my head away from Sadie I called out to Ti, "Are you okay? Did this bitch hurt you? Did Gus hurt you?"

"I'm fine, baby," she said, her voice snaking it's way inside of me, making me feel centered, grounded.

Complete.

Sadie looked down at Chop's handless body. "He's really gone?" Sadie cried, covering her mouth with the hand that wasn't holding the gun. A tear fell from her eye and ran down her cheek. "I mean, that's what I wanted. Him. Gone. But now…he really is."

"What the fuck did you think was going to happen?" I asked.

Sadie shook her head and took a step back. Her gaze went from me to Ti and then to King. "Don't know what you were thinking," I said. "But there ain't no way you're walking out of here," I said, and I meant it.

Sadie wiped her cheek with the back of her hand. "Oh, my Abel." she said, sniffling. "I never planned on walking out of here." She looked over to Ti. "Take good care of my boy," she said before placing the gun in her mouth.

Then she did what Chop was too much of a coward to do all those years before, and she ended it all.

CHAPTER THIRTY-FIVE

THIA

BEAR LIMPED OVER his mother's dead body and grabbed my face roughly in his hands. "Hey, Beautiful." He turned my chin from side to side and looked me over like he was inspecting me for physical damage.

"I'm fine, don't worry about me," I reassured him. "Just scrapes and bruises."

"Scrapes and bruises would be too much, but I call bullshit. Your cheeks are swollen and you just winced like I slapped you. What the fuck happened?" His nostrils flared.

I ignored his question, my teeth not seeming all that important. "Looks like I got off better than you," I said, pointing to the bloody hole in his thigh.

"Just scrapes and bruises," he said, repeating my lie. I rolled my eyes. "Now fucking tell me what happened to your mouth."

"I lost a couple of teeth. Just in the back," I added, like it would make Bear's eyes turn any less murderous. I instantly regretted telling him.

"Who?" he demanded. "Who the fuck did Gus leave you with?" Bear asked, like he needed to know whose name he could add to his list of people to kill. "How the fuck you even get out?"

Both questions had the same answer. "Jake." Bear's eyes went wide. "But it's okay," I said, grabbing on to his arm. "He rescued me." I left off the part about him being one of the people to pull those teeth.

"Fuck," Bear said, pressing his forehead to mine, grabbing onto the back of my neck. "That could have gone either way."

"But it didn't," I reassured him. "I'm fine. I swear."

"I'm sorry, baby. I am so fucking sorry," Bear said, pressing a kiss to my lips. He was covered in blood and from what I'd just witnessed I knew most of that blood wasn't his.

"Bear," I said, placing my hands over his. "You need to believe me when I tell you that I'm okay. Not just physically, but with all of this." I looked around the clubhouse. "You're alive. I'm alive. That's all you need to know."

Bear threaded his fingers up through my hair. "Why did you come here? You shouldn't of."

I shook my head. "You see, that's where you're wrong. I made you a promise that I wouldn't give up on you, and…"

"And?" he pressed.

"And so I didn't," I said, adding, "and believe it or not, there is no place else I'd rather be." Bear laughed and so did I because although it sounded ridiculous, it was true. Bear tugged on my hair. I stood on my tippy toes and pressed a kiss against the corner of his mouth. His lips didn't move and neither did mine. We stood there for a minute. Just feeling our connection, breathing each other in, reminding ourselves that we were together now.

Alive.

CHAPTER THIRTY-SIX

BEAR

"BEAR, COME LOOK at this," King said, putting an end to our moment. Without letting go of Ti's hand, I walked over to the balcony, dragging her with me, and looked down to what King was pointing at below. I was stunned at the sight before me. Surrounding the pool were Bastards. My former brothers, at least twenty of them, and they were all on their knees with their hands behind their heads while Munch, Wolf, Stone, and several older men I didn't recognize stood around them, guns at the ready.

Well, there was one guy I recognized in the group. It seemed I hadn't imagined seeing him earlier. "Ted?" I asked.

"Howdy, there!" Ted called up cheerily, covered in his own fair amount of blood splatter. Thor, who had been a prospect when I left, who was now wearing a member's patch on his cut, made a move to stand but Ted kicked him in the back of the knees and forced him back down to the ground, never breaking a smile.

I turned to Ti. "Was this you?" I asked, waving at all the unfamiliar men.

She shrugged with a little half smile. "I figured that if you were going to go to war, you should have an army." She leaned in, her breath tickling my ear. "So I called in an army."

Before that night I'd already known I was in love with Ti, what I didn't know was that I could love her more than I already did, but right there, standing in a pool of my parents blood, mixed with some of my own, I fell for her so hard my chest ached with all the love I had for her.

Ted saluted me. "Had more fun tonight than I have in years," he called up again, tucking one of his semi-automatics into the front pocket of his overalls so he could adjust his trucker's hat. "Was like rounding up pigs at the fair."

"What are you going to do with them?" King asked, nodding down to the men on their knees and I knew right away what he was really asking.

I shrugged. "I'm gonna talk to them first."

And then we'll discuss mass murder.

★ ★ ★

THIA

"THEY NEED YOU," I said, pulling away from Bear. I was relieved he was okay, but I wasn't ready to let him go just yet. I knew I had to though, because the men below needed him as much as I did.

He kissed me on the top of my head. "Don't go too far, baby."

King tapped Bear on the shoulder in one of those manly, reassuring, this-is-not-a-hug gestures and joined me by the top of the stairs.

Bear turned to his brothers, both current and former. From where we stood at the top of the steps I could see both Bear high up on his perch like an eagle stalking its prey, and the men below, all in different varying stages of dishevelment, all probably wondering what fate was in store for them.

I was wondering that too.

Bear looked down at Chop's lifeless body like it was offending him by even bleeding.

Bear tugged off Chop's cut and tore off the patch that read PRESIDENT. He spit on Chop's body, then, holding on to the railing, he used the boot on his good leg to kick it off the second floor and into the crowd, who gasped and shuffled around on their knees to avoid being hit by the lifeless body of their fallen leader.

"Listen up, motherfuckers!" Bear shouted, his voice booming across the courtyard like he was speaking into a microphone. He looked as if he was about to spit fire as he limped from side to side, pacing the second floor balcony. The single handcuff that used to be connected to Chop dangled from his wrist, clanking against the rusted metal of the railing as he slid his hand over the top.

Bear stopped and leaned over, glaring at the men who from the looks on their faces, had already come to the realization that there was a good chance they were already dead.

"This," Bear said, waving his arms around, gesturing to the walls of the building and then to the men themselves. "This was supposed to be brotherhood. Somewhere under Chop's rule, you monkeys turned this club into a fucking gang, and a fucking bad one at that. This is not supposed to be a dictatorship. You aren't motherfucking thugs. This wasn't supposed to be a fucking war zone." He grew more confident as the words came. Clearer. Stronger. "What this was supposed to be was a business." Bear looked back to me. "A family." He turned back around, the dried blood on his back covering his tattoos in a sheen of red.

He shook his head. Pausing. Thinking. "We've all been so caught up in who is doing us wrong that we haven't been able to look past the barrel of our own guns long enough to see who is doing us right." He looked back over to me again and the exchange between us was nothing short of electric.

"We've fallen so far," Bear said. "We were brothers. We *are* brothers," he said, closing his fist over his bare blood-splattered chest. "Family," he said, looking down to the bodies of both of his parents. "Not the kind of family that donated to your fucking DNA, but the kind that would gladly take a fucking bullet for you."

He cleared his throat like he'd made a decision, and I braced myself for what he was about to say. Although, good or bad, I knew Bear would do what was right for his family moving forward. Whether that meant that the men lived or died was completely up to him and either way, I'd support that decision. "You get *one* fucking pass. ONE," Bear said, followed by sighs of relief and bursting out held breaths. "And it's right the fuck now," he said, pointing to the ground. "If any of you pussy ass motherfuckers want out, now is the time to take it. This is your one and only chance to walk out that gate without the threat of the club on your back. Ted and his boys will gladly step aside and let you walk out, but if you choose to stay, if you choose to be in this with me, then you are not choosing to be Beach Bastard anymore." Again the crowd stirred but this time with 'huhs' and 'whats' of confusion. "That club is as dead as my old man. There is too much blood. Those stains are permanent. If you stay, you're choosing to start over with me." Bear paused while the crowd absorbed what he was saying. "So leave now while you have the chance."

Not a single man moved. Instead they all stared up at Bear and waited for him to continue.

"Holy shit, I can't believe he's really giving them a pass," King muttered.

"Did you really think he was going to kill all of them?" I asked out of the side of my mouth.

"Yep."

"As a brother of our new MC you will no longer forget what brotherhood means. *WE* will no longer forget who our friends are. We got into this life to live by our own rules. The rules of the club and the rules of the road. We are lawless. We are free. We are *FAMILY*," Bear said, pounding on his chest again. I'd never really known what pride was. I never had any major accomplishments of my own that I could boast about. But looking up at Bear there was no doubt that what I was feeling while watching him talk to his brothers was pure pride.

"Do you even know what is going on with your brothers outside this place anymore?" Bear continued. "Do you know if he's making his bills this month? Do you know if his kid wrecked the car last week or if his old lady's sneaking off when he's not home to fuck the little league coach? Because you should. And if your brother is going through any of those things, it's your job to help, and it's my job to help because help doesn't mean just when people need killing. Help means fucking *help* in any way you can put it in a fucking sentence."

He glanced down again at Chop's body, his blood outlined him in a halo at the bottom of the pool. "Get up off your fucking knees," he ordered. The men holding the guns stepped back and gave room to the men who now stood with their faces upturned, hanging on to every single one of Bear's words.

"Brotherhood means everything. Family means everything.

This time, don't fucking forget that." Bear pointed to King. "King is my brother, my family, and a friend of the club. Disrespecting him or my old lady will guarantee you a one-way ticket to hell. That goes for all of our families. Your old ladies, your kids, your friends outside the club." He leaned over the railing as far as he could, until he was practically bent at the waist. "Business used to be good because as a club, we used to be good for business, until people started looking at us as a reckless bunch of delinquents. That shit changes now. It *all* changes *now*. I am going to strip this shit down and take it back to what it used to be, what it was supposed to fucking be from the very beginning."

Bear shook his head. "This shit isn't going to be one-sided either. I will make you a promise right here and now that I will never ask something of you I wouldn't be willing to do myself. And I assure you that I would be willing to lay down my fucking life for you just as you would for me. I'm a member, a brother, just like each of you, and I will live and die as your brother. *That* I can promise you."

One of the men tossed something up to Bear and he caught it.

"My old cut," Bear said, looking at it with a mixture of hate and reverence.

"Here," King said, tossing Bear his knife.

Bear wiped it on his pants and dug into his cut, tearing the Bastards emblems off, and when he was done, he held up the blank scrap of leather. The once silent group of men erupted into whoops and cheers, whistling and applause. "Your turn," Bear said, tossing the knife down into the crowd where the men eagerly started tearing at their own cuts.

Bear leaned over the railing and smiled. He was in his element, radiating pure power. A rare smile spread across his face. Genuine. Real. Huge. Reaching all the way to his eyes. "Welcome to your new club. You are now brothers of The Lawless MC."

The crowd erupted into hoots and applause. Bear looked back at me, shrugging on his cut and flashing me a wink.

It was official.

Bear was now president of the Lawless.

And I was his old lady.

CHAPTER THIRTY-SEVEN

THIA

USING THE PALM of my hand I wiped off one of the plastic chairs surrounding the fire pit and took a seat. With my ankles crossed over the bricks I leaned back, tipping the chair onto two legs. I closed my eyes, soaking in the sun's last heat as it disappeared behind the tall trees across the bay.

It was that very spot where Bear first claimed me as his own. I didn't know that's what he was doing when he kissed and licked his way around my every wound and injury in his attempt to heal me with his beautiful mouth, but I knew it now.

I shivered at the memory, pressing my thighs together as another part of me also remembered that night.

"Hey, Beautiful," Bear said, making my stomach flip and my nipples harden with just those two words.

I opened my eyes to find Bear staring down at me. His sapphire blue pools hypnotizing me as he looked me over from head to toe. Maybe me and my woman parts weren't the only one taking a trip down memory lane.

"Looking fancy over there, Mr. McAdams," I said, with a low whistle. Bear was wearing something I hadn't seen him wear before. His new cut, which was actually his old cut, because as he had said "took me for fucking ever to wear the leather in." The patches over his right breast read PRESIDENT, THE LAWLESS, LOGAN'S BEACH, FLORIDA and their bright white color and lack of stains screamed of their newness, stiff with thick black embroidery.

"You ready, baby?" he asked, wagging his eyebrows.

"Yeah, but first, this came for you." I handed him the white envelope with no return address.

"What is it?"

"I don't know. It's addressed to you. The Mail America guy dropped it off a few minutes ago. There was one for King too. I gave it to Ray. I didn't open it. I don't know what kind of old lady biker code you guys have against postal fraud. Besides, it could be anthrax."

Bear looked at me and raised an eyebrow. "Thanks for saving the anthrax for me, baby," he said, planting a brief kiss on my lips. He sat at on the edge of the fire pit and tore open the envelope.

"I do what I can," I said, brushing an invisible nothing off of my shoulder.

Bear unfolded what looked like a two-page letter of some sort and as he read his eyes shifted from narrow to wide. His lips moving silently as he read. He stood up, walked a few feet and then reached behind him. When his hand found a chair, he fell back into it, never taking his eyes from the letter.

"What?" I said, watching Bear's reaction and wondering what impending doom was here to sweep away all of our newfound happiness.

"It's a letter," Bear said.

"Don't make me junk punch you Captain Obvious. Who is it from?"

"It's from…" Bear held up the pages. I stood up and snatched it. Resting his elbows on his thighs he dropped his head into his hands. "It's from Grace."

I scoffed, thinking that he was just joking until I began to read.

My Dearest Abel,

It's time I told you a story, one I should have told you a long, long time ago.

As far as the world is concerned, they think Edmund and I couldn't have children of our own because that is what we had lead everyone to believe, but that is only a partial truth. When people asked if we had children, we always said no. It was too painful to talk about then, and frankly, it's still too painful to write this now, but I owe you the truth and the truth you shall have.

As you know, my mother was old-fashioned and had arranged my marriage to my Edmund with his mother on the very day I came screaming into the world. I didn't care for him. I didn't want to be married. Ever.

I wanted adventure.

So a long time ago, in another life, I got my adventure.

I became a hang-around at an MC and got sucked into club life. I was the equivalent to the Wolf Warriors what a BBB is to the Bastards.

Shocking I know, but if you can believe it, I was quite a looker back in my day.

Rebellious as hell too, although I don't think that ever really went away. Age just has a funny way of tucking the rebellion in under loose and wrinkly skin.

I had a child, very early in life with Joker, VP of the Warriors.

A daughter.

We named her Sadie.

Joker was married at the time, and although he was never hateful, he never acknowledged Sadie as his own. I left the club life shortly before she was born, so I could raise her. I married Edmond after all, because I thought it was what was best for Sadie, and thankfully he agreed because although the beginning was rocky, we fell as madly in love as two people could possibly be.

But my girl, my Sadie, was a rebel from the word go, just like her mama.

By the time she turned fifteen, she was deep into drugs. The hard stuff. She'd run away at least once a month until the money ran out from whatever she'd stolen from us and sold.

One such time, she never came back. I tracked her down and it was no surprise where I found her. She'd taken in with the Bastards, who'd kept her comfortable and knee deep in her drug and party lifestyle. I stormed over there many times, but never got further than the gate. I called the cops, but it never yielded anything because, as you know, the cops in Logan's Beach wear badges during the day and cuts at night. I even called Joker and begged him to help me, but the epic on-again-off-again war of Bastards vs. Warriors, was on again, and there wasn't anything he could do.

I didn't even know my daughter was pregnant until I saw a glimpse of her at the Stop-N-Go one day with a rounded belly. I tried to talk to her, but she pretended like she didn't know me. Around the same time, Edmund and I found out that because of my daughter's difficult birth, that I would never be able to have any more children. Not only did I lose my daughter, but I lost my grandchild, as well as the possibility of creating life again.

Months later a picture showed up in the mail with no return address. A baby picture. It was you. I don't know if Sadie had sent it or if Joker had somehow gotten a hold of it and sent it to me. Either way that picture was the very first time I'd ever laid eyes on you and I loved you right then.

I never stopped trying to get to my Sadie. Joker had called me to tell me that rumor had it that Sadie had gone missing. I practically drove my car through the gates of the Bastard compound and demanded to see you, but the only thing I accomplished was being led out by gunpoint. Chop said that if I ever came back he'd not only kill me, but you too. I didn't even know that he was the father until he told me at gunpoint. And when I accused him of killing Sadie, he didn't even have the courtesy to deny it.

I slipped into a depression, nothing Edmund did could pull me out of it. He cleared the house of all evidence of Sadie's existence, thinking that it was the memory of her that was making me that way even thought it was much, much more than that. However, he did let me keep your picture as long as I promised to tuck it away somewhere, so I did. Eventually with no hope in sight I became bedridden with grief, my only solace was a glance at your beautiful face once a day when Edmund would leave for work.

Until Brantley.

When he came into my life, he started to fill the

gap in my heart. Thankfully, Edmond was able to get to know him for a short time as well, before he passed. Brantley was my little blessing, wrapped in anger and emerald eyes. Then Samuel came along, and I started to feel almost whole again.

Or so at least I thought.

Because on one hot summer day, you showed up on your bike. The spitting image of your father with your blond hair and sapphire blue eyes. I nearly fell off the porch.

There you were. My grandbaby. All grown up and right in front of me.

I wanted to tell you then. I tried so many times after that day too. But my overwhelming fear that Chop would cut you off from me... I couldn't lose you.

Not again.

Not ever.

However, he did find out eventually, because he showed up at the house with a half dozen other Bastards and stormed through my roses. The first thing he asked me was if you knew who I was, and when I told him that you didn't, he was relieved.

I would have shot him right there if I'd had a gun within my reach for what he did to my girl. He told me to stay away from you and that it was my last warning. I asked him why he was so hell bent on not allowing you to have a family.

"Because he has a family, the Bastards are his family. He doesn't need his daddy, his granny, or some weed-dealing thug kids. He's got his brothers." He turned to leave.

"You might as well stay, so you won't have to make another trip to shoot me because I won't stop seeing him. I won't. If you are going to kill me for it then just kill me now because I will not give him up."

Instead of killing me, he laughed in my face and then we made an agreement.

One I'm not proud of, but one where I wouldn't tell you who I really was to you, and he wouldn't ban you from coming around.

Oh, and he wouldn't kill us, either.

It was selfish, I know that, but I finally had you in my life and the risk of losing you again was too great. So I kept you in the only way I knew how and I am so so, so sorry Abel. My baby. My boy. Just know that I love you with all my heart and that I did everything I could to be a good grandma to you and protect you from the evil of your father.

You are so different from him. You are a good man. You made my heart and life so full and I would go through all the hard times all over again, as long as it all ended the same way.

With family.

My eternal endless love, forever and always,
Grandma Grace

"Holy shit," I said, covering my mouth. My eyes threatening to spill the tears that had been forming during the entire time I'd been reading Grace's letter.

When I'd taken it from Bear, I thought he was pissed or upset, but when he lifted his head all I saw was pure unadulterated joy. "I have a grandma," he said, sniffling and wiping the corners of his eyes.

"And it's Grace," I said, feeling his happiness.

"And it's Grace," Bear repeated, pulling me onto his lap.

"You have a grandpa too! Some guy named…" I looked back

down at the letter.

"Joker." Bear laughed. "You know I met him before. A long time ago. There was something off about him. No one wanted to talk to a little prospect, but he took the time. He was nice too, and trust me, nobody is nice to prospects. Said some shit to me that stuck over the years."

"Maybe he was there checking up on you," I pointed out.

"I think that's exactly what he was doing." Bear held me tight and for a moment we just sat there, content in each other's arms.

"Are you ready now?" Bear asked after a while. He lifted me up off the chair and set me down on my feet.

"Depends? Where we going?" I asked, standing up and taking his hand. Bear dragged me over to the driveway.

"I'm taking you for a ride," Bear said, gesturing to his bike. Before I could think of what he was asking, he was already shoving a big round helmet with a plexi-glass face guard onto my head.

"I bet you are," I said, my words muffled through the helmet. "But where are we going?"

"For fuck's sake, Ti, always with the questions," Bear said, and although his words were angry, I could tell he was trying to hide a smile. "Can't you just do what you're fucking told for once?"

"I could, but where would the fun be in that?" I asked, sticking out my tongue and inadvertently licking the inside of the helmet. I couldn't see through the face guard because the helmet was too far down on my head. Bear must have seen his error because he pulled it back up until I could see his beautiful face looking down at me and laughing as he adjusted the chinstrap. He tapped the top of the helmet when he was done and it echoed in my ears.

"Where's *your* helmet?" I asked through the enormous fishbowl surrounding my head.

"Right here." Bear lifted out a small black helmet that looked more like a plastic jock strap and set it on his head. His hair poked out the side when he secured the strap.

"How come you get to wear that small one and I look like I'm preparing for a moon launch?" I asked.

Bear chuckled. "You're precious cargo, baby. Gotta protect what's mine," he said smoothly, lowering his voice in the way that made me swoon like an idiot and want to offer him up anything I had in order to hear it again.

Damn him.

"Have you cleaned this thing? I don't want to catch some oral venereal disease from any of its former wearers."

"Baby, trust me, no one has ever worn that before," he said through a laugh. "I had Wolf pick it up this morning just for you." He winked because he knew exactly what he was doing to me, and I melted like the girl I was at the thought of him sending out his new VP just to get me a helmet for our ride.

Bear straddled the big shiny bike and patted the small space on the seat behind him. "I've never ridden on the back of a bike before," I admitted, unsure of how exactly to get on, or where to put my hands.

"Climb on behind me," he ordered, firing up the bike. I've heard Bear's bike before and I knew it was loud but standing next to it was an entirely different experience. The ground rumbled under my feet. My entire body hummed to life as Bear revved the engine in a way that had me pressing my thighs together. "Ti, Bike, now," Bear said, growing impatient.

I climbed on as best I could, but with Bear's big body already on the bike it was hard to maneuver my short legs over the wide seat, but I managed to do it without kicking him in the head or falling off the other side.

Winning.

"What do I hold on to?" I shouted. Bear leaned the bike to the side and kicked up the stand, he reached back and grabbed one of my arms, bringing it around his waist.

"Hold on to me, Beautiful." His words dripping with innuendo, made me want to get back off the bike and jump back in bed. Even over the noise of the engine, there was no mistaking the wicked intensions in his voice and I couldn't help but think what a long ride this was going to be.

I wrapped my other arm around him and settled my hands low on the bare skin of his hard stomach, right above his belt. His abs flexed under my touch and I felt him suck in a sharp breath.

It was my turn to chuckle.

Maybe it would be a long ride for Bear, too.

He started off slowly, easing us down the driveway at a snail's pace and keeping his movements slow. That's when I noticed Pancakes keeping pace beside us until Bear twisted the throttle and we rocketed forward, leaving poor Pancakes to watch us leave from where he'd stopped at the end of the driveway.

Riding on the bike was nothing like I'd expected.

The wind. The speed. The adrenaline.

It was too much and not enough all at the same time. "Woooooooohoooooo!" I shouted, unable to help the excitement bubbling up inside of me.

It ended as quickly as it started as I quickly recognized the route Bear was taking. I'd hoped it was just a coincidence and that at any moment he was going to take the next exit. But when we passed the familiar cross on the side of the road and the WELCOME TO JESSEP sign, the dread settled in.

It was the last place I'd ever thought Bear would take me. As we sped down the dirt road that led to the even smaller dirt road where the Andrews Farm Road sign had been eaten entirely by the overgrown orange tree behind it, my stomach began to twist. I clutched onto Bear's stomach tighter, digging my nails into his abs so he could feel how his choice of outing was affecting me. It was on this road where Bear had been shot and where he'd crashed his bike and killed two of his former brothers.

By the time we made it down the long gravel drive and parked in front of the little white house from my childhood, I felt downright nauseous.

The paint peeling off the siding seemed to have spread from just the side of the house that faced the sun, to every side. Most of the shingles were now missing. The grass below the front window now covered most of the dirty glass, completely blocking the fact that a window existed behind it. It seemed so much more rundown than the last time we'd seen it, but that wasn't possible.

It had only been days.

"Why are we here...*again*?" I asked, ready to move forward and so tired of being stuck in all the crap that the house represented to me. I didn't want to be there.

Bear got off and untied his chinstrap, setting his flimsily little helmet on the seat in front of me. He held out his hand for me to grab and I shook my head. "Nah uh," I said, unwilling to move off of the bike and fogging up my helmet from the inside. "Tell me why we are here first." I rung out my hands and nervously pulled on my fingers.

"Why do you think we're here?" Bear asked.

"Honestly? I don't know." I looked at the broken screen of the front door and took in the uneven front porch. "I hate this place," I said, and I meant it. There were very few things in the world I could say I honestly hated, and that poor excuse for a home, which held nothing but bad stacked on top of bad, was one of them.

"I know you do," Bear said, grabbing my hand and dragging me off the bike. I took off my helmet and set it on the seat next to his. "When you told me about Rage suggesting that you two burn it down, you seemed to like that idea." He shrugged. "So let's fucking do it."

"What?" I asked turning to him and searching his face for any signs of a joke.

There weren't any.

"This is your idea of normal?" I asked, suddenly feeling the heaviness start to lift off my shoulders.

Bear lit a cigarette and tossed me the lighter, which I caught in my right hand. "Yeah," he said, taking a drag and blowing the smoke out through his nose. Smoking isn't supposed to be sexy, but holy mother of sin did Bear look hot doing it. "You know. A little lunch. A little fooling around. A little arson. It may not be normal, baby, but I'm thinking we shouldn't use that word when it comes to us. 'Cause I'm thinking normal ain't something the two of us are ever gonna be." He was unusually quiet for a second, looking to the house and then back to me. "Let me ask you something, Ti."

"Yeah?" I asked as he came to stand in front of me.

"Is that what you want? Normal?" he asked, scratching the shaved part of his head with the heel of his hand that held his cigarette.

I shook my head. "No, I don't even know what normal is."

He pointed to the house. "I imagine that it's a house with a picket fence where the woman has dinner on the table every night at six thirty, and a man who is never late to eat that dinner and always places his napkin on his lap."

I scoffed at the idea. "I hate to tell you, Bear, but your idea of normal is like the fifties. Also, it's kind of sexist, and that entire scenario sounds really fucking boring."

"You know what I mean. I can't give you that. I don't even know what that looks like," Bear said, a crack of vulnerability breaking through the surface. "So tell me what you want. Be honest, because this might be the only time I ever ask you."

I shrugged because the answer was an easy one. "You. I want you."

Bear stubbed out his cigarette in the dirt and looked up to meet my gaze. "I'm no good for you, Ti."

The words rang in between my ears and bounced around in my brain, yet no matter how many times I registered what he'd just said, I still couldn't believe what I'd heard. "No good for me?" I asked. Heat crept up my throat as I stalked toward Bear, staring him down with everything I had in my little pink head. "Don't you think I'm the one who gets to decide what's good for me and what's bad for me? And why is good or bad even a factor? Good, bad, right, wrong. How about I'm a fucking adult, and the only person who needs to be good for me, is me. You're the man I love." I pushed against his chest. Hard. But he stood firm, his face expressionless. "You may not make me a better person, but you make me the me I want to be."

I turned around and Bear's arms came around my waist, pulling me back against him. "That's the last time I want to talk about that, okay?" I asked, in a much softer tone, now that Bear's beard tickled my temple and neck and I was surrounded by the comfort of his strong tattooed arms.

"Yes ma'am," he said, his deep voice rumbling against my throat as he used every bit of his southern drawl to do that thing he does when he says something and my point goes out the window.

"You know you lay on your accent thicker when you're trying to be sexy, right?" I asked, turning in his arms, asking him a question I knew he already knew the answer to.

"Oh, baby," he said, with a crooked smile. "I have no idea what the fuck you're talking about." His lips came down on mine in a kiss that was not meant to be anything more than a kiss, but still had me quivering and the hairs on my arms standing on end. I fit perfectly in his arms.

Surrounded.

Safe.

Loved.

"What do things look like from here?" I asked after he'd pulled back. I looked out into the grove, the trees were tangled with one another. The rotting oranges no longer smelled as the earth absorbed them. "With us."

"What's going on in that head of yours?" Bear asked, knocking on the top of my head.

"I just... I mean." I took a deep breath. "The entire time I've been with you, you weren't the Prez of an MC. You were just Bear. I don't know a lot about club life, what's involved or where I fit into all of that. So I just wanted to know, you know…what happens to us?" My confidence from only a few moments earlier faded quickly leaving me squirming in his grip, but he held me even tighter.

"Ti, nothing happens to us."

"Oh," I said, my heart sinking, my grip around his neck

loosening.

"No." Bear rolled his eyes. "I meant that nothing changes. It's still me and you, baby."

I didn't say anything. I knew I would learn what being an old lady was all about, but I didn't want to disappoint Bear in the process. "I just don't know a lot about the lifestyle. Or about my place in it."

Bear smiled and ran his thumb over my bottom lip. "That one's easy. Your place is right here by my side. All the other shit you'll learn. I'll tell you something. A lot of guys in the Bastards kept their biker life and their family life separate, almost like they were two different people. Wives at home, whores in the club. I know how it feels to be a biker, and not a man. I know how it feels when you find the person who makes you realize you can be both. I don't want to be two people." He sighed. "For a while there, I didn't have you or a club, and now I've got both of you, and I'm not keeping nothing separate and I'm not hiding you away. You're it for me, baby. We're family. Me, you, King, Ray, their crazy-ass kids, and now my brothers."

"It's all that simple, huh?" I asked, raising my eyebrows.

"I'm not gonna lie to you. There will be times I won't be able to tell you shit. Certain secrets are kept only between brothers. But if I can't tell you shit, then I'll just tell you I can't," Bear said. "I'll be as honest as I can and I expect the same from you."

"Okay," I agreed. Simple enough.

"I promise I won't shut you out. Not now. Not ever. Not gonna lose you again." He tipped my chin up so he could look me in the eyes when he said, "You're mine."

"And you're mine," I said. Bear closed his eyes like I'd just hit him with something hard and when he opened them again, they were the color of the clear sky overhead.

"I think what I was just trying to tell you is that it's okay now, you know. You've protected me. You've already fulfilled a promise that you never meant to keep. I don't want to hold you back. You've got your club. You've got your brothers. I'm safe. It's okay. No matter what you want to do," I said, needing him to know that his obligation to me was over. If he wanted to let me go it would hurt. It would be something I'd never recover from.

But I'd live.

Because if I'd learned anything in the last year it was that I was a survivor.

I AM a survivor.

"Hold me back?" he asked, pressing his thumb and forefinger against his eyebrows like he had head pains. "You're not holding me back. What do I need to do to make you get it? I've already asked you to marry me for Christ's sake. Don't you see it?"

"See what?"

"I can't believe you don't fucking get it," he said, the fire returning to his eyes. "You're not holding me back because you're the one moving me forward."

My heart leapt at hearing the words I needed to hear. I was now completely ready to start this new life. With Bear. "I was afraid you were bringing me here because you were taking me home for good," I admitted.

"Home?" he asked, pounding on his chest with his fist. "This," he said. "This is your home." He lifted my hands by my wrists and pressed my open palms to his chest. "This is your home."

I felt a tear spill out of the corner of my eye and roll down my cheek before I could stop it.

"I'm your home baby, just like you're mine, and if you want brutal honesty like you say you do, then I'll tell you right now that even if you wanted to leave, I wouldn't let you. You're mine now, so unfortunately for you, it's not an option," Bear growled.

I sniffled, because I'm a stupid girl and my beautiful man was telling me beautiful things and I couldn't help myself. "I don't want the option," I admitted.

"You said you'd marry me and since you have made me a man of my word and all, we need to get you a ring," Bear said, running his fingers around the empty space of my ring finger on my left hand.

"No," I argued.

"No?" Bear asked, looking worried. "Why the hell not?"

I tugged on the chain around my neck. "Because," I said, pulling his skull ring from my shirt, dangling it in front of him. "I already have one."

Bear smiled and reached out, grabbing the ring and using it to tug me closer. "I'm so glad I found you," he whispered.

"I'm so glad you found me too."

CHAPTER THIRTY-EIGHT

THIA

WE BARELY UNDRESSED, just moved clothes away from the important parts. Bear shoved my shorts and panties to the side, undid his belt and fly without pushing them down. He sat on his bike and pulled me down onto him, fucking up into me like he was solidifying everything he'd just told me.

"Wait, what's this?" I asked breathlessly, running my fingers over the new ink right above his right ear that his hair had been covering.

"That? That's just my old lady's name," Bear said grinding me down on top of his lap, causing me to cry out. He stood and carried me with him, only severing our connection long enough to turn me around. "Hands on the seat," he ordered, slamming into me.

I was his forever.

He was mine.

He was never going to let me leave.

He loved me.

"Watch," he growled into my ear, pulling back on my hair so I had no choice but to watch the house I hated burn to the ground as Bear fucked me from behind. By the time the roof collapsed, I was coming, calling out Bear's name in a guttural scream until he followed me over, practically roaring as he pumped his release deep inside of me.

We made our way back to Logan's Beach, leaving behind the wreckage of my childhood in a plume of smoke and ashes.

I'd never felt more free.

More alive.

Bear turned up the intensity on the ride home, weaving in and out of traffic at speeds that called for arrests, not tickets. I found myself loving every second of the freedom, of the rumbling machine underneath of us, and of the biker between my thighs.

"You like that, baby?" Bear called back, turning his head slightly.

"Hell yeah!" I shouted, holding him tighter. I tilted my head back and took a deep breath.

The first deep breath I'd taken in what seemed like forever.

Maybe the first one in my life.

We're not given forever. We're given just a finite amount of time on this earth. It's up to us to decide how we are going to spend that time, and who we are going to spend it with.

I decided on the back of Bear's bike that my time would be spent having more moments like this.

More moments with Bear, feeling like the world is at our mercy, instead of the other way around.

Bear was right. Home wasn't a place. It wasn't Jessep and it wasn't Logan's Beach. Home is where you feel the most like yourself. Home is the thing that makes you happiest during this very short life.

The *person* who makes you happiest.

I'd never known what a real home was, and now that I'd

found it, I was never letting it go.

    Home for me would always and forever, be Bear.

    We started as a broken promise, one never meant to be kept.

    We ended on the promise of forever.

THE END

EPILOGUE

BEAR

IT HAD BEEN two days since I'd taken Ti out for a ride and burnt down the fucking shit house that had brought her so much grief.

For the first time ever, with no impending deaths or distractions on the horizon, I felt content.

Peaceful even.

Not just because my old lady seemed like the weight of the world had been lifted off of her shoulders, and I helped alleviate some of that weight, but because things were getting back to business as usual.

Well, not usual. *Better* than usual.

Now that the war was officially over and Chop was officially gone from this world, the first order of business for The Lawless was church. I chose my officers from the best of the men and between Wolf, Munch, Stone, Craze, and Lock, we made the decision to reach out to the Bastards existing business connections and figure out which relationships we could salvage, and which bridges had been burnt beyond recognition.

The second order of business was fixing up the sorry excuse for a club that the compound had become. It was a shit hole when I'd left, but now it was like a bomb had gone off.

Plus, it smelled like dead bodies.

Mostly because of the dead bodies.

We were in the middle of the most thorough "clean-up" in biker history. We tore down all Beach Bastards' memorabilia, for the exception of a small banner hanging above the pool table, which we kept as a way of remembering the past and where we came from.

A reminder of where we never wanted to go again.

Bodies were removed. Blood was cleaned.

By the end of the second day, Munch even had the pool converted from a mold pit into an actual working pool.

I wanted us to operate like a team. Like a unit. We needed time to do that, but I was sure it was going to happen. We needed to learn each other again, get to know one another and most importantly, remember how to be brothers again.

I considered a party but decided against it. There would be no parties, no celebrating, no nothing until the place didn't smell like death and we had something to actually celebrate again.

Maybe when I knocked up Ti we could have the first official party. Or when I made the shit between us legal.

My cock was getting fucking hard thinking about her being mine in every way.

The thought of strapping myself to someone forever, of having an actual old lady, used to make me laugh or at the very least, maybe a little fucking sick.

Now the thought of giving Ti my last name, which I planned on making a good one again, made my fucking cock strain against my fucking jeans.

I chuckled. Oh how the mighty have fallen.

An oh how I have loved every single stomach flipping second

of that fucking fall.

I walked around the compound all day, assessing what needed to be done and figuring how much it would all cost. It made me wish Preppy was there. Not just because I stopped hearing his voice two days ago, but because as bad as he was at holding a serious conversation, the kid was a wiz at numbers. It probably took me twice as long as it would him, but I got it done and I think he would have been proud.

With the cash I found in Chop's safe, combined with what I had buried on the island behinds King's place, there would be more than enough to make the dump a place we could be proud of again.

The Lawless Compound.

"I'm out for the night," I called up to Wolf who was helping Stone carry out a blood-stained mattress from one of the second story rooms. They tossed it from the balcony, a cloud of dust billowed into the air as the mattress landed on top of a broken chair, sending one of the legs skidding across the pavement.

I wanted to get home to Ti, but I also wanted to talk to King about what he'd designed to cover up my Bastards' tattoos. Ti had also asked Ray to draw her something for her first tattoo, and I couldn't wait to see what it was.

Her pale and perfect skin was amazing perfection.

The thought of marring that skin with a tattoo that represented us?

Holy. Fucking. Shit.

I couldn't get out of there fast enough.

"See you tomorrow, Prez. Call me if you need anything," Wolf called back. "We're going to take this to the dumpster."

"Check the back building. See if maybe there are some extra mattresses in there or lamps or whatever to replace the broken shit. This place used to be some sort of motel. Maybe there's shit back there we could use," I instructed.

"Ten four, Prez," Wolf said, wiping his hands on the front of his jeans.

I rode back to the apartment feeling more content than I had in my entire life. Pancakes greeted me in the driveway, but instead of his usual tongue-down, he was growling and focused behind me. I turned around to see a black van pull up behind my bike. I grabbed my gun and started walking toward the van, because if whoever it was, was bringing a battle to my front door, they were going to be stopped before they got anywhere near, Ti. King must have seen it on the security cameras, because he was beside me in an instant, his own gun in hand.

The driver's side door opened. "It's just me, boss!" Wolf called out, jogging around to the passenger side. He slid open the side door and Munch leapt out, colliding with Wolf who pushed him back and held him at arm's length.

"What the fuck is going on?" King asked as we both lowered our guns.

"Boss, we tried to call you right after you left, but you didn't answer your phone, so we got here as fast as we could," Wolf said, jumping back inside and shuffling around in the darkness.

"We went to the back building to see if there were any mattresses to replace the old ones out there, and that's when we heard screams. Not just one either, but a bunch of fucking screams. The entire inside was lined with mattresses to muffle the sound. In the floor there was some sort of manhole looking thing with a chain. We snapped it with some bolt cutters. Down inside were like…makeshift cells with dirt floors and zero light. There were tons of them. Some were empty and some had skeletons with skin rotting off their faces. And some Prez…were alive. Whores I ain't seen in a long time, even Lance."

"Lance?" I asked. Lance was the brother who Chop had declared a traitor at least five years back and who he claimed to have killed while out on a ride.

"It's gotta be where Chop was keeping your mom all those years," Munch said, waving his hands around in the air like he was painting us a picture. "Dude was sick and fucking twisted, but none of us knew he was running his very own Bastards' prison."

"Fuck," I said, "that's impossible…"

Munch stepped aside to make room for Wolf and Stone, who between the two of them were maneuvering something heavy.

"It's not impossible, because it fucking happened. Look," Wolf said, emerging from the darkness. Between him and Stone, was an emaciated body, his arms draped around their shoulders, his head down and wobbling from side to side as they walked toward us. His hair so dirty, I couldn't tell what color it was and his clothes were nothing more than blood-stained rags.

"What the fuck is going on?" I asked. "Why the fuck did you bring Lance here?"

"He alive?" King asked, crossing his arms over his chest.

"Oh, yeah, he's alive, all right," Stone confirmed, walking toward us with the man's head bobbing around loosely with their movements. They had to be lying. I've seen my fair share of corpses and this looked very much like one of them. Maybe even worse. There was no way a man in that kind of condition could still be fucking breathing, but sure enough I heard a strained gasp for breath as they approached.

King looked over to me. "Why would Chop…" he started, but I knew what he was asking and we didn't have to wait long for an answer, because Lance's head popped up and suddenly we were face to face…with a ghost.

Who wasn't Lance.

"As I said, there were dozens of 'em down there," Wolf said. "Only five or six alive though."

"No fucking way," King gasped, dropping to his knees in the driveway. I would have dropped too, but I was too stunned to move a single muscle. Too stunned to even look away.

Too stunned to fucking breathe.

The ghost looked between myself and King, and before passing back out, he managed to choke out a few raspy words.

The greatest goddamn words I'd ever heard in my entire fucking life.

"Miss me, motherfuckers?"

BONUS SCENE

THIA

FOUR YEARS LATER...

"Mama, tell me a stowy," Trey said, yawning and rubbing his eye with the back of his little hand.

"Which story, baby?" I asked, as though he didn't ask for the same one every night.

"The one of you and Daddy," he said, climbing up on my lap.

"Okay sweetie," I said, covering us both with the blanket and brushing his angel soft white hair out of his face, and as I did every night, I kissed the familiar freckles below each of his eyes. "When Mommy was ten years old she met a big biker…"

"Daddy!" Trey cheered, knowing the story well after hearing it a million times. That's when I noticed Bear standing in the doorway, wearing his cut, wiping grease off his hands with a rag, listening to our story time.

"Yes, that's right, it was Daddy. He was so tall and so strong. He walked right into the store where Mommy was, and the second he smiled at her she just knew…" I trailed off when Bear flashed me that exact same smile, bringing all the feelings flooding back to me in a rush.

"Knew what, Mommy?" Trey prompted, pulling at the collar of my shirt. "What did she know?"

Bear and I locked eyes. "She knew that he was her forever."

I finished the story and tucked Trey into his bed. I turned off the lamp and gave him one last kiss. "Mama, can you sing to me?" I looked up to Bear who had to cover his mouth to stop himself from laughing out loud. This is how it went every night. Just when I thought Trey was all settled in, he'd request just one more thing and just like his father, I found it very hard to say no to him.

"Sure, baby. What song do you want to hear?"

Bear chimed in, "Sinatra."

I sang my little boy to sleep that night singing "Fly Me To the Moon" as his father listened on and I couldn't help but feel a presence as the song ended and Trey's eyes finally fluttered closed. I knew Grace was there with me and my boys just like she promised she would be.

We were the family I'd always wanted.

A real family.

Ghosts and all.

Other Work by T.M. Frazier

THE DARK LIGHT OF DAY (Jake & Abby's Story)

KING

TYRANT

LAWLESS